UNCOMMON FAITH

BY TRUDY KRISHER

Holiday House / New York

Library of Congress Cataloging-in-Publication Data

Krisher, Trudy.
    Uncommon Faith / Trudy Krisher.—1st ed.
        p. cm.
    Summary: In 1837–38, residents of Millbrook, Massachusetts,
speak in their different voices of major issues of their day, including
women's rights, slavery, religious differences, and one fiery girl named Faith.
        ISBN 0-8234-1791-3
    [1. City and town life—Massachusetts—Fiction.   2. Women's
rights—Fiction.   3. Abolitionists—Fiction.   4. Christian life—Fiction.
5. Massachusetts—History—1775–1865—Fiction.]   I. Title.

PZ7 K8967Un2003
[Fic]—dc21   2002191919

For Joe Pici,
uncommon teacher

Contents

FAMILIES OF MILLBROOK

The Common family

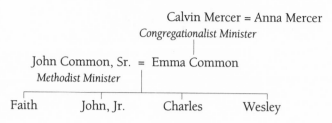

Calvin Mercer = Anna Mercer
Congregationalist Minister

John Common, Sr. = Emma Common
Methodist Minister

Faith   John, Jr.   Charles   Wesley

The Gordon family

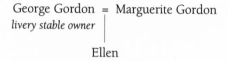

George Gordon = Marguerite Gordon
livery stable owner

Ellen

The Hungerford family

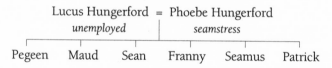

Lucus Hungerford = Phoebe Hungerford
unemployed   *seamstress*

Pegeen   Maud   Sean   Franny   Seamus   Patrick

The Putnam family

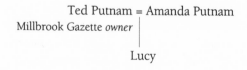

Ted Putnam = Amanda Putnam
Millbrook Gazette *owner*

Lucy

The Tanner family

Alberta (Birdie) Tanner = Ben Tanner

Frank Tanner = Abby Tanner
unemployed   *herbalist*

Celia

The Thomas family

Rufus Thomas   Jewel Thomas ≈ Jessie
handyman   *slave*   *slave*

Ruby Thomas
slave

The White family

Jacob White = Hetty White
carpenter

The Dorcas Circle

Miranda Callendar
Emma Common
Maggie Compton
Helen Cramer
Evangeline Fisher
Marguerite Gordon
Esther Grimes
Rebecca Kinder
Kate Loring
Sadie Martin
Amanda Putnam
Mildred Tyler

The Young Ladies Missionary Society

Amy Callendar
Faith Common
Vera Cramer
Betsy Fisher
Ellen Gordon
Liddie Martin
Lucy Putnam
Sara Tyler

Neither do men light a candle,
and put it under a bushel,
but on a candlestick;
and it giveth light
unto all that are in the house.
—Matthew 5:15

PART ONE

Summer–Fall, 1837

John Common

Truth to tell, most of what I remember about the fire was the sounds: the church bell clanging out warning; boots clomping across the wooden sidewalks; men barking orders; timbers crashing; pigs squealing; horses whinnying; and the splattering, sizzling, steaming sounds of water on flame.

Sometimes I climb up into the hayloft in the barn, trying to forget: the wailing of the singed and burned, their shrieks licking the air like tongues of fire. They were the sounds Grandfather had always warned us about: the sounds of the wicked moaning in hell. I try to forget the sound of ringing axes and breaking glass. I try to forget the haze of ashes and cinders and the young men like oxen, hauling buckets on shoulder yokes, heaving their watery cargoes at the flames. I try to forget the way the horses stretched on their sides in the middle of the road, flailing their graceful legs, men beating at their burning flesh with blankets. I try to forget the image of the mare, thundering toward me, her mane ablaze with fire the color of my sister's hair. I try to forget the way I ran, hiding under the rain barrel, cowering and afraid.

Hetty White

My Jacob was the carpenter around Millbrook, but when times got bad, he'd had to take up undertaking.

I was always my Jacob's right hand, but after the fire, Faith Common, dear Emma Common's girl, was Jacob's left. Faith helped him finish the coffins, passing him nails she held in her teeth, holding the boards steady when he sawed. I shined up the parlor, starched the curtains, and kept something buttery baking in the oven. Emma Common visited a lot more than usual. Her father was ranting worse than ever after the fire. Calvin Mercer bellowed that 'twant no surprise we'd been cursed like Job. 'Twas his belief we wicked heathens in Millbrook had brought the fire on ourselves by our sinful ways.

I don't know how my Jacob and I did it. Six funerals in two weeks and half of them laid out in our own parlor. We just kept going down inside ourselves and asking the Lord to give us the strength.

I'm not sure why they picked Jacob and me to bury the young ones: 'tis likely they knew how my Jacob and I felt about children. Out back is our woodpile and the extra coffins Jacob built and blessedly never had to use. Beyond that is the woods and our own quiet cemetery. 'Twas hard to think on little Charlie Curtis lying between Jimmy Sartoris, George Gordon's fifteen-year-old groomsman, and Pegeen Hungerford, the Irish girl who worked in the bathhouse above the livery. My Jacob said it was like to comfort Charlie to be between two older children watching over him like a big brother and sister. 'Twant no small honor when the Curtis family said they could trust us to keep an eye out for their boy.

I wrote my friend Sarah Grimke about the fire and the funerals. 'Twas nary but long faces all over town. She wrote back: "Dearest Hetty, May God bless their souls—and thine."

Biddy Bostick

They call me Biddy. Biddy Bostick. But Biddy's better'n some of those names they call a spinster, if you ask me. Thornback. Old maid. Stale bread. *Ha!*

One thing they oughta call me is *smart with a penny.*

Times turned bad in 1837, but only Biddy Bostick weren't surprised. I knew about bad times. After all, I was a woman, wasn't I? Knew a single woman paid taxes but couldn't vote. Knew a woman earned only pennies a day as a lace maker or shoe binder. Knew the banks was fixin' to fail when Jeffrey Sanborn, president of the Millbrook Savings and Loan, made his daughters sell their own china dolls. Biddy Bostick don't use a bank. Ain't no bank safer'n my own apron pocket. *Ha!*

From the porch of my boardinghouse I can see every-thing in Millbrook. I can see that Lucas Hungerford's the first drunkard in the tavern in the morning and that Albert Biggs's the last merchant in his store at night. I can see Lucy Putnam mooning with that Amos Read boy behind her parents' backs. Biddy Bostick can see more with both eyes shut than most folks in Millbrook with two blinkers wide open. *Ha!*

Biddy Bostick was also the first to see the fire in Gor-don's Livery that Monday morning. Rufus Thomas hadn't showed up to haul my slops away, and that meant I'd open the door to the root cellar so Rufus could stow my cargo when it came in. After I'd dragged the slop bucket out onto the porch myself, I set up my goods there like I do every morning: the Whites' eggs; Birdie Tanner's brooms and honey; Esther Grimes's crocheted purses.

I'd seen the bottle by the door of the livery and Charlie Curtis's feet flying into the livery to brush old Nellie. I hadn't thought much about it, for little Charlie hightailed it to that old mare near every morning.

Soon after, though, I saw the flames leaping through the windows and the horses bolting. Ran up the street to ring the church bell my own self. The clapper sounded like a mad-man banging his spoon against the side of his breakfast bowl. I was scardt near to death. What if the fire burned down my boardinghouse and a spinster's only livelihood?

Folks panicked, pushin' and shovin' and screechin' and hollerin' just like they did with the run on the bank.

We lost Ralph Underhill, Sr., Mattie Adams, Jimmy Sartoris, Pegeen Hungerford, Thomas Watkins, and Charlie Curtis. Nearly lost the Bruce twins and Eliza Peabody, too. Nobody ever really found out how it started, but I was sure as a snowstorm in January that it was little Charlie Curtis. Afterward, George Gordon said he suspected there'd been a bottle of Porter's Chemical Fluid spilled all over the floor.

Little Charlie Curtis liked nothing more than brushing that gentle old mare. I'm sure the child knocked over the bottle on the way. Ain't that just like a frisky boy? Anyways, I never told Charlie Curtis's family what I thought. Their hearts was broke into so many pieces, I couldn't add one more.

Celia Tanner

I started counting when I saw the fire. Eleven, twelve, thirteen. I always count when I get scared.

I was powerful worried about Birdie, my grandma. I didn't know at the time that I should have been worrying about Mama; she had gone to the woods to pick elderberries and I reckoned she was all right.

But when I smelled smoke all the way out to our farm that summer morning, my heart seized up. I knew Birdie was up in town. She had gone to speak to George Gordon about Pop. Pop had lost one job after another, and we was desperate to have the money he earned from mucking the stables at Gordon's Livery.

But when George Gordon fired Pop on that summer Sunday right before the fire, saying Pop would rather lift a bottle of whiskey than a hay fork, Birdie was furious.

"A true Christian, Celia, wouldn't strip a mother's son from his job on the Lord's Day." Birdie fumed so loud you'd think she was a believer.

Pop celebrated that particular Lord's Day by tipping back a bottle up by the river with Lucas Hungerford; Pop didn't come home until Monday morning, and when he did, he stunk so strong I confess Pop was like the drunkard the temperance folks warned about: so full of chemicals he's best out of range of a match.

Birdie threatened to march up to town first thing Monday morning.

"I'm fixing on giving that George Gordon a piece of my mind," she said. Then she turned around on her tiny bird's feet like a robin spotting tin in a bush. "No, on second thought, Celia," she said, "not just a piece. I think I'll give him the *whole thing*!"

Grandma was something fierce when it come to Pop. I was fierce about him, too, but for a different reason: Why couldn't he straighten up? Couldn't he see that his own mother, the only one who really loved him in this world, already had *enough* trouble with her heart?

Ellen Gordon

When I first saw the flames, I felt a forbidden thrill. To my mind, it was like sitting next to my aunt Thelma in the theater in Philadelphia, watching the red velvet curtains parting for a performance of *Maisie's Dilemma* or *Valiant Spring*.

I could feel my toes tingling. Nothing exciting ever happened in Millbrook. Sometimes Albert Biggs got a shipment of brocades or velvets that could only be found in places like Boston, but more often than not we settled for the dullness of coarse muslins. Sometimes bounty hunters thundered through, whooping and hollering and raising a fuss, but they kicked up little more than clouds of dust. My daddy's livery was more exciting than most places in town, what with the horses and the carriages and the stagecoach drivers sharing what little news there was. And once a week you could hear the post rider's bugle when he pulled up to drop the mail and change horses. But a bugle call in Millbrook was a far cry from a curtain call in Philadelphia. Daddy and I understood there was a world outside of Millbrook. Even if Mama didn't.

As I ran to town, my mama huffing behind me, the fire seemed like a play, a tableau in violet and red. At stage left were the men tossing barrels of vinegar and casks of salt out the window of the dry-goods store. At stage right were the firemen, slinging buckets of water from hand to hand to quench the flames. And then the terror dawned: at center stage was Daddy's livery!

As the fire licked at the face of the livery like a wolf's tongue, its red teeth took bites out of the rooftop above. Mama caught up to me, pulling me back. Through the smoke she pointed, and relief flooded my veins: we caught my father's shiny bald head and his strong arms struggling to hood the horses. But as the men pulled the frightened animals from the livery, one of the mares broke loose. Its mane was on fire, and it was heading straight for the crowd gathered on the apron of the stage. In spite of the smoke, I had a clear view of it all, just like I had when Aunt Thelma got us front-row seats to *The Picnic Lunch*.

The horse had panicked and reared. Ladies shrieked and gentlemen flailed their arms. Children clutched their mothers' skirts as they ran away. As the crowd parted, I saw Faith Common's brothers scattering like chickens in a flutter of arms and legs. And then Rufus Thomas lunged at a thin elderly woman whose face I could not see, knocking her out of the horse's path. Then I saw Faith Common standing her ground, facing the stampeding animal.

As the mare thundered close, my heart caught in my throat like it did that time I watched Amelia Robinson in *My Amiable Friend*. Faith ripped off the skirt of her petticoat, beating at the red mane with the white cloth until the fire was extinguished. Then, without flinching, she hoisted herself up on the back of the mare, her red braid flapping down the center of her back, heading in the direction of the river. As she flew past the coach maker's and the tavern, I felt my hands flying together as they did at the end of a performance.

After that, ashes and sulfur began to sting my nose, and I coughed on the smoke. Mama pressed her apron to my face and pulled me away. As I turned around, I saw something else. Something even more powerful than a performance by the famous Fanny Burney.

The Hungerford family was huddled on the ground in front of the burning livery, hunched together and crying. They kept looking up and waving at the window over the livery where the bathhouse was. More and more folks kept jumping out the bathhouse window onto what was left of the livery roof, streaks of flame behind them. The Hungerfords were hoping their oldest girl, Pegeen, who worked in the bathhouse, would soon come to the window to jump, too. Only when she did, her back was on fire.

I'd seen plays with heroines swooning on couches and heroes fanning them, begging them to live. But I'd never seen anyone die before. For real.

John Common

Father had been home at the time of the fire. There had been six dead and three injured; miraculously, my father had found words of comfort for them all.

I stood beside him at bedsides, in parlors, at the mouths of graves.

"Son," my father said, his broad hands on my shoulders, his eyes not on me but on a realm just above my head, which I could not see, "a pastor soon learns that grief expresses itself in different ways. And that the Bible has a verse for every one of them."

Truth to tell, Father was right.

At the home of Ralph Underhill, Sr., the father of our town auditor, I saw the family's stiff upper lips as signs of their sorrow. Ralph, Sr., had been trampled under the feet of terrified horses.

"God is the strength of your heart," Father said, sharing the comfort of Psalms. "He is your portion forever."

The Hungerford family had lost Pegeen, the young Irish woman who had worked as a laundress in Mattie Adams's bathhouse. I saw that the fiddling and the dancing at the wake was the Hungerfords' way of coping with grief.

To the Hungerfords, Father spoke of the mourning of the wine, the languishing of the vine, and the sighing of the merry hearted. "Isaiah 24:7," he pronounced soberly.

I saw that providing comfort at the home of Charlie Curtis, the six-year-old joy of the Curtis family, would be hardest of all.

I stood by Father's side as Charlie's mother sobbed uncontrollably, as Charlie's older brothers and sisters cried and pounded their fists, as Charlie's father blubbered out a confession: he had held a handkerchief to his eyes for so long that he had stopped wearing his spectacles and could only stumble absently about in his own house.

Truth to tell, it was then that my father stumbled for the first time ever. "The Lord is n-nigh unto them . . . ," Father said, his voice tripping on his words the way sightless Mr. Curtis stumbled about his house, ". . . who are of a b-broken heart."

Standing beside my father, observing him fit words like garments to the requirements of any occasion, I felt as I always did beside my father: far younger than my thirteen years.

Calvin Mercer

Can see with one eye as good as most folks with two, I can. So when I saw the flames, I knew it was just like the Bible said: Millbrook was a lake of fire, the lake of fire and brimstone predicted in Revelation.

But the fear of God struck my own soul. Saw Alberta Tanner teetering on her scrawny bird legs at the edge of the crowd outside the livery, I did. And Rufus Thomas, that stump-footed Negro, knocked Birdie to the ground as he leaped out of the way of a panicked mare.

Flung into the dirt, Birdie was. Stunned. It was how I felt when I realized that Congregationalists were deserting my church for the Unitarians.

Tried to turn Birdie Tanner into a Christian woman, God knows I did. Now that her skinny legs were splayed at odd angles like broken toothpicks, it was too late. Had converted the likes of Jonathan Tucker and even Evan Meeker, I had, but I never could figure out how a woman like Alberta Tanner could remain a stubborn heathen to her very soul.

I saw the flames behind her as a sign. Birdie Tanner was about to be drowned in the lake of fire. I'd warned her about this. Warned her, I had, years ago. I'd come to her side when Frank Tanner was born. Offered to baptize him, I did. I told that woman what the Bible said: *Except a man be born of water and of the spirit, he cannot enter into the kingdom of God.*

But she'd have none of it.

I told Birdie Tanner she was just like Eve. Her disobedience caused all the world's trouble, I said. After I said all the sins of the world pointed straight back to that first female, Birdie Tanner had put her face close to mine. She locked my eyes in the vise of her stubbornness and said, "If the sins of the world can be traced to Eve, Calvin Mercer, how do you account for the holiness of Mary?"

That's what caused all Birdie's trouble, it did. She allowed Frank Tanner to be born in sin. No wonder he was raised to the devil.

John Common

On the morning of the fire, I had run away from the flaming mare. I had crouched under a rain barrel while my sister extinguished the fire with her petticoats. I had watched from afar as my sister mounted the mare, heading toward the river. I felt ashamed.

Once the horse had been cooled in the river, Faith led the animal home, determined to care for it at our farm until the animal healed. Faith herself was wet and sopping, the braid down her back tight as wet rope.

Grandfather gave the horse one brief look. Then he leaped to a swift conclusion. "Thief!" he cried. "Don't you remember the sixth commandment?"

Quickly I bent beside the woodpile, safely huddling there. I knew to avoid my grandfather's thundering voice.

"Of course, I remember," Faith said, astonished.

"Then why have you willfully disobeyed it, girl?"

"I have disobeyed nothing. I was only trying to help the mare. Her mane was on fire! She was burning! I was planning only to nurse her back to health. Once she is well, I will return her to Mr. Gordon's livery."

Then Grandfather turned on her, full of rage: "Do not contradict your elders, girl." His white hair flew from his scalp like snow before a cold gust of wind.

She stood up to him; I crouched silently beside the woodpile.

"There is nothing in the commandments about contradicting your elders, Grandfather," she insisted. "They only speak about *honoring your father and your mother.* They say nothing about grandfathers who falsely accuse you of stealing!"

Then she turned on her heels to lead the horse away.

I looked up at the sky and tried to concentrate on the purple clouds and their promise of rain. The possibility of rain would help the efforts of the engine company.

Suddenly Grandfather smacked the ground with his cane. "On your knees," he ordered. "You have stolen a horse. From your knees you will ask the Lord's forgiveness. For your stealing. And for your insolent comments to me as well."

Faith thrust her shoulders back and her forehead up into his face.

Watching her stare into the cavern where his left eye had been, I shuddered.

"No, old man," she insisted. "I have stolen nothing. I will not kneel."

"*Like a jewel in a pig's snout,*" Grandfather growled, "*so is a daughter without discretion.*"

Jacob White

An undertaker's the only merchant in town who never hopes for more business.

Celia Tanner

When they laid Grandma out, I took her for dead. I confess I didn't even think of Mama. I didn't have time until later to notice that Mama hadn't come home.

Emma Common came right away. She swabbed Birdie's forehead all day and sat up by Birdie's side all night. I'd counted up higher than I ever had before. Got all the way to 14,094 before I realized: *Where was my mama?*

When Birdie came to, Hetty had arrived. She said she was in between funerals and knew her Emma needed some rest. Hetty always treated Mrs. Common the way she treated me: like the daughter she'd always wanted. Just then, Grandma blinked her black bird-shot eyes and asked for Pop. "Frank, coax me a tune out of your fiddle," she said in that bossy way she had. "It's too quiet in here, son."

It was then that I came back to life, too. And then just died all over again. On her way up the porch steps, Hetty had picked up the bag of Hunter's Red Drops and the note. They were from Mama. "Dockter Yr Gram with these, Celia, gurl," the note said. "And git yrself to skool. Yr plenty smart, Celia Tanner, and doant you fergit it. Yr Mama, Abby."

Hetty White

My Jacob and I've been spending most of our time since the fire with Celia Tanner. 'Twas a comfort to let her post letters to my friend Sarah or help her practice her sums. I'd let her hang the quilt out on the fence post or take it down as needed. I always sent her home with a dozen biscuits. 'Tis a shame my Jacob and I never had any babes of our own.

Celia was spending a lot of time in the woods like her mama had. 'Twant nobody for potions and doctoring like Abby Tanner. Ergot. Pennyroyal. 'Twant nobody for modesty, either. That poor woman wore her ragged sleeves down to her wrists and her collars up to her chin. 'Tis a pity when a woman has to hide her shame that way.

"Here's somethin' that's like to help Birdie," Abby Tanner said, pulling flower buds that looked like peonies from inside her wrist. Just under the hem of her sleeve I could see the yellow-and-green bruises in a circle like a bracelet. 'Twant hard to imagine the bruises at her throat. "Peony drops are good for Frank's mama's heart."

I got quiet. I went inside myself and prayed. I asked God to send Abby Tanner a potion for doctoring her own heart. And Celia's, too.

The hardest thing I ever did after burying those three children in our cemetery after the fire was to hold Abby Tanner's daughter's face in my old hands and say, "Celia, darling, I don't think thy mama's coming back."

I had to tell her the truth. Quakers don't go in for loose talk. And they don't lie, either.

Like I told Celia, "Sometimes thee just has to sit with the sadness. For as long as it takes."

I knew about sadness. Jacob did, too. Sometimes thee had to rock thy sadness for a long, long time. Just like it was a baby thee always longed to have.

"After a while, Celia," I told her, rocking her sweet fingers in the seat of my palm, "thee'll learn about faith. Not the noisy kind, the quiet. The quiet kind is harder. It may take a good long while, Celia, dear, but the light will come. 'Tis true what they say, sweet Celia. God provides."

Celia Tanner

I don't know what I would have done without the Whites or Rufus Thomas. The Whites gave Pop and Birdie and me a chicken a week. Rufus Thomas fetched the broomstraws from up in town for me and saved me the trip. Sometimes when I got up early to gather eggs at the Whites', I'd find Rufus had already gathered a full basket. "Go on, now, Miss Celia," he'd say, "you want to get these fresh eggs up to Biddy's before folks has their breakfast, don't you?" The Whites let me sell their eggs on Biddy Bostick's porch and pocket half their profit.

I confess I went to the woods when I could. It was my way of remembering Mama. I thought of her when I glimpsed the wild grasses and flowers. I reckon I started collecting them as a way of holding on to her. Mistletoe. Ergot. I doctored Birdie with potions like peony and burdock root the way I'd watch Mama do. I confess I felt proud when Rufus Thomas asked me to mix him up ointments for burns. Like many folks in town, Rufus had been burned by the fire. His black hands oozed patches of pink-and-white skin, and I mixed lard and arnica for them like Mama taught me. Biddy Bostick asked me for extra jars of honey to sell from her front porch, for folks all over Millbrook had learned the way a honey dressing can soothe a burn.

I missed my mama powerful hard, but I held tight to the blessing of Grandma Birdie.

"I'll be fit as a fiddle right soon," Birdie said when I worried over her. "A blackened skillet, Celia, makes for better corn bread."

It wasn't true. Grandma Birdie couldn't make brooms anymore. I had to make all of them myself. When I went to set them on Biddy Bostick's porch to sell like I did every morning, I passed Biddy a handful of the red drops Mama left behind. It was my way of thanking Biddy for all the years she let Tanners set up shop on her stoop. I don't know why Biddy dropped her jaw. Nobody'd ever seen surprise on Biddy Bostick's face for a single day in her life.

Emma Common

I thought I had known sorrow, but how narrow my learning had been! After the fire, the Lord sent me lessons in grief that I struggled to master. I learned that there was food, always food in the houses of the dead. I had seen common cakes in the huts of the poorer families, fancy cakes in the parlors of the richer ones. Tables brimmed with salt pork and beans, turnips and potatoes. Picnic baskets burst with dill pickles and lemon curd. Kettles bubbled with beef stews and mushroom sauces. Yet I found it curious: no one ever seemed to want to eat.

In my own family my husband was gone for hours, ministering to the families of the dead, my young son John by his side. Faith took to helping Hetty's Jacob, and my second son, Charles, took to muttering elaborate explanations for why the fire had started. Wesley, my youngest boy, cried into the milking pail, sobbing that he would miss Charlie Curtis. My own father almost drove me mad. He considered himself like Job whose servants were slain, whose sheep were burned, whose body was scarred with boils, and whose calamities were infinite. Incessantly he banged his cane, reminding us that God sent the fire to punish the wicked.

I redoubled my efforts at sewing. I called my Dorcas Circle to meet twice a week instead of once. I encouraged the women of Millbrook to produce three times the lap robes and jars of jelly as they had in the past. How generous they were with their time and energy! I agreed with my friends that the profits from September's Benevolence Fair should now go to purchase a new pumper and bell for the engine company, not slates and globes for the primary school. When my eyes blurred over my needles, I resisted the impulse to complain. How painful it had been to visit so many grieving families! How important was this healing work!

Biddy Bostick

Ha! The slop trough behind the haystacks in back of the livery had burned down, so Rufus built a new slop trough out back behind my boardinghouse. Built it fast as I can cipher, and that's lickety-split. And Rufus *still* showed up most mornings to dump my bucket.

"Any cargo due to arrive today, Rufus?" I'd ask. Sometimes I expected stock from out of town. New tablecloths. Some soup bowls. Two things true about boarders: they spill things and they eat. I could tell when the stock arrived because Rufus wouldn't dump my bucket that morning.

Then I'd just leave the door to the root cellar open so Rufus could make the delivery. *Ha!* It takes a powerful lot of merchandise to run a decent boardinghouse.

Which brings me to decency. And that lout of a father, Frank Tanner. Soon after the fire, I saw the signs that drunkard'd put up. He'd got a lawyer to write them for him. It was the only time Frank Tanner'd ever paid for something. *Ha!* When Frank Tanner nailed the signs up all over town after Abby ran off, it was the only time Frank Tanner'd stopped drinking to do a lick of work. The signs said:

Notice: Escaped from my bed and board, my wife, Abby, without my consent. As my rightful wife and property of fourteen years, she is bounden to my service. I will not pay any of her debts. All persons should be cautioned against aiding her escape in any way.

Ha! Most folks in Millbrook think it's the other way 'round: they're cautioned about *Frank,* not Abby. But ain't more'n a few see that a woman's no more'n a slave. A married woman can't make a will. Can't go to court. Can't own the kettle she cooks in. Even a free black like Rufus Thomas is better off than a woman. At least he has some papers.

I ripped down Frank Tanner's signs as soon as they went up. *Ha!* Biddy Bostick's always been one to outsmart folks.

But I'd thought I'd be better at sums than it turned out. Two dozen eggs at nine a dozen makes eighteen for twenty-four. Biddy Bostick can do sums like that lickety-split. You'd be surprised at how many women don't even know a dozen's twelve.

But I'd thought Biddy Bostick could always put two and two together, if you know what I mean. It took Celia Tanner to help me add it all up. When Celia passed me a handful of Hunter's Red Drops, I remembered that Clyde Harker, my boarder, was a patent-medicine salesman. Clyde just up and left. Slipped out of Millbrook right in the middle of the fire. He wasn't much to look at, but I'll say one thing for Clyde Harker: he got up to go to work every day. Got people to believe one little red drop could cure everything from dropsy to diarrhea. Likely got Abby Tanner to believe it could cure a troubled heart, too.

Celia Tanner

There's never much to remember about Wednesdays. Only one Wednesday in late July Emma Common appeared at our door. I confess she looked like an angel.

"I thought you might need some supplies. Faith and I came by to help you make up a proper sickroom, Celia, dear," she said. I liked the way she called me "Celia, dear." It made me feel like I still had a mother.

First Emma unpacked the small teakettle and the water pitcher. Then she set out spoons and tumblers and towels. Inside the towels were tucked lots of things. Bandages for cuts. Sweet oil for earaches. She laid them next to the plants I collected from the woods and used for doctoring Grandma Birdie.

While Grandma slept, Emma sent Faith and me outside to sweep the porch and beat the rugs.

When Faith got tired of beating, which was right away, she turned to me. She said, "Why do you always look down when anyone talks to you, Celia?" I confess Faith Common was bold as a boy in britches.

I leaned on the broom. I tucked my chin down into my chest.

"Pick your head up, Celia," Faith ordered. "Look at me," she barked.

I did not look up. I could feel my cheeks turning red.

Faith didn't quit. She was like swarming bees in summer, bound for the hive. "Why must you always keep your eyes cast down like that?"

I did not look up. I stared at my feet, at the sagging boards of the porch. "It makes it possible," I whispered, "to count the floorboards."

"The floorboards? Whatever would you want to count the floorboards for?"

I buried my chin deeper into my chest, but I told her this: "I float off with the counting, Faith."

Faith kept still.

"On this porch there's twenty-nine floorboards from one end to the other. Inside, there's forty-six floorboards from the hearth to the door," I said. "Counting back from the door to the hearth makes ninety-two."

Just then Pop called from out back. "Celia! *Ceee-Liii-Ahhh!*" A heavy rapping sound held hands with his words. Like it always does. I hoped Faith hadn't seen me shudder. I knew about those sounds. So did Mama. They were always made by something heavy. A rolling pin. An iron bar. I started counting. I knew I didn't have to come right away. In fact, it was better if I didn't. If I came right away, I got it. But if I waited, Pop usually just took a swig from his bottle and fell back to sleep. I knew what my grandma didn't: Frank Tanner was never going to rise up from his chair and coax a tune from his fiddle again.

By the time I reached 422, it was time for Faith and Emma to leave.

Emma bent over Grandma Birdie's bed, and Grandma waved a bony finger in my direction. "Go fetch that sack of walnuts for Emma, will you now, girl?"

I fetched the sack and looked down while I talked. "There's a hundred and eight hulled walnuts in there," I said.

"I counted. Every one. That's nine dozen, I think." I pressed the sack into Emma's hand. Emma didn't push the sack away like that lady from the poorhouse. Whenever I tried to give that lady something, she said Tanners needed their own gifts more than she did.

Instead Emma peeked into the sack, stuck her nose down into it, and inhaled the scent of the walnuts. "There's nothing to sweeten my apple cake better than a handful of walnuts, Birdie Tanner," she said. "And they take forever to hull, don't they, Faith? The fact that Celia's hulled them for us makes the gift twice blessed, don't you think?"

Emma Common didn't kiss the top of my head that time. I confess I was disappointed.

Faith nodded awkwardlike. She looked away.

I know that folks in town say the mother's got a charity that the daughter lacks. But I confess it: Celia Tanner's not so sure.

I only discovered it later, of course. After they'd both gone. Somehow Faith had slipped from behind the rocking chair where Pop lay snoring, his fiddle and his bottle at his feet. Somehow she had found his boots. Somehow she had taken the bootlaces into her own long fingers. Somehow she had knotted the laces together with a dozen knots, pulling the laces hard.

Somehow, after that, I decided that Faith Common, like her mother, had her own kind of charity. Faith just showed hers off in a different kind of way.

Calvin Mercer

I only went once to visit Birdie Tanner. Heard up in town that she'd gotten better, I had. Wanted to see for myself.

"Sorry Rufus knocked you down, Birdie," I said, holding the flowers behind my back.

"Not *down,* Calvin," she sputtered. "Out of the *way.* And I wouldn't be here jawing with you if he hadn't."

"Saw it with my own eyes, Birdie."

"*Eye,* Calvin. Not *eyes.*"

I could feel my fist tightening around the flower stems, I could. "My one eye's as good as most folks' two."

"Whether it's one or two's no matter, Calvin. Eye's not the only way to see things."

How could I have forgotten that talking to Birdie Tanner was like wrastling with the devil?

"Here," I said, laying the flowers across her spread. "Brought you some jonquils, Birdie."

She lifted one egg-shaped brow and a tiny black bird of an eye peeked out. "Are you courtin' me again, Calvin, or tryin' to convert me?"

Birdie Tanner always could stop a man dead in his tracks.

"A preacher never stops aiming for converts," I said.

She struggled to lift herself on one elbow. I took it as a good sign. "But how'd I ever know which church to join, Calvin? Millbrook's got more religions than hands have fingers."

I couldn't let that remark go. If there was anything I knew, it was the number of churches in Millbrook. I opened my right fist and started counting on my fingers, I did. "Well, there's Presbyterian, Congregationalist, Episcopalian, Methodist, Unitarian." I stopped and continued counting on the fingers of my left hand. "Then there's Quaker and Catholic. That's only seven, Birdie."

"You haven't counted Baptists yet," Birdie said.

"But that's just one more. That's only eight. You said there were more religions in Millbrook than hands had fingers."

She held up her own fingers and wiggled them. "Hard-shell Baptists. Soft-shell Baptists, Particular and General Baptists, Primitive and Freewill Baptists. Are you satisfied there's more than ten, Reverend?"

A smile of triumph spread across Alberta Tanner's face, it did, and her eyes sparked with the wit I remembered from years ago. "And they're not jonquils, Calvin. They're daffodils." Then she collapsed against the pillow.

I turned to leave, angry and happy at once. As I thudded down the rickety steps past the snoring body of her sinful son, I knew who Birdie Tanner reminded me of. The brawling woman in Proverbs. Like the Proverb says: *It is better to dwell in a corner of the housetop than with a brawling woman in a wide house.*

Hetty White

'Tis a shame Emma Common has nary a day of peace. Only a thin line separates the Commons from the truly poor. Their utensils 'twas made from tin; their seeds 'twas saved from last season's crops. Emma accepts the temporary plenty of her husband's temporary visits. When he is home, he trades funerals for cobblers or a marriage ceremony for a cord of wood. When he is gone, they have nary to trade save the fruits of a farm run by a stubborn old man, a headstrong young girl, and three half-grown sons who, together, hadn't the strength of one full-grown man.

When her husband John was away, I often asked Rufus Thomas if he would go over to help out. The few free blacks in the county were always looking for work, and Rufus was handy with tools and always willing. After Calvin's one eye was blinded in that accident, Emma was plain grateful. Her father could only do half as much work, but he caused twice the trouble.

'Tis a blessing Emma's husband was a Methodist. Where her Calvinist father saw a God of wrath, her Methodist husband saw a God of grace; where her father saw sin, her husband saw virtue; where her father saw punishment, her husband saw forgiveness; where her father believed salvation to be available only to the elected few, her husband believed salvation to be available to the converted many. Quakers don't come down either way. 'Tis the Quaker way to believe in quiet, in going inside to seek the inner light. But I was grateful John Common's Methodism. 'Twas comfort to his wife.

John Common

Truth to tell, when Rufus Thomas asked me to help him build a new slop trough behind Biddy Bostick's boarding-house, I was glad to oblige. He'd been helping me for years. I liked returning the favor.

I was not the strongest of the Common brothers, and the chores I was expected to do never came natural. With Father so often away, Rufus somehow taught me everything I was expected to learn: how to swing a scythe; how to run a furrow; how to repair the brick cisterns that held the water for the cows; how to build the big plank bins for keeping the rats from the grain in the barn.

From the time I was small, Rufus had been patient with a clumsy boy.

After I spilled the precious oil filling the lamps and my grandfather had bellowed about my wastefulness, Rufus caught up with me in the cellar. He grinned at me and whispered, "My, son, but you pour that oil like a rich man!"

When I mixed up the whitewash for the fences, using a whole bushel of lime instead of a half, my grandfather launched a stream of words about my absentmindedness. Later, Rufus peered over my shoulder as I mixed the proper amounts. "Did the same thing when I was your age, John. Ain't a bad thing to learn that a job half done's often double the trouble."

Truth to tell, it was always a pleasure to see Jacob White crisscrossing the landscape in his wagon, making deliveries of coffins with Rufus Thomas at his side. Sometimes after I'd mastered a difficult chore like cleaning the horses' hooves or repairing the roosting perches in the henhouse, Rufus would press something into my hands. A drum. A clapper. A pair of castanets. Things he'd made from the scraps in Jacob's shop. Things that made music.

When I helped Rufus with the slop trough, I saw that, thanks to him, I wasn't as clumsy with an ax as I once had been. But it pained me to see the burns on Rufus's hands. They were healing, more yellow now and not so pink. But they were still tender. Like the way I felt about Rufus himself.

Celia Tanner

I confess I didn't know too much about the Hungerford family before the sadness of the fire. I knew they were poor like me. I'd seen the twin boys up in Albert Biggs's store in town, picking up straw for plaiting like I did. You could plait until your fingers were good and sore. Then you could take your hats or mats or fans back to Albert Biggs, and he would give you a grunt and a few pennies. I knew that Phoebe Hungerford, the mother, stitched shirts long into the night. I knew she had another son. A big boy with long limbs and strong hands who hired out for jobs around town. I knew there were other children, too. Nobody Irish ever came from a small family.

I confess it: I didn't go to the Hungerford wake. I knew a visit would be better later on. After everyone left. When you were all alone with the pieces of your broken heart.

I wasn't expecting the place I saw. It was even worse than ours. Dirty mattresses on the floor for furniture. Candles in every corner, burned down to their nubs. Palm grasses and straw all over. There was only one chair in the room. Half a dozen finished white shirts hung on the back of it; stacks of unfinished sleeves and shirt fronts and collars were stacked up on the seat. Everything in that room was grimy and worn. Except for the goods that held a place of honor on the chair.

When I arrived, Emma Common and Faith and her brother John were there. In fact, John and the Irish boy, the big one, passed by me dragging a grimy mattress out into the street. They were followed by the two younger boys, the twins.

Emma Common was standing over a kettle of boiling water, pushing one of the mattress tickings down into the water with a laundry fork and looking like an angel. One of Mrs. Hungerford's girls was peering into the water and grinning. "Look at 'em jump," she said, pointing into the kettle. "Those bedbugs can jump out of water faster than Irishmen can dance a jig." Her freckled face lit up. "You know, Mrs. Common, I think I'm going to miss those bedbugs. We'd had 'em so long we'd got used to the scratching."

Emma Common grinned. Then she spied me in the doorway. "Celia, dear. Why, it's a pleasure to see you! Do you know everyone, Celia?" she asked. Just as if I was family.

Emma Common introduced me to Mrs. Hungerford and to Maud, the oldest girl, and to Franny, the young girl who had been joshing about the bedbugs. Emma said that John and Sean had gone into the street with the twins to empty the mattresses of straw.

Then, when I stuck out my hands to offer my gift, Emma exclaimed, "Cherries! And pitted, no less, Phoebe!"

I confess it: when Faith's mama sets her velvet gray eyes on me, I feel like I've been looked on by an angel. "All that work, Phoebe," Emma said, turning to Mrs. Hungerford, "makes the gift twice blessed." Then Emma kissed the top of my head.

I hung my head and looked down. I'd pitted 157 cherries. With my own hands. I confess I felt proud for someone to notice. I figured Mrs. Hungerford could make a pile of pies out of that many cherries. It felt good to be kissed.

Suddenly a big man with a few days' growth of whiskers flew into the room. He grabbed Mrs. Hungerford by the hand. Roughlike. Scattered my cherries every which way. He flung Mrs. Hungerford into a corner of the room. Shook his fists at her.

Phoebe Hungerford's hands gathered into fists that covered her face. The man shouted. "Open your hands, woman," he ordered.

After a struggle, finally she opened her hands. A fistful of coins jangled across the floor. The man fell to his knees. He crawled across the grimy floor, grabbing coins. He ran by us out of the room. Same way he came in.

What I saw made me think of my own mama. Seven hundred seventy-nine. Seven hundred eighty.

"That's me pap," said Franny, the freckle-faced girl. "Me mither earns the money, and then me pap peels the coins out of her hands. We broke custom when we buried Pegeen. It's a habit to put pennies on the dead one's eyes, but me mither said no. She knew me pap would steal the pennies off his own daughter's corpse."

"Shush, Franny," ordered Maud, her older sister. "Stop your chattering now!"

The girl shrugged. Then she and Maud and Mrs. Common rushed over to comfort Phoebe Hungerford.

But Faith stood still. Then she seized my hand and put her mouth up to my ear. "Celia," she said, whispering loud enough for anyone to hear, "why's a drunken husband entitled to every penny his sober wife has earned?"

I confess I couldn't quite tell whether that was a question or a statement. I knew about drunken husbands. Sober wives, too.

When we finally left, the big boy had his arm around his mother and Maud. His little sister Franny said, "Thank you, Mrs. Common, for helping out with the bedbugs. You're not anything like that lady who comes from the poorhouse and acts like we're not a proper family."

Emma Common blushed, but I knew what Franny meant. When Emma came to my own house, I felt thankful in the same way.

Ellen Gordon

I was planning on becoming an actress. Daddy sent me to visit his sister in Philadelphia every summer, and Aunt Thelma gave me the cast-off clothing of her elegant friends.

I'd practice before the mirror wearing the white satin bonnet with the gold braid or the lady's top hat with the trailing veil. I could manage the haughty speech of queens, the rough speech of fishwives, the innocent speech of coquettes. To my mind, the only way a girl ever got to be something other than a mother or a wife was by pretending.

I could make my face look worried or pleased or surprised, but I struggled to capture the faces around me in

Millbrook. Understanding the folks right next to you always seemed harder than understanding folks from far away.

When the bounty hunters galloped into town only a few weeks after the fire, I tried to capture their faces, too: the heavy jowls, the knitted brows, their swagger as they paraded their reward papers before the magistrate. They were demanding the return of two slaves escaped from Virginia.

It was harder to depict the gestures of the townsfolk as the bounty hunters tried to ransack our village: Amelia Simpson biting her gold locket as the men strode through her millinery shop; Robert Kinder stamping his boots as he watched them turn over his soap displays; Jonathan Hardcastle fuming when they asked to peer into the beer barrels in his tavern.

But most difficult of all was imitating the gestures of my own daddy.

When the bounty hunters even showed up at the tax assessor's office, I saw my generally peaceful daddy change. He'd been in line to talk to the assessor. He'd come to beg for an extension on account of the fire.

As the strangers began to search the office, Daddy stepped up to them.

"Why don't you go back where you came from, gentlemen? Can't you see that Millbrook's suffered a fire and that we've hardly had a decent time to mourn our dead?"

Something about the way Daddy carried himself made me proud. I tried to capture that posture before the mirror: a head held high, a chest full of pride in spite of the humiliation of his losses.

Suddenly I saw my mama's reflection in the mirror. She was standing in the doorway, watching.

I'd just opened my mouth and raised my arms, practicing an imitation of Biddy Bostick. When the bounty hunters approached the steps of Biddy's boardinghouse, she had bellowed at the strangers and beat on their backs with a broom.

Now Mama pulled me away from the mirror. She said no self-respecting female would ever get up and speak in public and that only strumpets turned to the stage.

After that, I practiced in secret.

Hetty White

'Tis true that Emma was exhausted from work, so I was worried when I heard that September's Benevolence Fair raised nary enough to cover the cost of the new fire pumper and bell. 'Twas Mayor Girton who had loudly promised it to the town in the first place. Now he was loudly pledging to raise more money to have the pumper and bell in time for the anniversary of the fire next June. I'd nary a doubt about what would happen next, and I was right: the mayor asked Emma to chair the subscription campaign. I tried to talk her out of it.

"Has thy John got the corn in yet, dear?"

"Did thy father get the fences mended?"

"What about the cistern for the cows? Are thy boys up to fixing it yet?"

Emma shook her head. The corn, the fences, and the cistern still needed attention, and her husband John was soon to depart again for the West.

"But, Hetty, dear," Emma said, her dove gray eyes full of mercy, "how can I say no when I've seen what the Curtises and the Tanners and the Hungerfords have suffered?"

Amanda Putnam

Frankly, my husband Ted's *Gazette* is just like our sewing circle: one round of local gossip followed by another.

"I hear the tavern in Worcester calls itself a 'hotel,' now," Marguerite Gordon said, poking at a loose thread in a collar.

"Frankly, ladies," I said, "the only building to qualify as a hotel in my mind is the Tremont in Boston. It has eight water closets." Ted and I were the only people in Millbrook to have ever stayed in a hotel. Or visited Boston. Or frequented a water closet, for that matter.

Frankly, I found the ladies' conversation tiresome. "Ladies," I began, determined to elevate the conversation, "again I offer you the opportunity to sign my petition."

Rebecca Kinder's as blunt as her darning needle. "My, Amanda," she said, "how you *do* love to cause a *stir*. First it's your temperance society. Now it's your petition campaign."

I lifted my needle. "I for one think the 'stir' is important, Rebecca." I was not one to be outdone by the likes of Rebecca Kinder.

None of the women responded.

Now I stuck my needle into the collar I had been repairing. "Frankly, my aim is simple, ladies. I merely intend to circulate petitions opposing slavery and present the signatures to the legislature. The bounty hunters that swoop down on Millbrook are an abomination. We will not tolerate them."

"*We*, Amanda?" asked Kate Loring. Her head was bent over an infant cap.

"No self-respecting female would participate in petition activities, Amanda," Rebecca's voice snapped. "It's unfeminine to go door-to-door soliciting signatures like a common peddler."

"Politics is unseemly work, Amanda," Marguerite Gordon said. "It is better left in the hands of the men."

"Frankly," I said, picking up my sewing again, ignoring the looks of disapproval that circled the room, "once you recognize a wrong, you commit another wrong by not attempting to right it."

Then I returned to my collar in earnest. I was visiting my sister Jane in Boston in a few days and wanted to hold my head up in her presence: Boston had four or five different abolition societies to choose from.

I was jostled from my reverie by Emma Common. "I agree that slavery's a pity, Amanda," she said. "But why should that mean I need to join an *abolition* organization or *sign a petition* in order to help?" Emma Common's fingers fluttered over her cloth. When she spoke, she did not look up. "I'd much prefer bringing a poor widow a supper or her children some thick wool blankets," she said. "My duty is to *help* the suffering, not agitate the public on *behalf of them.*"

Bent over her needle, Emma looked like a sister of charity fumbling with rosary beads. Frankly, that was the problem with women: they never looked up from their laps.

My husband, Ted, is as addlebrained as my women friends. The fire last June was the biggest story he ever tried to cover. His headline was accurate enough: FIRE THREATENS MILLBROOK. SIX DEAD. Only he got the date mixed up. He wrote it as JUNE 25, 1837. I had to reset the type at the last minute myself. Ted was too lazy to change it to June 26.

There was only one good thing about the fire: it finally got some civic spirit going. I'm sick to death of the way the selectmen let the pigs romp through the streets and the Commons' cow wander through town. Because of the fire, the selectmen finally passed an ordinance. Now every building in Millbrook's required to keep two buckets of sand and two of water on the premises at all times. Imagine that! Politicians in Millbrook actually *doing* something!

Mayor Girton determined to get a new fire pumper for the village after I finally got Ted to write an editorial about it.

But after the Benevolence Fair failed to raise enough funds to cover the costs in September, the mayor asked Emma Common to be in charge of collecting more subscriptions. After all I'd done! The mayor wanted to have the new fire equipment by the one-year anniversary of the fire. Frankly, I can't see why the mayor didn't ask *me* to chair the campaign, and I said so to the ladies of my sewing circle.

"Can't Ted and I reach more people through *The Millbrook Gazette,* ladies, than Emma can by going door-to-door?"

I was annoyed by the attitude of my women friends.

"Don't you know, Amanda," huffed Kate Loring, drawing her thread through the thread waxer, "that folks are more likely to respond to Emma's requests than yours? They get tired of all your *isms!*"

"My *'isms,'* Kate?"

"Yes, you know. Like abolitionism." Mrs. Loring took a final stitch on her infant cap. She often made and sold these caps for a few pennies in Albert Biggs's store. They were embroidered with fleurs-de-lis. "I still need to pickle the beets, and I can't even keep up with my own mending, Amanda. How do you find time for *abolitionism?*"

The ladies tittered.

Now Esther Grimes joined in. She had finished hemming a skirt held in the beak of her hemming clamp. "And another *'ism'* like *transcendentalism,* Amanda," she said.

"And Christian *perfectionism,*" said Marguerite Gordon, returning each of her pattern pieces to its proper bag.

"And *vegetarianism,*" offered Rebecca Kinder, sweeping the floor for stray pins with the tip of her sewing magnet.

Frankly, I was annoyed. "Well," I huffed. "There's one *'ism'* that you ladies find quite *enough* time to support: your own *provincialism!*"

Lucy Putnam

Well, I declare, the fire had changed nearly everything in Millbrook.

Because of the fire, I singed the flounces on my skirt and the tulle ribbon on my bonnet that made such a sweet little ruff under my chin. Because of the fire, all my mama's Dorcas sisters stitched more furiously than ever to raise funds for the engine company. Because of the fire, Mama harped on about Millbrook's civic pride and hounded Daddy about the contents of the *Gazette* from breakfast to supper. Worst of all, because of the fire, I had to stop meeting Amos Read behind the bales of hay at the back of the livery.

It was easy slipping out of the house either early in the morning or late at night. But I declare, everything happened so quickly that morning. Amos had finished telling me how I smelled like fresh cream, and he was just about to kiss me when we heard a shuffling over by the slop trough. After Amos peeked around the hay bales, he pressed his index finger to my mouth instead of a kiss. He'd seen a couple of figures huddled over the trough and then Rufus Thomas appeared, signaling them to hurry away. After that came the huge flash and the explosion, and after that the flames.

Because of the fire, lots of things had changed in Millbrook. But I declare the only thing that hadn't changed was Faith Common.

Faith Common's the sauciest girl in town. Her hair's a matted bird's nest of strings and tangles. She chews with her mouth open and slurps at her spoon. Everybody says the only time she ever behaves is when her father's home from a mission in the West.

Our latest sewing circle took place at the Commons' house. Faith spent most of the time making fun of all the teachers we'd had in the primary school who'd up and left. Why in the world couldn't Faith see that talk like that would encourage my mama to send me away to school? I wanted to stay put right here in Millbrook. I'd finally mastered what I couldn't learn from a moldy old book: how to gather up Amos Read on the crochet hooks of my eyes.

While my mother's friends discussed the prospects for the new teacher this fall, I witnessed one of the only times in my life when I saw Faith Common concerned about how she herself acted.

"Do you think," Faith asked, waiting for Miss Grimes to add two lumps of sugar to her teacup, "the new teacher will know where the Indian Ocean is? Myra Scroggins couldn't find it on the map—even after we gave her the hint that it's right near India."

The other girls tried not to giggle as they thought of Myra Scroggins.

"Or do you think she'll end up scratching herself out of town like Sophie Butterworth?" asked Faith. "Cream, Mrs. Loring?"

The other girls' shoulders began to jump with laughter as they thought of Sophie Butterworth. After the young teacher boarded at the Brookinses', she caught fleas from their dogs.

"Or do you think this one'll be as fond of tobacco as Reilly Bell?" Faith put down the tea tray and picked up a stray square of fabric from the floor. She wadded it up and stuffed it into her lower lip. Now she looked just like Reilly Bell, the schoolmaster who lectured with his tobacco quid stuffed into his chin.

The other girls put down their needles and threw back

their heads. Tea slopped into their saucers. Even their mothers began to laugh. Reilly Bell had been a poor excuse for a schoolmaster.

"Perhaps the teachers seem incompetent, Faith Common . . ."

I was startled, and so was Faith. She had wrapped her fingers around the edge of the tea tray to pick it up again when the voice caught her up short. She pulled her fingers quickly from the tray, watching the teacups sway in their saucers.

"Perhaps the teachers seem incompetent," the voice continued, "because their pupils are unmanageable."

Faith straightened immediately. She had recognized the vibrations of her father's voice.

Quickly Faith removed the wet swatch of fabric from inside her mouth. She stuffed it into her apron pocket.

"Clamorousness does not become a young lady," her father said soberly. "Proverbs 9:13, Faith."

I'd never before in my life seen Faith Common blush. Or shut her sassy mouth, either.

PART TWO

Fall-Winter, 1837

Ellen Gordon

Of course, Faith Common is a few years older than most of us girls in the sewing circle. I'm thirteen, closest to Faith in age. Betsy Fisher's twelve. Sarah Tyler's eleven, and Vera Cramer's only seven. Faith's the worst seamstress among us, but Mrs. Common's patient with her anyway.

Nobody hates stitching more than Faith Common, but to my mind, her boldness is the only thing that makes sewing circle worthwhile.

Once her mother, Emma, held her silver needle high, watching it catch the light. "Ah, Faith." Mrs. Common sighed. "If only I had a snatch of time to work on a bit of embroidery." Then she looked at her daughter and brightened. "Perhaps you, Faith, dear, will one day enjoy the leisure for such fancy-work."

Faith scowled as she fumbled with the sampler under her fingers. "Only if I can pay a needlewoman, Mother."

The other girls tittered. Sarah Tyler's mother's lips turned down. Betsy Fisher's mother bit her tongue.

I didn't glance over at my own mother. I didn't have to. I knew Marguerite Gordon's scowl. I'd secretly practiced it a million times before the looking glass.

"The first thing Adam and Eve did in the garden was sew, Faith," Emma said, attempting to adjust Faith's temper. "They stitched garments out of fig leaves."

The words gathered behind Faith's lips like powder down a musket throat. "And if God wished to punish them for their sin," she shot back, "He could not have chosen a more fitting occupation."

The other girls now giggled outright.

Their mothers shushed them.

To my mind, Faith Common was the only reason to attend the sewing circle. I would never have told Mama, of course, but I was fascinated and frightened by Faith Common all at once. One time, when I'd been sent to Jacob White's for a fresh chicken, Faith was out back hammering some boards. When Faith saw me she squealed with delight. She tossed aside her hammer, jumped onto an empty coffin, and pulled me up after her. When she began to dance, I didn't resist. There we were, high off the ground, our shoes tapping out rhythms like raindrops on a roof. Of course, I never told Mama about the shivers of fear and pleasure that surged up my spine. I never told her I felt like an actress high on a stage. I never told her how much I liked that feeling.

Amanda Putnam

When school's not in session, a few of the women bring their daughters to sew along with us. Frankly, the girls' conversation's just as claybrained as that of their mothers.

"If you smell your stockings after you take them off," Sarah Tyler whispered, "you won't have nightmares."

"That's not true, Sarah." Faith Common corrected her.

"Is so," said Sarah. She held out her hands. "Here, Faith," Sarah said. "Just look at my fingernails."

Faith grimaced. "What in the world do your fingernails have to do with it, Sarah?"

"Look. There's not a single white mark."

Faith looked. "So?"

"So the number of white marks on your fingernails says how many lies you've told," said Sarah. "My nails haven't a single one, Faith, so what I said *must* be true."

Faith snorted.

Frankly, I wish my Lucy and my women friends had Faith Common's kind of spunk.

I keep trying to bring more enlightenment to Millbrook. Once I tried to raise a discussion with the ladies about the woman who refused to pledge to *obey* in her wedding vows, but all they were interested in was the shame of her serving wine and spirits at the reception. I'd tried to interest people in booking lyceum speakers, but all they wanted to see was a Bengal tiger pacing in a cage or that huckster who claims to make electric sparks. Imagine that! People in Millbrook think entertainment is the same thing as culture.

I tried to spread the news about the Grimke sisters, who'd been traveling our countryside to speak out against slavery.

Hetty White's knobby knuckles paused over her knitting needles. "My Jacob is taking me to Worcester next week, ladies. To hear my friend Sarah and her sister Angelina. All of thee," Hetty continued, "are invited to join us when the Grimke sisters speak there."

Frankly, I was pleased that *someone* picked her head up when she spoke.

Kate Loring's mouth swung open like a door with a missing hinge. "A woman is speaking *in public*? And holding forth with her views *like a man*?"

Rebecca Kinder scoffed. "Haven't you heard of Sarah Grimke and her sister Angelina, Kate? They've been traveling all over the countryside speaking against slavery before audiences. And *mixed* audiences at that! It's a *scandal*."

"Hummph," snorted Esther Grimes. "The Grimke sisters. I hear they are both horrid-looking frights."

"And I hear they long to grow beards and take tobacco," said Miranda Callendar.

My Dorcas sisters hooted.

Hetty interrupted. "Well, friends, the Grimkes don't even mind the ridicule," she said, "because it's in the name of a cause they believe in."

I fumbled in my pocket for some coins. "I would go with you to Worcester to hear your friend," I said, "but I will be away in Boston visiting my sister Jane. Here, Hetty," I said, passing her a handful of coins. "Add this to your friend Sarah's cause. Freedom for the slave is certainly a cause *I* can subscribe to."

"Hmmmph," scoffed Rebecca Kinder. "If I may say so, Amanda, you may as well admit how much you love to cause a stir. Your agitation is bound to help your husband sell more copies of his *Gazette*."

Frankly, I was disgusted. "If that's so, Rebecca," I said, arching my left eyebrow, "a newspaper's far cheaper than the ignorance it attempts to replace."

Hetty White

'Tis such a pity for a father like Calvin Mercer to heap such shame on a daughter like Emma.

'Twas rude of him to interrupt our Dorcas Circle. Calvin had a musket in his hands. Said he was going out to check the barn. He'd heard all about the robberies hereabouts of late.

The ladies had heard about them, too. 'Twas one of the main subjects of conversation at the Dorcas Circle. Maggie Compton had heard noises downstairs, and her husband Thomas ran somebody off with a fire tong. The Kinders noticed that their flour barrel was down by half, and Rebecca Kinder swore someone was stealing even the corncobs from her pigsty.

But I expect 'twant the robberies Calvin was worried about. What he'd really wanted was to keep us from going to Worcester. What he'd really wanted was to rant about the letter he waved in his hands. His words were still ringing in my old ears.

I knew all about the letter. Sarah had written to me about it. It was from the General Association of Congregational Ministers of Massachusetts. They were trying to keep Sarah and her sister Angelina from speaking.

Calvin scattered his words like buckshot.

I waited until he finished. "They say, Calvin," I offered, "that thy letter has only served to increase the size of the crowds."

When he turned around and stomped off to the barn, shouldering his musket, a bright flush appeared on Emma's cheeks, and I knew she wouldn't be traveling with me to Worcester.

Calvin Mercer

Quakers are no more than wolves in sheeps' clothing. Not only is slaveholding permitted by law, it's supported by the Bible, it is. *Servants, be obedient to them that are your masters.* Ephesians 6:5.

Ellen Gordon

It was crowded in the Whites' wagon as we drove to Worcester, but I didn't mind a bit. To my mind, it was like being elbow to elbow at a Saturday matinee in Philadelphia. There was Hetty and Jacob, of course. Mama and Mrs. Compton wouldn't be attending the speech, but they sat up front between Hetty and Jacob. Mrs. Compton's daughter Grace was getting married, and they would be looking over the superior selection of laces in the dry-goods stores in Worcester. Jacob was carrying an order for two coffins in the back of the wagon, and I rode on top of one, tapping out rhythms on the wood with my feet and hands all the way to Worcester.

The neighboring fields were crowded with wagons and carriages and stamping horses when we pulled up outside a large barn. We arrived just in time, for a throng had gathered inside the barn, and the seats had already filled up. I begged Mama to let me stay and watch, and when Mrs. Compton reminded her that it was easier to shop without a child in tow, Mama agreed. Jacob dropped us off and then went to deliver Mama and Mrs. Compton to the dry-goods store and the coffins to someplace in town.

Inside the barn groups of men hung from the hayloft and perched on the rungs of ladders ranged against the walls. Hetty and I had to take seats on barrels. I felt the press of bodies and the smell of sweat. It wasn't anything like the theater in Philadelphia.

Soon Hetty's friend Miss Sarah Grimke joined us, and Hetty and Sarah hugged and kissed. "Here," she said, "sister and I have saved some stools for thee up close."

Sarah Grimke moved us closer to the platform to hear her sister speak. Even though it wasn't anything like having front-row seats at the matinees with Aunt Thelma, it still seemed a privilege.

I overheard Sarah whisper hoarsely to Hetty, "They'll forbid a woman to speak in public. They'll claim it is *unscriptural*."

"But if she dares to defy them," Hetty replied, winking,

"they'll line up like folks on Market Day, eager to see their first Bengal tiger."

I watched Angelina Grimke approach the makeshift platform of stacked hay bales. From my stool I could see that Angelina was tall and slender, prettier and less shy than her older sister Sarah. Chestnut ringlets sprang from under a plain Quaker cap just like the one Hetty wore. In fact, everything about Angelina Grimke was plain. Unlike the actresses in Philadelphia, there were no bands of fur around her face or feathers in her hair or gold necklaces dangling little bottles of perfume.

When she mounted the rustic platform, catcalls and hoots arose from the crowded loft. I searched Miss Grimke's face for signs of fear, but saw none. It was hard for me to imagine how she stood her ground so calmly. When the audience began pelting the actors in *The Vain Virago* with tomatoes last summer in Philadelphia, Miss Charlotte Kincaid had fled the stage in a flood of tears. In the face of those crude noises, however, Angelina calmly turned her clear blue eyes to the crowd, and it grew quiet, holding its collective breath. I held mine, too. I can scarcely remember all the things she said about slavery and abolition and freedom. But what I remember most is this: for the first time in my life I heard a woman speak her own lines. And not from a theater, but from a public platform.

Afterward, on the ride back to Millbrook, Jacob White seemed tense and irritable. When I beat out rhythms on the lids of his coffins, he called for my silence. I think he was disappointed. His customer in Worcester had changed his mind, and Jacob's boxes would have to return to Millbrook.

I was still stunned. Angelina Grimke was nothing like the heroines I had seen on the stage. How was it that a woman in plain gray Quaker dress found herself upon a platform? How could a woman in such plain clothes make such a powerful impression? And why was my mind racing so hard, imagining new ways a woman might *be*?

Biddy Bostick

If you ask me, running a boardinghouse's nothin' but complaints about the food. Either the ham's too salty or the corn bread's too dry or the turnips ain't the way their mama cooked 'em. Boarders raise up a protest at the same time they're pickin' their teeth and belchin' satisfaction.

Which brings me to satisfaction. *Ha!* A spinster don't get much of it. Far as I can tell, a spinster's treated like a porcupine with quills, and she can't turn a living wage without running a few side businesses. I let Miss Esther Grimes sell her butter from my front stoop, and she gives me two cents a day for the privilege. Celia Tanner brings her brooms to sell, and the Whites let Celia sell the eggs from their henhouse. Sometimes I slip some extra coins in Celia's hand; most of the townsfolk had healed from their burns, and the run on her honey had dried up.

Far as I can tell, everybody in Millbrook knows they can get the finest eggs they ever counted straight from Biddy Bostick's front porch. Which brings me to counting. *Ha!* Women in Millbrook can't count money half as good as they count stitches. And the menfolks likes it that way. It's a good thing I'm an honest woman. Edna Barrow come by this morning for a dozen eggs. Her Henry's family's coming over from Lynn, and she's fixin' on makin' her deviled eggs. Told her for the millionth time they're nine cents a dozen, but Edna don't know that a dozen's twelve. Thought it was ten. I could have cheated her straight off. *Ha!* After that she said she'd be stepping across the street to Albert Biggs's store. She was fixin' to buy three yards of ribbons for the braids of Henry's nieces. *Ha! There* Edna likely *would* get cheated. Ribbon's a half copper a yard. And Edna Barrow don't know how many half coppers it takes to make three yards any more'n she knows how many eggs make a dozen.

Which brings me to knowing things. I know that new schoolteacher they've been squawkin' about can't get here soon enough.

Emma Common

Oh, how I dreaded John's leave-takings! I can still feel the sharp ache of his parting on that damp October morning.

I had stitched him a cloak as a farewell gift. "You'll notice the double row of stitching under the arms, John Common," I said, laughing lightly.

John stared in his kind but absent way at the cloak seams. He was unfamiliar with the intricacies of woman's work. "Indeed, Emma," he said blankly, "it has been doubly stitched."

"That's because, husband," I said, "you wear out your arm seams with all your gesturing and pointing. I want your ministry to wear a cloak that stands up to your enthusiasms."

My husband laughed broadly. His straight white teeth gleamed bright against the black wool.

Over the years we had developed family rituals around John's departures. Our son John whistled out a tune on his flute, hoping to dispel the gloom. Charles offered arguments for why his father might change his mind and stay. Wesley made himself useful by adjusting the bridle and saddle on Onward, John's horse. Faith was always the one to offer the final good-bye, throwing her arms around his neck as he leaned down to her from the saddle. "Be a dutiful daughter now, Faith," John said. Reluctantly, she released her grip and then handed her father's hat up to him.

More and more, especially after my father's accident with the pruning hook, I had come to rely on the help of Rufus Thomas whenever John was away. He never asked for anything in return, although his eyes told me he was grateful for the bushel of apples or the mended shirt I'd send his way.

Years ago, even before Hetty had asked him to help with our haying, he had earned my gratitude. Rufus had been passing by on the way to do chores at the Ferrises' farm, and Faith, only a child, had climbed out the attic window into the branches of our apple tree. Terrified, I had watched from the ground as she crawled out the ledge and onto the sturdy branches. My heart leaped to my throat as she cleared the shingles, swinging from her hands, her legs flinging themselves across the yard.

Suddenly I felt her brother John by my side. Grasping my hand, he stared—wide-eyed—as Faith seated herself on a sturdy branch, cupped her hands around a ripe red apple, and sank her teeth into its skin.

But it was Rufus Thomas who calmly hauled her to safety. Ted Putnam even wrote the incident up in the *Gazette*. I came to know the piece by heart:

> Mrs. Common's daughter Faith climbed out the attic window into the family apple tree on washing day last. The child stubbornly refused to come down and gorged herself on apples. Although Bishop Common was away in the West, Rufus Thomas hauled the disobedient girl down. When her daughter was finally pulled to safety, Mrs. Common fainted dead away.

What I remember most about the incident was that Rufus introduced himself only after I had revived. "Rufus Thomas," he said, pulling out a paper embossed with a gold seal. "Free black, miss," he said. "Always looking for honest work. I've been a stevedore, a bonesetter, a coal smelter, a watchman, and even an orchard hand. But I never thought I'd find myself harvesting a young girl from the trees." I saw that he suffered a limp as he shifted his weight and grinned.

Before he left, he entertained the pouting Faith. Her brother John stood at his shoulder as Rufus spread a checkered cloth on the ground. Then he pulled out a penknife and began to slice a handful of apples in half, pointing out the pattern of stars on the pulp until I could gather my wits.

Then, after my father's dreadful accident, Rufus helped out more and more. I was thankful for the intercession with my father that Rufus often provided when my father impatiently rebuked my children.

How hard Father was on the children! He had become like that verse from Isaiah: *Obstinate. Thy neck an iron sinew. Thy brow brass.* He admonished my children at every turn, especially John, my most awkward and sensitive child. Often Rufus trailed along beside my children, setting to rights the damage my father had done.

How difficult it is to tolerate the behavior of my father! Yet something within me understands. Father had lost his wife, my own dear mother, to an untimely death. He had lost his pulpit, he believed, to Unitarians and Methodists. He had lost his eye to an accident in the barn with a clumsy child. He had lost the agility of his youth to the plague of rheumatism. He imagines himself like Job, singled out for adversity. Worst of all, he had lost the ability to seek and ask for God's help. How I prayed for his change of heart! How difficult were things without my husband!

Lucy Putnam

What in the world was wrong with my mama and daddy? They'd got a bee in their bonnet after they went to the Family Night at the district school last fall. Mama hired a driver to take me to Troy in the carriage every day. I hated learning those dead old languages like Greek and Latin that didn't have one bit of use. But I did like being ten miles away from Mama. And I liked it that handsome Amos Read helped out the master in Troy. When Amos bent over my history book with me, he said I smelled like lilacs.

Why couldn't Mama and Daddy ever mind their own business? They came back from Family Night mad as hornets.

They paced the floor in front of me.

"Did you hear the way that master introduced the Widow Simpson as the '*Widder*' Simpson, Amanda?"

"Yes, Edward, I did," Mama said, stomping her foot. Mama's face turned beet red as she repeated parts of the master's speech for my benefit. "Did you hear him, Lucy?" she shrieked. "Did you hear your master say that it was a *farvant* wish of *hizen* to *garrun-tee* a good *eddicashun* for *these-here chilrun* of *ourn*?"

Then my daddy swarmed with fury, too. "You'd think since it was ordered by law and supported by taxation that a parent could expect a good deal more from the district school! I've never seen such a sinkhole for a taxpayer's dollars!"

Then my mama piped up. "And you'd think a town like Troy could find better than that Master Thatcher. He needs to be sent back for an '*eddicashun*' himself!"

Mama and Daddy wagged their heads up and down

together. They were taking me out of the district school right away. Whether I liked it or not, next fall I'd go to some other school. And I didn't like it one bit.

Soon after that, Mama whisked me off to look at that new school she'd heard about in South Hadley. It was a school called Mount Holy-Yoke, and Mama and I arrived the day before it opened. We had to step around paint pots and over a man who was still laying the front threshhold. Groups of girls were hemming linen in the parlor, and the trustees' wives were washing dishes in the kitchen. When a woman named Mary Lyon asked us to join in, Mama clapped her hands with delight. I said I had a headache from the racket of driving over roads no better than logs tossed across ditches. Mama slapped me on the wrist in front of everyone and said we'd be happy to help.

It turned out that Mary Lyon, who'd been washing dishes like a common servant, was in charge of the school. After she introduced herself, I thought she was too countrified to run much more than a dairy. Miss Lyon talked with her hands, her cap strings flying. How could Mama be so impressed with a woman who was as plain as lye soap?

Besides, if I went to Mount Holy-Yoke, I'd never see Amos Read again. He'd made me a kind of promise. "Miss Lucy Putnam," he said, "if I'm ever able to enter Harvard College, will you wait for me while I'm gone?"

Worst of all, when we left Mount Holy-Yoke, Miss Lyon pressed a mathematics text into my hands as a parting gift. She said I could get started right away. Being as how Mama even invited Miss Lyon to Millbrook to tell her Dorcas sisters about that silly school, I cried all the way home. Mama told me to straighten up. She wouldn't bear with a silly twit for a daughter.

Ellen Gordon

I practiced for hours before the looking glass, trying to capture the expression of Miss Samantha Sprinkle. The new primary school teacher wasn't much to look at. She had bristly whiskers for eyebrows and a thin mustache on her upper lip. The boys whispered that she was secretly a man.

From the first, it was clear that the children, not Miss Sprinkle, held the reins in the classroom. Of course, every new teacher we'd ever had was tested from day one by Ethan Loring. First of all, as outsiders to Millbrook, the teachers were unfamiliar with Ethan Loring's fat cheeks and his reputation for trickery. They could not have known that he had slipped whole bulbs of garlic into the butcher's sausage grinder; they could not have known that he stole the clothes left on the bank by children swimming in the pond, selling them back to their owners and pocketing the change.

Samantha Sprinkle's experience would be no different.

Our newest teacher sat down while the children made their introductions to her. Quietly Ethan Loring crept up behind her chair and pinned her cushion to her skirt. When the children had finished with their introductions, Henry Stump, in cahoots with Ethan, rose and asked, "Now that we've made our introductions to you, Miss Sprinkle, will you stand and make one to us?"

We children covered our mouths, stifling giggles as Miss Sprinkle rose on her bowed legs to introduce herself. We convulsed with laughter as our teacher waddled before us, a cushion pinned to her broad backside.

Soon Miss Sprinkle's routine became predictable.

The day began with complaints. Miss Sprinkle was boarding with the Tanners, whose meals were among the poorest in town, so our teacher began the morning with belches and complaints about the food there. Celia Tanner looked down as if she was trying to count the planks in the floor.

Those complaints were followed by sighs about the woodpile. Since our school term began the first Monday after Thanksgiving, it was always cold, and a full woodpile was essential. Even after a fire had been built, the stove itself presented problems. It heated unevenly and ineffectively. Each day Miss Sprinkle wailed that the schoolroom was either too hot or too cold or too smoky or too dry.

After the complaining, the sighing, and the wailing, Miss Sprinkle tried but failed to teach. To my mind, learning in Miss Sprinkle's classroom was a drudging round of rote memory, recitation, and practice in penmanship followed by more rote memory, recitation, and practice in penmanship.

Of course, we heard that the district school in Troy owned a globe and slates, but in Millbrook's primary school, we had to share primers that were badly damaged by careless pupils. In one of the primers, Henry Stump had filled in all of the Os with lead-pencil marks. In another, Tommy Brookins's scribblings appeared on the flyleaf:

> If my name you wish to see
> Look on page 103.
>
> If my name you cannot find
> Look on page 109.
>
> If my name you cannot find
> Shut up the book and never mind.

Faith Common, at fourteen, was the oldest pupil in the primary school. Unlike other girls her age, she was not sent to the district school in Troy, for she could not be spared at home. It was ten miles to Troy and back on foot, and her father was away in the West until spring; with Bishop Common away, Faith's mother needed another pair of working hands by her side. I knew that Faith's attendance was conditioned on a promise. Faith could go to school in proportion to the amount of time she devoted to her sewing. Under Miss Sprinkle, Faith's sewing improved more than her learning.

Of course, I was glad whenever Faith did come, for she kept the classroom lively. Faith swore Miss Sprinkle couldn't count past ten, and when I saw our teacher's toes moving under the tips of her shoes when Ethan Loring asked her what five times three was, I finally believed her.

Faith soon discovered that there were spaces between a student's question and a teacher's answer that could inspire chaos.

"Miss Sprinkle," Faith began during one especially dull mathematics lesson, "if you take *e* from the word *hope,* how many letters would be left?"

Miss Sprinkle's eyes held the dull and placid look of cows grazing in the pasture. By the time she'd figured out the answer, the classroom had exploded in a noisy round of hopping. We watched with glee as Miss Sprinkle turned to the corner, blew her nose into her apron, and wiped her eyes with her apron strings.

Afterward, when the girls and I were playing together at indoor recess, sharing the kerchief dolls we had made, Faith approached Sarah Tyler, Betsy Fisher, Vera Cramer, and me. Faith's lips were knotted in thought. "What do you girls think?" she asked us directly. "Do students hate a stupid teacher more than a permissive one?"

Then Faith turned on her heels and skipped away. Over her shoulder she said, "I suppose it doesn't matter. I can always tell when a schoolteacher's about to quit. And Miss Sprinkle can't last much longer."

John Common

I, like the rest of my family, missed my father, and my flute, truth to tell, was a comfort to me. In Father's absence, I often slipped off somewhere to practice. More often, I'd head out to the river and sit on a rock ledge, fingering out tunes. Everything in the world can be described in music. The sloshing sounds of water as the bucket rose from the well. The billowing clothes on the laundry line, running the rapids of wind.

At other times I took comfort in the letters sent by my father. When they arrived, I watched the pulse throbbing in Mother's throat as she read about the hundreds he was introducing to the promise of Methodism. Miss Paula Kincaid, a schoolteacher he had converted, had her piano shipped from Philadelphia to use during his camp meetings. "'I will never forget the sight, Emma,'" Mother read, "'of that piano sitting atop a wagon pulled by oxen and swaying across the plains.'" He was heartened by the simple spirit of the people on the frontier. "'Tell Faith,'" Mother read, "'that a westing woman needs only one plain calico dress and a single sunbonnet. And tell your Dorcas sisters, Emma, dear, about the settlement near Columbus, Ohio. There the women had to share a single darning needle for six months until a peddler finally passed through.'" I saw my mother's chest rise on the harmony of two words: "Emma, dear."

Father's letter reminded me how much we all missed him.

But I, the firstborn son, knew my limitations, and when

Father was gone, they seemed more visible. Charles was stout and smart; Wesley was handy with tools. I was unequal to many a task. One thing I could do, however, that neither of my brothers could, was set Mother at ease. While she prepared a meal with cheap cuts of liver or slit cornhusks for mattresses, I often coaxed sweet music from her voice with my own whistling instrument. At those moments, I am certain, Mother was happy.

Still, like me, Mother could hardly wait until Father returned to us in the spring.

One of Father's most memorable letters arrived from western Pennsylvania just before Christmas. It was bundled in a brown paper package that looked as weary as a traveler arrived from a distance. The enclosed letter said only: "A remembrance, dear family, of my steadfast love for you. Especially at Christmas." The package itself contained separate items wrapped in burlap. They were gifts for us all. We could expect only the smell of evergreens and spices of mulled cider in a year as forlorn as this one had been. Instead we were surprised by separate packages from afar from the father we loved: a sachet of lavender for Mother, a sharpening stone for Grandfather, a compass for Charles, a knife with a pearl handle for Wesley.

Faith examined the wrapping on her gift before she tore off the burlap. First she felt of it. "It's long and thin," she said. "Perhaps it's a ruler."

"Yes," I offered. "A ruler would be handy. You could use it when you worked beside Jacob."

Then she wrinkled her brow, changing her mind. "I know. A new quill!" she said.

As she peeled the burlap from the bundle, Faith was savoring her anticipation. As the cloth fell away, the anticipation turned to disappointment. From beneath the burlap she had pulled out a new pair of scissors dangling from a long black cord.

Mother was delighted. "Look, Faith," she said, pointing to the tips of the scissors. "They are very sharp. That means a fine quality." She pricked the end of her finger on the point.

Faith stubbornly looked away.

"And you can wear them 'round your neck to keep them well in reach," she said, slipping the black cord around my sister's neck. "I will greatly appreciate the help you can give me with these," Mother said, beaming.

My sister's face was ashen. And then suddenly she ran from the room, scattering the rest of the family, once again disturbing their peace.

Mother hesitated, then followed her up the few short stairs to the loft.

"It is important, Faith, to practice tolerance," she said. "To embrace the gift you have been given."

I heard the scowl in Faith's reply. "I will try to *tolerate* this gift, Mother," my sister said. "But I will never *embrace* it!"

Later, I crept up the steps to join my sister. She hadn't heard me come, so absorbed was she in her copybook. When she finally saw me, she had looked at me absently, still engrossed in her thoughts on the page. Then she had asked solemnly, "Do you agree with Mother, John? That you must embrace the things you hate?"

I was silent before her question. My sister had that effect on people.

I seated myself on a corner of her pallet, my own Christmas gift heavy in my hands.

Faith looked up. She put the quill in the inkwell. "Father doesn't *see* me, John. It's like I'm hidden. Do you ever feel that way?"

I couldn't say out loud how I felt. I felt the weight of my

own gift in my hands. Truth to tell, I had feigned pleasure when I opened it. It was a Greek textbook. Father intended for me to start learning Greek. It would aid me when I became a minister one day. Fine sermons, Father believed, were produced by those who understood the New Testament, especially the words of its original Greek.

I did not answer my sister.

But I understood what she meant.

Hetty White

'Twas over tea I often watched dear Emma's dove-soft eyes hovering over a letter from her husband. Emma was tired. 'Twant just her family she cared for, but she performed many kindnesses on behalf of our community. Anna Landis, a spinster who 'twas old like me, had been a lifelong member of Calvin Mercer's church. For years she had lived alone, earning her living by knitting. Now she was too old to do even that. Every winter, dear Emma made certain Miss Landis had a store of firewood.

Evelyn Bruce had followed her husband out to Minnesota with their four daughters, giving birth to twin sons along the way. After that, Mrs. Bruce's husband George had been struck by lightning. After she returned home, her twins had been injured in the fire. 'Twas a marvel at the stories Evelyn could tell when she visited with Emma and me. I'd met nary a woman who could shoot a wild turkey with a bow and knock down beehives without getting stung. But Emma knew Mrs. Bruce needed help. 'Tis a fact that after Emma spoke to Lionel Neely, the Methodist foreman at the mill, Mrs. Bruce got work as a wool sorter.

'Twant nary a day went by that Emma invited me and her son John on her fund-raising visits for Millbrook's new pumper and bell. "If I bring my apple cake and you bring your flute, John, dear," she told the lad, "we can make parting with pennies a bit less painful for everyone."

'Twas good for me to get to town with them now and again. Jacob and Rufus usually tied up the wagon making their deliveries all over the county. In town I could post my letters to Sarah Grimke myself, and I could save Jacob the trouble of collecting our egg money from Biddy Bostick. I could look over the goods on Biddy Bostick's porch, too.

"My, Biddy, but thee has got the best-looking brooms in Millbrook."

"That's for sure, Hetty. Dust runs off of its own accord when they see one of my brooms headin' their way."

Biddy had a gap between her two front teeth through which her laughter escaped.

"Hope you'll be in town in the morning, too, Hetty. I'm expecting some new stock right soon." She winked.

I squeezed Biddy's hand, thankful for the egg money she slipped into my apron pocket. "I'll keep my eye out for it, Biddy," I said.

Watching Emma, I learned 'twas the rich who were the most stingy with their money. When Emma approached Amelia Campbell on Water Street, Mrs. Campbell had a heavy parcel in one hand and her daughter Bettina in the other. Mrs. Campbell was heading to her carriage at the curb where her driver was holding the reins.

"Excuse me, Amelia," Emma said. Then she began her well-practiced pleas, emphasizing the importance of the new fire pumper and bell to the security of Millbrook. 'Twas I who caught her boy shuddering as his mother recalled the sounds of the fire.

Mrs. Campbell fumbled with her package as she listened. 'Twas sure the package contained something expensive. While Mrs. Campbell thrust her package first under one arm and then under the other, avoiding a contribution, Bettina skipped beside John. She had spied his flute.

"I quite understand, Amelia, dear. Perhaps you'll be able to contribute at a later time."

'Twas the lad who then lifted his flute to his lips and whistled out an air. Bettina clapped her chubby hands and grinned. Suddenly Mrs. Campbell reached into her purse for some change. She pressed it into Emma's palm.

'Twas hard to watch Emma's shoulders sagging under the weight of constant work, and I wondered if caring for thy own child could cause any more worry than caring for someone whom thee loved like one.

Emma Common

I remember the day most clearly. It was one of those rare January days when the sun shines as brightly as it does in June. We were about to cross Exchange Street when Faith yanked off her bonnet. Then she lifted her forehead to the noon sun.

"Faith, dear," I corrected her gently. "Your bonnet."

The golds and reds and coppers of her hair glistened in the winter sunlight. I tried to concentrate on the beautiful colors. Not on the twisted strands. In her brown eyes was a familiar fierceness. It appeared whenever she asked a sharp question. "Why, Mother? Why must I wear this wretched bonnet? It keeps me from *feeling* things. The sun on my cheeks. The wind on my neck."

I frowned. Mildly, I hope. My stubborn daughter still

had many things to learn: to stay on the narrow path, to sew with devotion, to bear with a bonnet.

As I lifted my skirts before the slush of the winter street, I admitted how tired I was. Daily I prayed for God to restore my energy and my flagging spirit. I seemed to find solace only in my son's music.

I paused for a moment to gaze up at the sign of the store that came next: Albert Biggs's Domestic Staples and Dry Goods Store. With relief, I stepped inside. Here was a welcome diversion from my anxieties about John's absence, Faith's boldness, my father's stubbornness, and Amanda Putnam's impertinence. Whenever I entered Albert Biggs's store, I violated the tenth commandment: *Thou shalt not covet,* saith the Lord. Here were displayed the bolts of cloth that arrived daily from Worcester and Lowell and Boston. Here were the calicos and muslins, the silks and taffetas that I tried, unsuccessfully, not to desire. Here in the window display was the handiwork that flowed from the fingers of my own friends: Kate Loring's embroidered infant caps; Esther Grimes's fine tablecloths; and Rebecca Kinder's collars, which revived the spirits of women who could not afford an entire dress.

Inside the store I was greeted by the mingled odors of vinegar, wood shavings, barley seed. Albert Biggs himself, straightening goods behind his counter, nodded as I moved down the makeshift aisles to the dry-goods section in the back. Lemuel Cooper and Samuel Endicott, friends and former congregants of my father, sat on stools playing checkers in the middle of the store.

I saw piles of crisp white shirts, stitched by the many seamstresses making their living in and around Millbrook. Displayed on dressmaker's forms in each of the corners of the dry-goods section were shirts. I didn't need to see Phoebe

Hungerford's monogram on the tail of a shirt to recognize the crisp pointed collars and the neatly tucked bodices as hers.

Faith and I dug into a variety of baskets for a dozen needles at a good price. I looked through the notions. Finally, Faith held up the packet that we needed. Together we proceeded to the front counter.

A young man had stepped up to the counter ahead of us.

In his arms he held a few shirts, neatly folded and pressed. The white shirts gleamed against his strong arms, brown with a laborer's tan.

"I've come with me m-m-mither's shirts, Mr. Biggs, sir."

Once he spoke, I recognized the young man: Phoebe Hungerford's son Sean.

Now Mr. Biggs acknowledged Faith and me. "You're a good customer, Mrs. Common. I apologize for the delay. Let the girl help herself to a lemon drop from the barrel there," Albert Biggs said. "I'll just be a minute. Perhaps a candy will sweeten your daughter's wait."

"Thank you, sir. How kind of you!" I tried to suppress a shiver of pride at his recognition of my value as a customer.

Faith dived into the barrel of sweets, picking out the largest one she could find, popping it into her mouth.

Meanwhile Sean laid the snow white shirts on the counter. "It's s-s-seventeen cents a shirt, sir," the boy stuttered, "but they're b-b-beauties, and I'm asking again if you'll give eighteen."

I knew Phoebe's shirts were worth far more than a mere seventeen cents.

Albert Biggs's heavy hands riffled through the shirts. His eyes squinted over them. "I'll give only a nickel for a shirt like this one here," he said, holding up a shirt that looked flawless to me. "It's careless work. Look at this loose thread."

Albert Biggs scowled. The Irish boy hung his head.

Suddenly Faith stepped up to the counter. Her chin was thrust forward, a sign that meant trouble. I pressed my hand against Faith's arm, restraining her. She shrugged it off.

Then I witnessed what I never in my life would have believed. Faith placed her fingers at her collar and began to pull something forth from around her neck. How surprised I was to recognize the black cord and scissors of her father's gift!

"Ah, that's easily fixed," my blunt daughter said.

Then Faith inserted her fingers into the loops of the scissors, pulled the shirt from Albert Biggs's hands, and snipped at the offending thread.

"There, Mr. Biggs," she said. "Completely mended." She grinned over at Sean Hungerford.

Albert Biggs scowled at Faith. I could hear stool legs dragging across the wood floor. The sound meant Lem Cooper and Sam Endicott were moving forward to listen.

I was shocked by my daughter's boldness. At the same time, I was pleased by her use of her scissors.

Then the Irish boy, recognition dawning, turned to Faith, beaming broadly at her.

Faith nodded while Albert Biggs fussed over the shirts. "All right," Mr. Biggs conceded. "That's two I'll take today," he said, rejecting the rest of the pile. He bustled about, adding up what he owed. "That's thirty-two cents, young man. Twice seventeen," Mr. Biggs announced. "Here's your money, boy," he said, counting out the change into Sean's huge palm.

"Excuse me, Mr. Biggs," Faith said, interrupting the transaction. "Shouldn't you add it up again? Two shirts at seventeen cents each. Isn't that thirty-*four* cents for the both?"

62

I caught the blank look behind the Irish boy's eyes.

Mr. Biggs was not just annoyed; he was outraged. The veins on his neck bulged. The whites of his eyes swelled like eggs as they begin to cook. "See here, missy. They always said Calvin Mercer's granddaughter was stiff-necked. And now I know it for myself."

"See here *yourself,* Mr. Biggs," Faith retorted. "I think you've made a mistake in your ciphering."

I winced at Faith's conduct. Out of the corner of my eye, I could see Mr. Cooper and Mr. Endicott nodding in agreement about the character of Calvin Mercer's granddaughter.

"Faith," I insisted, desperate to rein her in. "A proper lady does not insert herself into business dealings."

"This isn't a *business dealing,* Mother," she insisted. "This is a *swindle.*"

She stood stubbornly at the counter, crossing her arms across her chest, sucking loudly on her lemon drop.

Albert Biggs glared at Faith as he recounted the change. The top of his head was as bald as my darning egg.

The Irish boy turned away, red-faced but grateful. He gripped the coins in his giant fist. Faith followed him merrily out into the street.

Quickly I laid my needles on the counter, eager to have my transaction completed. I unknotted the handkerchief in which I had wrapped my coins and laid the proper amount across the counter. "I apologize for my daughter's behavior," I said briskly. Then I headed awkwardly out the door, hoping I hadn't looked as flustered as I felt.

Across the street Faith conversed with Biddy Bostick. The Irish boy had disappeared. Faith had slipped her bonnet into her apron pocket. Her head was thrown back, the red strands snarled like twisted thread. She was laughing with

Biddy, likely recounting the scene in Albert Biggs's store. As I approached, I watched my daughter poise her tongue behind the lemon drop in her mouth and thrust it wildly into the street. Then she and Biddy Bostick clapped their hands together, laughing with delight. Faith doubled over in merriment, her scissors swinging madly from the cord at her neck.

As I crossed to join her, I wished more than ever that John would hurry home.

Amanda Putnam

I'd made the introductions all around. "Ladies, meet our special visitor, Miss Mary Lyon. She's come all the way from South Hadley in this dreadful cold. I imagine she feels as dented as a steamer trunk!"

Frankly, I was annoyed. Not one of my friends had looked up from her stitching until Miss Lyon herself began to speak.

"Mrs. Putnam tells me, ladies," Miss Lyon said in that quiet but firm manner she had, "that you've a need for decent teachers here in Millbrook. I'm hoping that once I graduate some talented girls from my college, you'll have a surplus of qualified teachers from which to choose."

That was when the ladies of the Dorcas Circle looked up. They had never before heard the word *college* linked with *girls*.

"Yes, that's right, ladies," Miss Lyon continued, "a college." She seemed unfazed by her audience's astonishment. "Most people are surprised by my plan, but I opened my college this November past. And dear Amanda here was on hand with her Lucy to witness the merry confusion. My school has been a long time in the making. But it is a college for young women. I'm calling it Mount Holyoke Female Seminary. I'm hoping you ladies will see fit to make a contribution."

Then she held open her green velvet purse and smiled.

While the ladies hesitated over her request, I stepped in quickly. I explained that women from tiny towns all over Massachusetts, towns like Ipswich and Shelburne, towns just like Millbrook, had put gifts of two or three pennies at a time into that very green bag. I informed them that over the years Miss Lyon had collected thousands of pennies, enough for the opening just last November.

The Dorcas sisters looked too astonished to speak.

When they did speak, it was with skepticism.

Marguerite Gordon said she thought Miss Lyon's plan was frivolous. "A girl's best education for the world is a knowledge of her domestic duties," Marguerite declared.

Kate Loring remarked that book learning was unbecoming in a female. "It leads to crossed eyes and spectacles. It frightens off any decent marriage prospects."

"Besides," said Miranda Callendar, "men are clearly superior in reasoning, Miss Lyon. Their province is the head," she observed.

"Of course, Mother," agreed Miranda's daughter Amy. "And women are superior in tenderness."

"Devotion," said Mildred Tyler's Sarah.

"Sensitivity," said Helen Cramer's daughter Vera.

"Thank heavens we are *not* like the men, ladies," Emma Common said. "A woman's province is the heart, and she does not need schooling to remind her of this."

Emma Common usually spoke for the group. She was their quiet leader, and I could not allow her to have the last word.

As I turned in Emma's direction, I concentrated on my eyebrow. The left one. I understood the power of its arch.

"Perhaps, Emma," I said as sweetly as I could, "a woman's province is the heart because of necessity, not destiny. Isn't it possible that women must nurture relationships because we are totally dependent on them for survival?"

Emma Common squirmed in her chair. She was agitated by heated discussions and difficult questions.

Miss Lyon had been listening quietly, sipping her tea. "Dear ladies," she said calmly, "the only kind of survival I'm hoping for is the survival of my school. I'm trusting people to be attracted to its possibilities. I intend my school to be different, ladies. My girls will study chemistry and Greek and Latin. I plan to challenge their minds with physiology, rhetoric, astronomy, and logic. I believe young ladies are capable of learning every bit as much as a man."

Rebecca Kinder harrumphed, "Well, if you ask me, the rich can *always* afford more education for their daughters if they wish. Those so-called seminaries give their daughters silk embroidery and French in exchange for a hefty sum. The wealthy can buy a girl any kind of adornment that they want."

Miss Lyon set her teacup pointedly down. "An adornment, Mrs. Kinder," she said firmly, "is not the same as an education."

There was another awkward silence while the ladies busied themselves in their workbaskets.

Miss Lyon waited quietly. Then she said, "But my focus is not on the wealthy girl, ladies. I'm opening my school to poorer girls and girls of the middling classes. The girls will live plainly. I will require them to work in the laundry and the pie room. They will not shirk domestic learning. I'm interested in devoting my school to the more common young lady. Who has few advantages. But who has an interest in learning."

Frankly, it was time for me to step in again. I opened

the thick printed circular Miss Lyon had distributed all over Massachusetts. It had been written and printed by Miss Lyon herself. It stated that her college still needed furniture and bedding for dormitory rooms.

I passed the circular around the room. The ladies eyed it suspiciously.

When Miss Lyon rose to leave, she held out her green purse. A few pennies were tossed into it; they clinked together in the bottom of the bag. "Thank you, dear ladies," Miss Lyon declared. "Your contribution will mean the world to your daughters. I am doing a great work," she explained, turning to the door, "on behalf of them." At the door I slipped some extra coins into Miss Lyon's bag.

Mary Lyon departed as quickly as she had arrived. Immediately my Dorcas friends raised objections.

Kate Loring said, "It's improper for a woman like Miss Lyon to travel about the countryside unescorted."

Miranda Callendar added, "It's scandalous for a woman to solicit money from strangers like a common peddler."

"Frankly, ladies," I said, indifferent to their complaints, "I plan to enroll my Lucy at Miss Lyon's seminary in the fall. She's entitled to a common sense education. And that's that."

"But, Mother," I heard Lucy protest. "I don't *want* to go to Miss Lyon's school! What about a school like Miss Tisdale's? It's not nearly as far away, and she teaches both plain and ornamental needlework, and both formal and informal curtseying!"

Frankly, I sometimes think my Lucy is a ninny. And I was grateful for the presence of Faith Common. The girl jumped from her chair. "Yes, Lucy, isn't that one of those silly schools that teaches girls never to walk in a straight line but to move only across a room in curves, like figure eights?"

Faith jumped from her chair, lifted her skirts, and

swept around the room making figure eights. Emma Common frowned in her daughter's direction. Faith ignored her, and soon the other girls joined in, jumping from their seats, lifting their skirts, and prancing riotously around the room in curves.

Watching them, Emma Common's face turned serious. She put down her needle, turned to me, and whispered hoarsely, "But, Amanda, dear, if a girl traipses off to college, who will help her mother bake the pies?"

Celia Tanner

I'll confess it: folks couldn't know how lonesome it was without Mama. I escaped on long rambles in the woods more and more. I came to know the tall masts of the sourwoods and the tiny bells of the lilies of the valley. Once I learned to tell ragwort from motherwort and the roots of blue cohosh from horseradish, I came to make a collection. I had twenty-seven different petals and leaves and seeds so far and nine yet to label.

I came often to the woods that lined the river. I liked hiding behind the trees and listening to the sweet sound of music. Whenever I followed the sound, I discovered John Common sitting on a wide flat rock overlooking the river, his knees folded Indian style. He never sees me, but I listen to his flute playing from a distance. When spring arrives, his music comes all in a rush, just like the ice breaking up. In summer the notes trip like the brook spilling over rocks. The breathy sounds of John's piping reminded me of Mama's lullabies.

The way John's sister, Faith, treated me in school was soothing, too. What Faith did that winter helped me to lift my head straight up in public.

It was never easy getting to school. Pop was never

much for it, but I'd promised Mama, and because Miss Sprinkle boarded with us, I always had a ready reason for being there.

We'd killed our only pig when we heard Miss Sprinkle would be boarding with us, and it had been the only meat we'd had all year. Still Samantha Sprinkle complained about it right enough.

When the pupils filed in of a morning, Miss Sprinkle started up. She'd make a fist and press it to her mouth. She'd give a long wet burp. "Oh, my aching belly," she'd wail. "Pork, pork, pork. I'm just sick to death of it. If I have to eat another mouthful of pork, I am going to *die!*"

I looked down then, fingering the dirty cloth into which I had tossed a few scraps for my own lunch. Six hundred fifty-five. Six hundred fifty-six.

I confess it: the primary schoolroom's nothing to look at. The ceiling plaster's cracked. Stools pass for desks, and bending to write's a strain on the back. One window's been repaired with a scarf tacked over the broken pane, and a few ragged pictures and maps try to hide where the wall's been grimed by smoke.

But then the teacher's not much to brag on, either.

I can't say I was sorry to see Miss Sprinkle leave Millbrook. But the way she went allowed me to hold up my head for a spell. It wouldn't have happened like that without Faith.

When January arrived it was the most bitter month in recent memory. Hot tea cracked china cups. Pie dough froze on the board. Miss Sprinkle's students spent their days shivering instead of studying. Many stayed away altogether.

Still, in spite of the cold, the boys still found the energy to test Miss Sprinkle. First, Ethan Loring lured her outside. He said he wanted to introduce her to a traveling salesman from Sturbridge with an offer for cheap blackboards.

"Help me, Celia," Faith said, throwing on her coat and following the teacher outside into the snow.

Quickly Ethan signaled to the boys inside, and from the snow-banked road, Faith and I could see the younger boys scurrying across the schoolroom, bolting the doors and sealing the windows against our return. Then Ethan streaked off, hooting and jeering at our sputtering teacher.

Miss Sprinkle ran on her thick ankles to the schoolroom door and set to pounding on it.

Faith pulled her cloak tightly about her chest. "Celia," she said, heading for the porch, "help me."

My jaw dropped as I watched Faith climb onto the rickety porch railing and shinny up to the porch roof. Standing on the eaves of the roof, Faith called down to me. "Hand me one of those falling clapboards, Celia. Quickly, now."

I gripped firmly and pulled hard. The clapboard gave easylike, and I handed it up to Faith.

I confess it was a jaw dropper to watch: Faith climbed higher, avoiding the patches of ice on the roof, finally placing the clapboard firmly over the open chimney.

It took only ten minutes to smoke them out. They came pouring from the front door, hatless, mittenless. Henry Stump. Tommy Brookins and Nate Tucker. All the girls and Faith's brothers. The girls were sputtering and angry. The boys were coughing pledges of future good behavior.

Miss Sprinkle, her hot tears glistening in the frozen air, said she was quitting right then on the spot.

"Do what you want, Miss Sprinkle," Faith declared, shrugging her shoulders. Then her voice turned fierce: "But if you quit, don't you *dare* blame it on Tanners' pork!"

Somehow I could feel my head lifting. Just a tad.

PART THREE

Winter–Spring, 1838

John Common

Faith had always hated Amos Read. She had never made any bones about it. Truth to tell, I had always kept what I thought about him to myself.

Now, without a teacher for the primary school, I saw a great deal more of Amos Read. Mother worried about her sons' lack of progress in school. Anticipating the arrival of my father in the spring, Mother employed Amos for extra hours of tutoring for my brothers and me.

"But why should *my* pennies go to help my *brothers* learn?"

"Because you will learning with me, dear. While they are studying things proper to a man, you will be studying things proper to a woman. You will learn to season a new brass pot with salt and to recognize a poor fish by a thin tail."

"But I don't *want* to learn about fish tails, Mother!" she shrieked.

When it came to the wishes of my father, my pliant mother could be as hard as stone. Calmly Mother replied, "Sour beer is only good in pancakes, Faith."

When Amos Read arrived for tutoring, Faith often managed to participate in a quiet, secret way. Sometimes she pulled a chair within hearing distance, shelling beans or darning socks within earshot.

Charles was the best student among us, but Wesley and I only half listened to Amos Read. Usually I polished my flute during the lesson, and Wesley absently whittled a stick. Charles was the only one who bent his head over Amos's open texts, usually a Greek or geometry book. Charles often paid attention solely for the delight of poking holes in his teacher's arguments.

"What's a quadrilateral?" Amos asked when the lesson for the day was geometry.

No one spoke. I could tell my sister might have known the answer by the way she bit her lower lip and dipped her neck more deeply over her sampler. She was stitching a motto picked out by my mother:

There's nothing near at hand or farthest sought
But with the needle may be shaped and wrought.

Impatient, Amos repeated his question. "What's a quadrilateral?"

There was a haughty tone to Amos's voice. It suggested he'd be just as pleased if his pupils *didn't* answer; then he could swell up on the hot air of his own superiority.

I watched as Faith raised her eyes from her lap. "Quadrilaterals are figures with four sides and four angles," she announced sharply. Then she bent to her stitching again.

Amos's pale blue eyes narrowed. "Well, yes," he agreed. "But can anyone give me an *example* of a quadrilateral?" He pointedly ignored Faith. He directed his question to my brothers and me.

The room was silent. Even Wesley stopped scraping his knife across his stick.

"They're squares like table napkins. Or rectangles like our vegetable plot. Jacob White taught me all about quadrilaterals in his workshop. A coffin, for instance, is a quadrilateral."

Now Amos Read's eyes glared openly at Faith. He had received the right answer from the wrong student.

"I am paid to see that your *brothers* receive a fitting education, Miss Common," Amos said. "*Your* interruptions are not welcome."

"Nor are your insults, Amos," she barked. "Especially when it is *my* pennies that allow *you* to sit here and give them."

Then she pushed up from her chair, threw down her sampler, and flew out of the room, her thread unraveling behind her across the floor.

I missed her presence, for Amos now turned to the Greek lesson, using the book my father had sent me as a gift. Although it was a simple beginner's version, with the Greek text on the right-hand page and its translation on the left, I was confused and frustrated. The letters swam before my eyes.

After our lesson, I escaped with my flute to the rock ledge above the river. Of late, I had become frustrated with the music it created. A flute was sprightly, antic. The music I now heard inside me was plaintive, melancholy.

Sometimes I heard a rustling in the trees around me as I played, and I imagined rabbits and frogs attending my concert, perched on stumps to listen.

But I discovered instead that my concert had been attended only by a listener of one, a human listener. She had given herself away when she fell from a stump as she reached for a twig of hackberry.

"Celia Tanner!" I said, astonished. "What are you doing here?"

She stood up and brushed herself off. Then she opened a box on the ground beside the stump and placed the twig carefully inside.

She seemed to steady herself by looking around at the branches of trees. Almost as if she were counting them. "I just come to the woods whenever I can," she said.

"I do, too." I was afraid of talking too much, of frightening Celia away.

Celia looked at me and took a breath. "When it's quiet, I can finally hear the sound of my own thoughts."

I nodded.

"We don't have music in our house." She pulled at a thread in her dirty dress. "At least not anymore. Pop has a fiddle. He hasn't picked it up for years."

It was only when Celia turned to go that I realized I didn't want her to. I tried to think of a way to delay her. "What's that?" I asked, pointing to the box at her feet.

"Oh, that's just my collection." She shrugged.

"Can I see it?"

She bent down slowly and picked up the crude metal handle of the battered wooden box. I could hear dead leaves crunching under her feet as she moved closer and passed it to me. "You can open it if you want."

I opened it carefully and peered inside. I saw assortments of vials and bottles, packets of leaves and berries, bundles of twigs tied up neatly with string.

"What's that, Celia?" I said, pointing to a stalk that had flowers like a paintbrush on its tip.

"That's plantain."

"And this one?"

"That's ragwort."

"And this?"

"Comfrey."

"How can you tell, Celia?"

"Well, ragwort has those small, daisylike flowers. Comfrey flowers look like bells."

I was astonished by her ability to remember such details. My mind always drifted away when it came to details.

"Can I tell Faith about your specimen box?"

"My *what*?"

"Your *specimen* box."

She turned away from me now, as if she were ashamed, not proud, of her collection.

"Celia, those things you've collected. They're specimens. You're doing exactly what scientists do who collect things from nature. Naturalists, they're called. The things they collect are called specimens."

I caught the tiny smile flickering across her lips.

"Can I tell Faith about your specimen box, Celia? Faith is curious about everything in the world."

Celia shrugged. "I guess so. Besides, she's like to find out anyway. Faith's powerful nosy."

When she grinned shyly, I saw the way one front tooth slipped crookedly over the other. It made me want to help her. I grinned back, agreeing. "What got you interested in these specimens, Celia?"

"There's uses for all these things, John. I can use my collection for doctoring. Rufus and Hetty White still order my lard and arnica salve, and Grandma Birdie can get awful sick."

"And how do you doctor your grandma, Celia?"

"Well, for boils I use a tincture of burdock root. Grandma gets boils from lying in bed too long." She pointed to a vial filled with a hairy root. "But mostly Grandma Birdie has trouble with her heart."

"What's wrong with her heart, Celia?"

"It races, John. Her heart just seizes up and beats real fast like a hummingbird's wings. When that happens, I dose her with a potion from the flowers and roots of peony. Some days she takes as many as thirty drops."

Suddenly she returned to her specimen box. "You got anything that needs a salve, John?" she asked me. "A sore or hurt somewhere?"

I don't know why I said it, but it slipped out easily in her presence. "Only on the inside."

Celia looked straight at me then. Her pupils narrowed and focused: like our cat when he smelled cheese. "Don't have any salve for that, John. Still trying to find it. Mama called it 'heartsease.' When Mama left, she said she'd gone searching for it. I reckon I'm still trying to find it for her." She bit her lower lip with her teeth. "And for you, too, John Common."

I couldn't see the crookedness now. Her teeth were hiding behind her lips.

"*Me?*"

Celia nodded. "You could use some heartsease, too."

I was puzzled. "How do you know, Celia?"

"I can hear it, John. I can hear it in your music."

Ellen Gordon

I was surprised that a new schoolteacher had been found to finish out the winter term. In fact, I was overjoyed. With a schoolteacher in place, I could be out from under Mama's watchful eye for several hours each day. On the teacher's very first day, I wore a new collar I had embroidered with sheaves of wheat.

Ethan Loring mistakenly assumed that any new teacher would be a dupe for his tricks. But on the master's very first day, Ethan learned that this master was different.

Ethan had begun a commotion among the girls by teasing Liddie Martin. He stole her bonnet, tossing it over her head into the greedy hands of his comrades.

"Come here, Mr. Loring," the new teacher insisted.

Grinning, Ethan had skipped over to the new master.

"I see that you admire Miss Martin's hat, Ethan."

Ethan had nodded, gloating with the boys who had been his partners in crime.

"Well, then," the new teacher said. "I believe you should keep it. I do believe Liddie's bonnet should be yours."

The children looked astonished. The girls protested on Liddie's behalf.

The master wagged a finger at Tommy Brookins, who was clasping the bonnet in his grimy fingers. Tommy gave up the bonnet to him.

Then the new teacher began to pass the bonnet into the hands of Ethan Loring. Ethan's greedy hands opened wide to receive it.

"One thing, Ethan," the teacher then said, snatching back Ethan's booty when it was just out of the boy's grasp. "The condition," said the new teacher, "is that you wear the bonnet all day." Quickly the master clapped the bonnet over Ethan's bewildered head and yanked the strings tight.

I watched admiringly. All of the children giggled and pointed at the crimson face of Ethan Loring. The new master had certainly set the troublemaker to rights.

Then the new master quickly added, "After all, everyone knows you're a mama's boy, Ethan. You may as well dress like one."

The pupils drew a collective breath. The boys seemed especially astonished by the daring of their master. Perhaps they were afraid. After all, there were a few other "mama's boys" in the classroom besides Ethan Loring. Henry Stump, for one. Tommy Brookins. Maybe even John Common. But then the boys quickly recovered, slapping one another on shoulders and backs, doubling over, shaking with uncontrollable laughter.

Red-faced and ashamed, Ethan Loring was never much trouble after that.

Like the other children, I was impressed by the new master. Unlike Miss Sprinkle, the master *did* govern the classroom. He set Henry Stump to hammering nails to the walls for coat hooks; now the children could not jump into the piles of coats as if they were feather beds. He persuaded Charles and Wesley Common to carry an old dented pew all the way from the basement of the Congregational church to use as both seat and table for the schoolroom; now at least a few pupils at a time could avoid sitting on stools, balancing work in their laps. He enlisted John Common to entertain the children on his flute when it was too chilly for recess outside. To keep the hearth clean and safe without any effort on his part, the new master developed a system of rotation for putting out sparks from the stove. Anyone who jumped up out of turn or stomped out the sparks without sweeping them away lost recess privileges.

I was in awe of our new master's ability to control our unruly classroom, and I was in awe of the teacher himself. He was tall and fair with blue eyes that sparkled behind a pair of spectacles. With the handsome new master in charge, it would matter what I wore to school again. Yet I was also surprised: I hadn't expected the kind of competence that came from our new teacher, the master named Amos Read.

John Common

Now and again Celia Tanner visited me out by the river.

Often I didn't say anything. I knew that the best way to encourage Celia Tanner to talk was to keep quiet.

When she bent down to open her collection box one afternoon, she dipped out a muddy mixture of something I had never seen before and placed it in my palm.

I shrank back: Celia's potion was gritty and gray and uninviting.

"I was hoping this potion might work on Pop," she said. "Until I could find some heartsease."

The potion felt damp and clammy in my hand.

"It's a combination of these three things," she said, pulling specimens out of her box and passing them to me. "It's a dab of wine," she said, holding up a vial, "and a lot of dandelion fluff," she said, bringing forth a seed package. "Plus some drops of whiskey."

Then she grinned her slip-toothed grin, and as she handed me the vial of whiskey, it slipped from my hand. The glass vial broke against the rock ledge. The smell of sour oak casks drifted under my nose. "Oh, Celia, I'm sorry," I said, cursing my clumsiness.

"Oh, John, *look*!" Celia said, pointing to the rocky ledge on which the whiskey had spilled. "The whiskey's melting the ice!"

I looked down at the silver crystals forming on the ice as it melted.

"But it's still wasted," I said. "You've no more whiskey in your collection now."

Celia grinned. "I've no trouble replacing whiskey in the house *I* live in, John Common."

The lazy tooth drifted over the sturdy one, reminding me of the slipped stitches in my sister's sampler.

"Besides, my potion didn't work," Celia said, opening her palm so I could return the lumpy and lifeless substance to her.

"I put some of this stuff in my pop's potatoes. He never noticed. Gobbled it right down. Didn't change him a lick."

I winced. It was hard for me to imagine anyone eating such stuff.

"I was trying to invent a potion to help him. If one of my potions can help Grandma with her heart, maybe I could invent something to help Pop. To help him with his drinking. Only my potion didn't work, John. Maybe it *is* true: there's no salve for hurts inside."

When Celia looked at me then, her teeth had disappeared behind her sober mouth.

Ellen Gordon

Although I was pleased that the new master managed to govern the classroom, I came to recognize that his was a government of manipulation and tyranny.

Under our new master, the atmosphere in the schoolroom made me uneasy, for Miss Sprinkle's short-term replacement developed a strategy for ruling his pupils: he made use of their weaknesses. He quickly learned that Ethan Loring was famous for trickery. He learned that Celia Tanner was ashamed of the moldy ends of bread that passed for lunch and that Liddie Martin was proud of the doughnuts and gingerbread she dined on at noon. He learned that the Lukens brothers were poor by the cut of their pants. They passed trousers through their family, and when Michael's pants got too short on him, the same pants were worn too long by his brother Marvin. He learned that Henry Stump was a follower, easily duped. He used this knowledge to establish order through the tyranny of shame.

Escaping from under Mama's watchful eye was not as pleasant as it had once been. In fact, I was shocked at the way the master treated the lumbering lad with the shock of red hair who appeared one morning at the schoolroom door.

His name was Sean Hungerford. I'd never seen him before. Mama never allowed me on the west end of town. "I've c-c-come . . . ," he said haltingly, leaning on first one big foot and then the other, ". . . to learn my s-s-sums."

A smirk crept up the master's face. "Oh, you have, have you?"

The master looked around at the boys who served as his lords-in-waiting, inviting their participation in his taunting of the Irish boy. "But *everyone knows* that the Irish can't learn, boy," he said. "At least that's what everybody says in town. Isn't that right, fellows?"

To my mind, the boys behaved like pups, wagging their heads in agreement. Sean's cheeks turned red as the locks that fell down his collar and across his forehead.

John Common stood awkwardly apart from the other boys, fidgeting with the sleeve of his shirt.

"I doubt, boy," the master offered, "that you'll prove them liars."

The master grinned. The other boys sniggered.

I watched as Sean slowly turned to leave. He moved his feet with great difficulty. As if his boots had been filled with lead weights.

Suddenly the Irish boy recognized Faith Common. He blinked, blinded like someone coming from a dark room into sharp light. Even from a distance I could see that the boy's eyes were gray blue, ragged at the edges like fingers of sky gathering a storm. Inside, my heart suddenly felt sore.

"I don't know what they say in town about the Irish," Faith said, stepping up to the master's desk. "But I do know that the Irish know how to work. They have strong backs, and you, master, have a woodpile in need of order."

The master raised his eyebrows.

Sean Hungerford turned disbelieving eyes on Faith.

"I'd be g-g-grateful, master, for the chance to h-h-help with the woodpile," Sean stammered.

The boys in the schoolroom sighed with relief. It was obvious that the strapping lad was up to the backbreaking work of the woodpile. But in the frame that towered over him and the muscles that powered the frame, our new master recognized something that alarmed him: the Irish boy's superior strength. The new master would need to keep this brawny lad in his place.

"You can s-s-stay if you keep the woodpile, boy," the master said, mimicking Sean. "But you'll have to s-s-sit with the girls for your lessons."

While the boys tittered and the girls looked sheepish, Sean Hungerford looked surprisingly pleased, but I was angry.

I recalled the question Faith Common asked when she'd become disgusted with Miss Sprinkle. About whether a stupid teacher was worse than a permissive one. At the time I hadn't been sure how to answer. But now, under this new master, I was sure of one thing: I would have preferred either a stupid or a lax teacher to a cruel one.

Celia Tanner

I was happy to return to school. Grandma Birdie had been sick for weeks, and she had no one but me to care for her.

The middle of March was almost as cold as January had been. Cows huddled together in the barn. Horse blankets were thrown over pump handles.

I'd hoped to slip into the classroom. Quietlike. Without the new master noticing. I confess it: I was never one to bring attention to myself.

As I peeked around the schoolroom door, I saw the master grumbling over the pens and setting copy for the day.

Suddenly the master looked up. Just as I was slipping in the door.

"Miss Tanner, I believe?" the master said. "Miss *Tardy* Tanner?"

I nodded and ducked my head. I felt frozen as ice.

"Although I couldn't be sure, now, could I?" he asked. I heard the scoff in his voice. "I hardly recognized you. After all, you've been shirking your studies for three weeks now, isn't that right?"

I began counting the tops of the heads of the pupils in the room. Tommy Brookins. Eliza Loomis. Liddie Martin. That's three. Four, five, six. That's Ethan Loring, Ellen Gordon, and Faith Common.

"Answer me, girl," the master commanded, rapping his ruler on the table. The sound reminded me of Pop when he picked up a hammer or an iron bar. I confess it confused me. I shook my head up and down and then side to side. I didn't know what I was doing. Seven, eight, nine, ten, eleven.

"See here, now, Amos Read," a voice said. "She's been caring for her grandmother. And she's no trouble as a student. Celia Tanner's smart as a whip."

I recognized the voice as Faith Common's.

The master glared at Faith. "Well, Miss Common, I'm afraid your friend Miss Tardy Tanner cannot stay today." The master's voice had turned from scoffing to sneering. "I've already got more pupils than I can manage. I couldn't possibly take on one more. Besides, it's so cold the ink's frozen in the wells. We can't even enjoy the wretchedness of penmanship practice," he grumbled.

The master then turned his back and returned to his work.

I confess I didn't hear much of anything after that. I was busy counting. I'd finishing counting the twenty-seven children in the room. Now I turned to the logs in the wall. Seventeen. Eighteen.

I turned to go.

Then I heard Faith speak up again. "Excuse me, Master Read," she said. "But Celia's brought you something special."

I confess I was confused. I didn't know what Faith meant.

Then she pointed to the box I gripped in my hand.

"Celia's brought her specimen case," Faith declared.

I felt embarrassed when she called my battered box a "specimen case." In front of everyone.

I looked down. I recognized the hand clutching the metal handle of the box as belonging to me.

The master looked interested.

"In fact, Master Read," Faith said respectful-like. She had moved beside me and was peeling my frozen fingers from around the metal handle. "Celia Tanner's a gifted naturalist. A botanist. She knows every leaf and flower in the woods. And she catalogues them like an expert."

I could feel my cheeks glowing red as Faith began to lift my vials and envelopes from the collection box. I confess I couldn't tell if the red glow came from embarrassment or pride.

The children gathered around as Faith named the plants and herbs.

"Oh, yes," Faith said, explaining about the collection to the children while she searched. "This is pennyroyal," she said. "And that's hawthorn."

Then Faith stopped talking and began to root around in my collection as if she was looking for something.

The master was growing impatient. He was tapping his foot.

Finally she found what she'd been looking for. "And *this*," Faith said, "is the solution to your frozen ink, sir."

Faith held up the vial of whiskey. Then she quickly turned and called over to her brother John. "My brother's the one, Master Read, who can solve the problem with your ink."

I stopped counting and concentrated on John. He stared at his sister, dumbfounded by the remark.

"This was John's discovery," she babbled. "Out by the river." While she talked, John moved closer, ducking his head like he often did so he wouldn't be noticed.

Faith held the vial of whiskey high. Then she passed the vial to her brother.

John shyly opened the glass vial and tapped a few drops of brown liquid into one of the inkwells. Master Reed moved closer, peering down his nose into the well.

"See," said Faith, "the ink's already beginning to thaw. Ink freezes up when it's cold, master," she said. "If you put some whiskey in, the ink won't freeze."

"*Whiskey,* did you say?" asked Master Read.

"Well, it's just a few drops, sir."

Then I heard Faith Common say that Miss Tanner could teach the master's students about nature. Then after that she said that Miss Tanner could help his pupils make specimen boxes of their own in the soon-to-be spring weather.

After that, I stopped counting. I had finally heard Master Read give in. I could stay.

Later, after school, John told me that the best way to deal with the master was to make myself of use to him. I followed his advice. With my specimen box in hand, I confess that making myself of use wasn't difficult, for many of Master Read's pupils came to school sick or tired or bruised or scratched. One morning when Arnold Smith appeared with a toothache, I fished a bud of clove from my specimen kit; sucking on it eased Arnold's tooth pain. When Nate Tucker fell in the yard, scraping the flesh from his knee, I reached for some ergot to stop the bleeding.

I confess I was grateful for what John and Faith Common had done for me. It wasn't the first time a Common had helped a Tanner. I felt like what Emma Common said: twice blessed. But I was sorry for what happened to John afterward. On my first day back when John Common unthawed all the inkwells to keep me in school, what the master did to John after that made me more sorry than I could ever explain. What the master did to John set me to finish counting the logs in the wall. Nineteen. Twenty.

Ellen Gordon

I never would have said a thing to Mama, but I was beginning to hate our new master. I no longer cared whether I wore new ribbons around my sleeves or the slippers with the ties around the ankles. Now there were days I thought staying home with Mama would be more fun than going to school.

Lately Amos had even found a way to shame us girls even more. While he gave the boys more challenging lessons in mathematics and geometry, he banished us to sew. When he ordered the girls in front of the hot stove and set them to stitching, Lucy Putnam complained of the heat, and Master Read pulled a special chair up to his desk for her.

"Why can't the girls learn geometry, too, Amos?" Faith challenged him. "We get plenty of stitching at home."

Then Lucy Putnam stuck her tilted nose into Faith's business, looking up from a picture she'd done up in embroidery stitches. "Why would girls *want* to learn geometry? It's boring and complicated."

"Why *wouldn't* they, Lucy?" Betsy Fisher countered. "Maybe it sounds interesting to a lot of us."

Then Betsy turned to Amos. I saw that she'd put her

hand on her hips the way I'd seen Faith do so many times. "Why shouldn't girls want to learn about something that's interesting?"

Even Celia Tanner picked up her head to listen.

"Well, they just can't, Miss Fisher. It's not done," Amos Read said, dismissing Betsy.

"Well, *why not?*" asked Faith. She moved close to Amos, thrusting her face right up to his, right next to the glasses and the milky blue eyes.

Amos Read cleared his throat. "You see, Faith," he said, parading before the boys. "Studying geometry requires logical deduction."

Now Amos waved an arrogant finger in the air. "One must be able to see that one thing leads to another. From a plane figure, say, to a quadrilateral and then to a square or a rhombus. And so forth. Geometry's logical. It makes sense."

"So why can't the girls learn to make use of its good sense, too?"

Amos turned sharply to face Faith. His spectacles glinted harshly against the light. The master was growing angry.

"*Everybody knows* why not," he said haughtily, backing away from Faith and nodding at the boys. "Women are flighty. Illogical. *Everybody knows* they haven't the logical capacities."

Faith bristled. "*Everybody knows?* I *hate* those words. Can 'everybody' *prove* that girls don't have this logical capacity?"

"Well, they don't *have* to prove it. You don't have to prove things that everybody knows!" Now Master Read stamped his foot. I knew what the stamp meant: Amos was dismissing her. "Obviously, it's quite *impossible* for girls to study geometry," he said, warming to his own words. "*Com-*

pletely impossible, in fact. Besides," Amos added with authority, "the kind of learning you are asking to acquire is even forbidden by the Bible. The prohibition is in First Timothy."

Lucy Putnam had been watching us all the while. She brought the classroom's Holy Bible over to Amos. I hated Lucy Putnam. She had spent her days either reading a silly book about manners or stitching a stupid sampler verse:

Why should girls be learned and wise?
Books only serve to spoil the eyes.
A studious eye but faintly twinkles.
And reading paves the way to wrinkles.

Lucy had already opened the Bible to First Timothy.

Master Read's finger went straight to the passage. "Here it says that women are to learn *in silence with all subjection.* Verse Eleven. Chapter Two."

The master paused and looked around, intending to impress us with his learning. Faith Common's face said that she was not the least bit impressed.

Then Master Read went on. "The chapter *further* says, young ladies, that a woman is not to teach, *nor to usurp authority over the man.*" Now the master glanced over at Lucy Putnam, who was nodding her black sausage curls.

Amos warmed to Lucy's encouragement.

"Teaching a girl geometry," he said, smirking, "would be like teaching a mule to dance, wouldn't it, boys?"

Immediately the boys rallied around the master's insult. They got down on all fours. They pranced around the room. They made hee-hawing noises. They wiggled fingers that flapped at their temples, imitating donkeys' ears. Henry Stump climbed on Ethan Loring's back, and they began to gallop around the classroom. Even Faith's brothers, Charles and Wesley, joined in the uproar, but her brother John stood apart.

I saw the anger scalding Faith's cheeks, and I felt it burning my own as well.

As I watched the edges of Amos Read's mouth twitch in victory, I heard Faith's solemn vow.

"I'll show *you*, Amos Read," she said. "I'll show *everybody*, in fact."

Somehow I was certain that Faith Common would manage for the mule to enjoy the last laugh.

John Common

I'd come to the river to think. I'd had words with my sister after school. I felt guilty for not standing up for Faith against Amos Read.

But I had trouble enough of my own now with the master. After that day when the ink had unthawed and the master had agreed to let Celia stay, Amos had made me pay for the act of helping a girl.

What Amos Read said was this: "Well, now, Mr. Common, since you're obviously so loyal to the girls—and a mama's boy at that—why don't you just sit with the ladies every recess until the end of the term?"

The other boys began to titter.

Quickly Faith stepped up to the master. "You can't treat John like that."

Amos Read didn't even bother to answer her.

Daily I felt the red-hot sting of shame. At recess, when the other boys played ball or climbed trees, I was banished to sit with the girls while they played hopscotch or jumped ropes.

After school on that day when Amos and the other boys

had mocked the girls, hee-hawing and prancing around the schoolroom, Faith stomped right over to me.

"Why didn't you *say* anything, John?"

"I'm sorry," I said lamely.

"I thought you were different, John."

I laid my hand on Faith's shoulder. Under my fingers, I felt her shoulder tense.

Suddenly she shoved my hand from her shoulder, turning blurry eyes on me. Her bottom lip was quivering. "Sorry's a cousin to pity. It's like the mercy Mother distributes when she visits the sick."

Then she stomped off.

After I'd had words with my sister, Celia had found me at the river, trying to play my flute. But the whistling notes could not capture the sounds of guilt and shame.

Celia had crept up quietly, keeping her hands behind her back. As if she were hiding something. "I knew your heart would be sore about everything, John."

Then she pulled something from behind her back.

She handed me her pop's fiddle. "I wanted you to have it, John. Pop hasn't played it in years."

Then, just as suddenly, she turned and left.

Jacob White

I supposed the wee one and the lad were hungry when they came by that time, and Hetty and I were always happy to feed them.

But there wasn't much of peace between the two of them. It had something to do with the schoolteacher.

"You know what I hate most in this world, Jacob?" Faith said, the fiercest of gleams in her eyes.

I didn't know. But I was sure that, by the by, the wee one would tell me.

"What I hate most in this world," she said, "are all the things folks believe in that just aren't true."

Hetty was pulling the biscuits out of the oven. The room smelled buttery and warm.

"Well, there's dumb things folks believe in, first of all. Liddie Martin says if the cabbage you pull up has a lot of dirt on the roots, you'll marry rich. Rufus Thomas says you can carry a potato in your pocket to cure the rheumatism."

The wee one was like an arrow flinging toward a target. She hadn't even noticed the heaping plate of biscuits Hetty set down in the middle of the table.

Her brother stayed quiet.

"But those kinds of things are harmless, Jacob. What *I* hate are the things folks believe in that are *not* so harmless." She took a deep breath and fanned her anger with it like a bellows on a fire. "Like saying that teaching a girl's like trying to get a mule to dance."

The lad stared at his plate while the wee one failed to notice hers.

"And I hate it that a girl can't depend on a single one of her brothers to stand up to someone who says so!"

Finally the lad looked up and linked eyes with her. "I *said* I was sorry, Faith."

"Thank you once again, then, John Common," she said, but she didn't sound grateful.

I suppose I was impressed with the new master. Hetty and I had heard the rumors about Amos Read. We knew his family history had been a study in contrasts. We knew Amos had a respected grandfather, Duncan, and a dissolute father, Isaiah. In town they whispered that it remained to be seen whether Amos Read would fill his grandfather's shoes or his father's, but Hetty and I didn't pay much mind.

Besides, the woodpile proved the naysayers wrong. I could see plain as day that the master's woodpile showed promise. The wood had been stacked neatly into three piles: one for wood that still needed splitting, a second for wood split and ready for the fire, and a third for kindling. A big strapping boy usually worked beside the three piles, busying himself with a fourth pile of stray twigs and chips.

Now Rufus Thomas peeked his head around the door. He laid a new jar of salve on the table. The children were so lost in their own thoughts, they scarcely noticed him.

"Thanks, Rufus," I said. "Will thee join us?"

"No, thank you, Mr. Jacob. Just came to deliver the salve and air the quilt out on the fence for you."

Hetty pushed up from her chair and picked up the quilt. The threadbare cloth had been darned and patched in scores of places over the years, but it still had its uses. She passed the quilt to Rufus, and I stared greedily at Hetty's biscuits. They wore crusts like golden bonnets. The lad's stomach was rumbling. So was mine.

But the wee one pulled a black cord from around her neck and stabbed at the air with the scissors at the end of it. "Jacob, why must every woman be a needlewoman if not every man must be a carpenter?"

I said I didn't rightly know.

"Well, now, Faith," my Hetty said, trying to soothe the closest thing we had to a daughter. "It takes uncommon faith to sit quietly with a question. To trust that the answer will one day come."

Faith fidgeted in her seat. She wasn't much for sitting quietly.

"Sometimes it helps, dear," continued Hetty, "to think about what we've got to be grateful for from above instead of what disturbs us down below. Could thee join me in prayer?" Hetty asked.

Faith and John and I bowed our heads.

"Dear God, Father and Mother of us all," Hetty prayed. "Bless this food and those who eat of it. May we be ever mindful of the great gift that is the nourishment of thy tender love."

While my wife prayed, I thought of the great gift that was Hetty's own tender love. As the years passed, I liked looking at her gray head more and more.

When Hetty opened her eyes, she smiled at the wee one. I always liked the way my Hetty prayed. Because Quakers felt free to heed the inner light, sometimes Hetty was inspired to add her own special message to the end of a prayer. "And," she added, winking at Faith and John, "may we be ever mindful of the great pleasure of the company of our young friends."

"Amen," I said.

Then I passed the lad the honey pot. His eyes were drooling. John took a big bite of biscuit, and Hetty smiled as she watched him eat.

"Goodness, child," she laughed. "Thee beat Jacob's record. He eats one of my biscuits in three bites. Thee took just two."

While her brother sucked at the sticky spots on his finger, savoring the last licks of sweetness, Faith didn't touch her food. She was pelting me with questions: *Why, Jacob, is John encouraged to master Greek when I'm encouraged only to master the roasting pan? Why is Charles taught to stitch up an argument like Aristotle while I'm only taught to stitch the pocket handkerchiefs?*

Her questions were so perfectly formed I could tell she'd been thinking about them for a long while. Likely she'd been confiding them to her copybook.

I scratched my head to give myself time to gather my

own thoughts. I told the wee one I'd have to think on things awhile. One thing I've come to know about that girl: it's more than food she's hungry for.

Lucy Putnam

I declare Faith Common was up to some kind of trick. The girls whispered together all the time: at recess, at lunch, especially while they sewed together before the fire.

Mostly I just pretended to read my book. *Rules of Politeness for Proper Young Ladies* was filled with all kinds of useful advice: Never appear in the parlor with your hair in papers; always avoid satin shoes in cold weather; never sing more than two numbers consecutively in public; always seek information from a man, even if you must pass for a simpleton.

I declare it was easy to tell Faith and the other girls were up to something. It was harder figuring out what it was. And not letting them know that I was one bit interested was the hardest part of all.

Jacob White

I had been working late in my shop. I had just finished sanding the door to a curio cabinet the Putnams had ordered.

The wee one came in all of a rush. She kicked up the wood shavings at my feet into miniature whirlpools. "Jacob," she said, opening her copybook and sticking it right under my nose, "are you familiar with any of these passages?" The wee one had a way of getting right to the point.

"Whoa, wait a minute, wee one," I said. I saw the

urgency in her eyes, so I fixed my attention on the copybook right away.

She had filled most of the pages in the back of the book, pages which had been blank just last August. In her neat firm hand, she had written two lists of Bible verses. They marched down the page in two long columns like soldiers on parade. On the left-hand column were the following verses:

O woman, great is thy faith,
The woman is the glory of the man.
Give her of the fruit of her hands; let her own works
    praise her in the gates.
A virtuous woman is a crown to her husband.
Dorcas, this woman, was full of good works.

On the right-hand column, in opposition to the words on the left-hand side, were these:

Let the woman learn in silence with all subjection.
God created Man in His own image.
Let your women keep silent in the churches, for it is
    not permitted for them to speak.
Suffer not a woman to teach, nor to usurp authority
    over the man.

"Jacob," she asked again, "are you familiar with these passages?"

"Well, yes, I suppose I am. A Quaker knows his Scripture like a carpenter knows his tools."

She smiled. She looked satisfied with my answer. I was pleased. It had been a long time since I'd answered one of the wee one's questions to her satisfaction.

"And do you know what all of those words mean?"

"Surely do," I said. "Lots of them. They're just common ordinary old words. 'Woman.' 'Man.' 'Church.'"

"But look again closely, Jacob. Are there some words you're *not* so sure of?"

"I guess I could look again." I saw that was what she wanted, so I dipped my head back into her copybook and ran my finger over every word. "Well, maybe 'virtuous,'" I said, stopping to read again. I had read over the passage that said, *A virtuous woman is a crown to her husband.*

"And why might you not be so sure about that word?"

I stared into the candle flame, thinking. Somehow the light opened my mind to clarity. "Well, wee one, virtuous can mean a number of different things. Thy mother is a virtuous woman. She does everything for everybody without expecting a word of thanks. She's been raising all that money for the fire pumper and bell ever since the fire. But I think thee could call Mrs. Putnam virtuous, too. Even though she's mighty different from thine own mother and not everyone in Millbrook would think so. I guess it depends on what thee means by virtuous."

"Well, what do *you* mean by virtuous, Jacob?"

I stared into the candle flame again. The image of my wife's hands rose up. I could see the knuckles of her fingers, like knots in wood, struggling with the needle. I knew I loved those fingers as much now as I did when I first saw them. "Well, I suppose I think of virtuous as someone like my own Hetty."

Faith smiled. She seemed satisfied.

"Now, Jacob," she said with urgency. "What about that word right there. '*Silence.*'" She poked her finger in the copybook, pointing out another passage.

I mumbled the words under her finger to myself. "Hmmm," I said, lingering over each phrase. "Let the woman . . ." I paused. "Learn in silence. With all subjection."

"What do you think the Bible means by silence Jacob?"

"Well, maybe that depends, too. I suppose everybody's got their own notions about silence. Like they do about virtuous."

She nodded, encouraging me to go on.

"Well, Calvinists, for one. Like thy grandfather. I suppose Calvinists have their own notions of silence, wee one."

"I think they do, too," she said, laying the chisel down. "I think Calvinists think of silence like this."

She closed her lips tight together, making a ruler-straight line above her chin with her mouth.

I had to laugh. I wished Miss Ellen Gordon could have seen the wee one. Ellen had a gift for mimicry. She often entertained Hetty and me with her imitations of Albert Biggs or Biddy Bostick or Amanda Putnam.

Then Faith scolded me. "Don't laugh at me, Jacob. I'm serious."

I could see that she was.

"I think that Calvinists think of silence as something absolutely mute. Completely wordless. Something like a punishment. Something you are ordered into. Not something that you choose willingly."

"But what about Methodists?" I said.

Now she put her ruler-straight mouth back on. But next she loosened her lips, turned the ends of her mouth up gently, and made a quiet, soft smile.

"From the look on my face, Jacob, how would you say that Methodists think of silence?"

"Well, I'd say they're not as strict as Calvinists. I'd say Methodists might think of silence as something quiet or reverent or thoughtful. More like an attitude a person might *choose* for herself."

She picked up the hammer, pounding lightly at an

imaginary nail in her palm as she gathered her thoughts. "I think so, too. So would it be fair to say that Calvinists and Methodists mean different things by silence, Jacob?"

I nodded. I believed her conclusion was right. But Faith wasn't satisfied until she'd hammered a conclusion flush with the wood of a question.

"What, *exactly,* does the Bible mean when it speaks of *silence,* Jacob?"

"I don't rightly know, wee one," I said. "Learned folks, scholars and preachers and such, think that to understand things like that, a person's got to go back to the original."

"The original *what,* Jacob?"

"Greek. The original Greek. In order to understand, preachers often follow the words all the way back to their beginning. To the Greek that the New Testament was first written in."

The wee one didn't stay long after that. When she left, the wood shavings swirled at her feet like miniature whirlpools, just as they had when she arrived.

Emma Common

I began with the needles. I separated the darning needles from the blunts and the sharps. Ah, how hopeless was the muddle of my sewing basket!

Out of the corner of my eye, I watched my daughter. She was sprawled on the floor before the hearth, and her brother John sat beside her. Piles of newspapers and scraps of paper were strewn around them. How focused she was on the task at hand!

"This letter's *what,* John?" she asked her brother. Faith held up a letter she had scissored out of newspaper.

John looked confused.

I was surprised when Faith began reviewing John's Greek with him. She used the textbook my dear husband had sent my son for a gift. How thrilled I was to witness my daughter's more pliant spirit! How thrilled my husband would be to witness his son's learning!

"Remember?" she asked, shaking the newspaper letter in John's face as if to jolt his memory. "This letter looks like the willow. At the south end of the brook. It soars upward through the trunk and then swoops downward through the branches."

John turned a blank face to her.

Faith sighed. "Epsilon, John. This is the letter *epsilon*."

While I separated the common buttons from the nicer ones, Faith picked up another newspaper cutout. "And this one?"

John looked blankly again.

"Well, what does it *look* like, John?"

"It looks like a horseshoe, Faith."

"Good. Yes. You're right!"

John's face lit up, remembering. "Omega," he said.

"Good, John," she said, picking up another newspaper letter. "Now this one. It looks like the two columns that hold up the bank in town."

John scratched his head. He was not remembering.

"Pi, John. That's the letter *pi*."

He grinned at her. "Cherry or apple?" he teased.

She swatted him with a rolled-up newspaper.

Often I had chanced on them while I busied myself about the house washing the hearth or melting the lard for filling the lamps. Faith had gone about teaching her brother the Greek alphabet the way she went about everything else in her life. Fiercely. In contrast to her attitude toward stitching, in these lessons Faith held her standards high. She refused to give her brother the answers to the passages he stumbled through. She insisted that he write his own corrections to his errors.

John was easily bored with his learning. As a diversion, Faith offered him a variety of ways in which to learn. Often she turned his attention to the maps in the text, and sometimes they drew pictures together of the places they identified: the Aegean and Ionian Seas, the islands of Crete and Rhodes, the cities of Athens and Delphi.

Yet I often overheard John pleading with her. "Why, Faith, must I spend all this time on Greek?"

"You *know* why, John. If you are ever going to be a minister, you need to be able to understand the truth of the words in the Bible. You have to go back to the original, to the source."

John frowned. I knew he'd rather be playing his instruments.

John reached for his violin. It was a sign that he wished his lesson to be over.

I sympathized with John myself. I was eager for him to learn Greek, but I often found Faith's lessons about it confusing and dull.

What I liked best was when Faith simply read John the stories in the back of the text. I gathered up my sewing to stitch quietly in a corner and listen. Often John interrupted her, entertaining his sister—and me—with his instruments and his interpretations.

"Listen, Faith," he said, plucking ominous notes from his fiddle. "Can you hear the Cyclops, thundering across the ground with his one eye?"

I shuddered, thinking of the puckered hole in my father's face where his left eye had been.

Then John would switch to his flute, creating airy notes that shuttled back and forth across the room. "Can you hear the Trojan women at their looms, Faith?"

After Faith nodded, she added, "And don't they remind you of Mother's Dorcas sisters?"

I sometimes heard John turn the tables on his sister, playing a game he created. When he became the teacher and she the learner, I enjoyed their lessons most of all.

John picked up his fiddle, making raw, scraping sounds with it. "Which story am I playing, Faith? *The Iliad? The Odyssey?*"

Then he'd switch to his flute, and ask again, "*Now* which is it, Faith? *The Odyssey? The Iliad?*"

In the threads of his music, I instantly recognized either the warlike sounds of *The Iliad* or the peaceful sounds of *The Odyssey*. The fiddle squealed the sounds of clanging swords and snorting horses. The flute piped the sounds of fields sparkling with golden thatch and women pouring water into basins. It took Faith a bit longer to answer correctly in John's version of a lesson.

Once John looked at his sister and said, "I'll guess you like *The Iliad* better than *The Odyssey*, Faith."

The look on her face told him she disagreed. "Why should you think *that*, John?"

"Well, you're the more warlike of the two of us. I should think you'd prefer the crested helmets of the soldiers in *The Iliad* to the weaving fingers of the women in *The Odyssey*."

"I like both of the stories equally well," she responded. "And for the same reason."

"The same reason?"

"Yes, John. Both of them are filled with clever tricks. In *The Odyssey*, I like the way Odysseus and his men escape from the Cyclops guarding the cave by hiding under the fleecy bellies of the rams. I like the way Odysseus helped defend against the Sirens whose singing lured sailors onto rocks by filling his crew's ears with beeswax. In *The Iliad,* I liked the way the Greeks tricked their enemy by sending the Trojans a huge wooden horse as a gift: only the Trojans didn't know that Greek soldiers were hiding inside, ready to spring."

As I began to measure tucks in a shirt front with a paper measure, I saw that John had grown bored with her chattering. So had I.

Amanda Putnam

"Well, I have definitely decided to withdraw my Ethan from the primary school. His last day will be next week." Kate Loring looked up from the baby bonnet in her lap; her needle stopped moving.

"Is that so, Kate?" asked Marguerite Gordon.

I pricked up my ears. Frankly, this was news I hadn't heard.

"Absolutely. I should have done it sooner," said Kate, returning to the bonnet that would likely find its way into Albert Biggs's display window. "How that dear boy of mine has suffered at the hands of this master!"

My Dorcas friends bent forward, eagerly listening. I spied Faith Common rolling her eyes.

"Ethan comes home *filthy*! He says he was sent to wallow in a mud puddle when the children forced him to act out the part of the Prodigal Son. Imagine! Irreverent playacting about sacred Scripture! Ethan reports to me about the most ridiculous activities! I've never *heard* of such carrying on!"

"Well, Kate," inserted Rebecca Kinder, "Evangeline Fisher, Betsy's mother, told me that her daughter's been crawling around in the charcoal dust on the floor, playing with some kind of contraption to adjust the heat of the stove. No, that school does not sound like a fit place for a good boy like Ethan, Kate."

Now I spied Faith Common biting down on her cheek. She appeared to be tamping down a grin.

"Well, Kate, I hear the master's made a success of the woodpile, at least," said Esther Grimes, squinting across the table at Mrs. Loring. "I spoke to him in town just this week. He's had a difficult job, poor boy. Said he's had to arrive early to chop every morning. This winter that stove's consumed more than a cord of wood a week."

Frankly, I was suspicious of Miss Grimes's positive report.

Kate Loring huffed. "Woodpile or no, ladies, I ask you: Is it necessary for children to come home from school dirtier than when they arrived? Is it appropriate for them to be lying on a dirty floor, making dangerous experiments with a stove? Can we afford to ignore such incompetence?"

Faith Common halted in the midst of her mending. She seemed as if she were resisting the urge to speak.

Now Faith's mother piped up. "A Christian woman knows to withhold judgment until the truth is known. I doubt that incompetence is the issue with Master Read, Kate," she said. "In fact we're lucky to have him."

I had no respect for Emma Common's opinions about that boy. She was not interested in interrupting the education of her sons for a single minute.

"Didn't you see, Emma," I asked, "Ted's recent report in the *Gazette* on the problem of unruly schoolchildren?" While Emma sputtered for words, I filled in the silence. "Yes, dear. He reported that nearly three hundred schools in Massachusetts were broken up last year by mutinous pupils."

"With all due respect, Amanda," Emma asserted, "I've witnessed this master's competence firsthand. The mathematics my boys have learned in a very short time under Master Read has been astonishing. John still struggles, but Charles's logical reasoning abilities have soared. Wesley's not very far behind him, and he's young. He'll catch up in time. I am certain that the mutinous conditions of which you speak would have kept my sons from progressing so rapidly."

"Your *sons*? But what about your *daughter*?"

"What do you mean, Amanda?"

Frankly, Emma Common could be dull as the daily gossip. "Your daughter, dear. Faith. Can you be satisfied when your daughter Faith knows only enough chemistry to boil water, only enough botany to identify weeds in the garden, only enough mathematics to count the places for supper?"

Emma struggled to respond. I don't think she entirely understood me.

"Now, Amanda," Miss Grimes said, coming to Emma's rescue. "I hear even Faith's made progress, too, under this master. Didn't you tell me, Emma, that Faith has greatly improved her sewing?"

"Yes, Esther," Emma said, struggling to recover. "That's true."

I looked over at Emma's daughter. She had a sour twist around her lips.

"Go get your quilted blocks, Faith, dear," her mother said. "I'm sure Mrs. Loring and the other ladies would be delighted to admire them."

Faith complied. But, frankly, her eyes were frowning.

Ellen Gordon

I both liked and didn't like what was happening.

I liked it that some of the ladies were opposed to Master Read.

I didn't like it that the opposition was on behalf of Ethan Loring.

I liked it that Mrs. Putnam was concerned about the girls' learning.

I didn't like it that the evidence of it would be Faith's stitching.

With reluctance Faith brought her quilted squares down from the loft.

When she passed them around the circle, she caught my eye. Her look told me that she felt like I did: she both liked and didn't like what was happening.

Miss Grimes admired the unusual patterns: Saw Blades, Fence Posts, Cornstalks.

Mrs. Tyler admired the colors: Gold Rings, Red Barns, Pink Tulips.

But none of them could admire what Faith and I and the other girls were most proud of: the fact that we had defied Amos Read with our stitching.

Banished to sewing before the fire while the boys learned geometry, Faith had her own plan for revenge and we girls followed it.

Faith often confessed her disappointment to me.

"It feels terrible, Ellen. Like an ache in the belly that won't go away. We can only learn if we do so in secret."

At the Dorcas Circle, Mrs. Common herself praised what she admired most of all in her daughter's work: Faith's neat hemming stitches, running stitches, chain stitches, and backstitches. Finally she had a daughter who could sew.

Mrs. Putnam raised one eyebrow sharply. "I suppose you consider improvements in sewing as a kind of educational progress, then, Emma?"

"Well," said Mrs. Loring, "I'm happy to have withdrawn

my boy Ethan before it's too late. I'm convinced that Master Read's school can come to no good. Yes," Mrs. Loring whispered conspiratorily, "I have it on good authority. They have had *spirits* in the school."

The women put down their needles and leaned forward in their seats.

"Whiskey and wine," Mrs. Loring announced with self-importance. In the plump pillows of her cheeks and the fleshy swags of her neck, I recognized her chubby son Ethan.

I bit my tongue against the words banging against my teeth. Surely Mrs. Loring didn't mean the whiskey that had thawed the inkwell or the dab of wine Celia used to soothe Mitchell Palfrey's sore throat?

"Perhaps there needs to be an investigation, Kate," offered my own mother. I wondered how to capture my mother's expression before the mirror, her lips quivering, her words barely concealing her outrage.

"There certainly does," declared Mrs. Loring. "In fact, an investigation is already under way. The committee that oversees the district school in Troy will arrive week after next. They've determined to examine our students. They want to find out what kind of youth Master Read intends to send to them."

Now I didn't know whether I liked or disliked what was happening.

I liked it that Master Read would be put under a microscope.

But I didn't like it that, should our school be found wanting, our learning would be abandoned.

I looked over at Faith, wondering what she thought about this new development. But I could not read the gleam in her eye.

Hetty White

'Twas nary a day went by that Jacob and I didn't try to comfort Celia Tanner. I'd listen to her practice her ciphering or help her make her brooms. She didn't seem to mind it when an old lady rocked a young girl like a baby. But Jacob and I insisted on paying her for the jars of salve, even though that poor child tried to give them to us.

Ellen Gordon

I never admitted to Mama that a schoolteacher could be lazy. Mama would not have believed it anyway, but Mama had never met a master like Amos Read.

Mama probably didn't know that half the time in school was spent not on learning itself, but on *preparing* to learn.

The classroom had no blackboards and no slates. Only Betsy Fisher and Lucy Putnam owned lead pencils. Preparing to write, then, took more time and effort than Master Read was willing to give.

Each family was expected to provide its own ink, but poor children like Celia Tanner and the Lukens brothers could not afford ink powder like I could. Their homemade ink was usually so pale that the master had to spend extra time making up ink for them, frowning all the while.

The goose-quill pens we used were always breaking or losing their points. They required constant mending by our surly teacher.

Paper was rough, dark, and expensive. Those who could not afford it—like Celia Tanner—wrote on birch bark they gathered and dried themselves. Even the lucky children, like me, who could afford paper, had to fold the paper up into copy- and sum-books and watch our master tap his foot impatiently at our slow pace.

Even after the books were made, we then had to rule them for writing in. Using rulers and lead plummets, we children ruled the paper ourselves, and we could not work fast enough to suit our master.

At the end of each day, the master stayed late, setting the copy for the next day's penmanship practice in each pupil's copybook. To my mind, it required a great deal of time and patience and energy, qualities our master possessed in very short supply.

For beginners, the master copied letters and short phrases: "waste not; want not." For more advanced students, he copied longer epigrams and verses: "Be ye doers of the word, and not hearers only."

But Master Read was now under a great deal of pressure. The committee from Troy was due to arrive; there was much work to be done.

And Faith Common knew it.

She had told me of the proposal she would offer. She would promise to take over supervision of *all* the work of the girls in the class. And the Irish boy, too, of course. That would include trimming the pens, ruling the lines, and setting the next day's penmanship practices into the pages of their copybooks. She would also hear our recitations and help with the teaching. Her plan would allow Master Read to focus his attention more sharply on the boys.

Nodding his head, Amos Read agreed.

After that Faith engaged us girls in simple projects we could display around the classroom for the committee. She'd picked up a book from Mrs. Putnam's library, burying her face into *Lessons for Little Fingers,* coming up with all kinds of ideas for teaching. We built magnets from iron bars. We pressed fossils in damp clay. Faith supervised our mapmaking, helping the younger children sketch the European rivers with long snaking lines or the Appalachian forests with sharp-roofed carets. Soon Faith was helping us older girls make looking glasses of glass, mercury, tin and tinfoil. Then, with Celia's help, the younger girls assembled specimen boxes filled with insects, leaves, wildflowers, stones, and grasses.

We continued, of course, our work by the fire with our quilt blocks, but Faith spent even more time practicing mathematics with the girls and Sean Hungerford. She gathered brown nuts for addition and subtraction practice. She invented new riddles to keep the lessons lively. "How many letters in the name Sarah Tyler?" "If a girl plays three days a week, how many did she work?"

Betsy Fisher and Sarah Tyler made especially good progress, and Celia Tanner's progress was outstanding. Sean Hungerford's motivation made up for a slow start. He caught up rapidly, but when it came to multiplication, Faith saw that he was stymied by the nines. She taught him a trick that worked most of the time.

True to her promise, Faith stayed late every afternoon to set the copy in our copybooks. I looked forward to the school-yard visits with the other girls before school each morning. There we would huddle together and wonder about what Faith Common might have in store for us today. And soon we girls were creating even newer ways of seeking revenge on Amos Read, discovering that trickery wasn't a trait possessed *only* by Faith Common.

Emma Common

How hard they had worked to prepare for the visit of the committee! The children and their master had spruced up the building and yard. Jacob White had hammered up falling clapboards and shored up the sagging porch. The children had swept and cleaned and arranged displays of their schoolwork around the perimeters of the room. And how proud I was of the needlework on display, much of it stitched from my daughter's own fingers!

The committee arrived on an April morning, its members sitting behind a long table, which had been placed across the front of the classroom. Reverend Jonathan Norcross, pastor of the Congregational church in Troy, led the delegation. He was accompanied by Master Jeremy Thatcher, who had served as schoolmaster in both Troy and Bradbury for a number of years. Local representatives from Millbrook had been asked to join the group. They included Mayor Samuel Girton; the *Gazette's* Mr. and Mrs. Edward Putnam; and Lionel Loring, a seed merchant and brother-in-law of Kate Loring.

My children's classmates shone like freshly polished windows. The boys' hair was slicked down. Their boots were well greased and shiny. The girls had cast off their quilted hoods and winter-weight pantalets for gingham or calico bonnets, many of them gay with ribbon streamers. Each shiny face took its appointed place before the committee like gems in a rock collection.

After Amos Read called us to order, he began with a prayer that was followed by a hymn. Then the examination began in earnest.

First Vera Cramer, the youngest girl, and Seth Wilkins, the youngest boy, stood on matching stools and together recited a piece they had learned about the vowel sounds:

"Short *a*: man, hat.
Broad *a*: ball, tall.
Flat *a*: ask, part."

Then Peter Burbage read Betsy Fisher's composition on George Washington; I recalled Faith's grumbling about that at home: she did not believe a girl should be thought too modest to read her own good work in public.

Finally the class recited the verses from Ecclesiastes, the boys and the girls alternating lines: *a time to be born;* a time to die; *a time to get;* a time to lose; *a time to rend;* a time to sew; *a time to embrace;* a time to refrain from embracing; *a time to keep silence;* and a time to speak. I recalled all the happy times when my John had returned to us and read these verses before the fire. My son John must have remembered, too: his fingers were tapping out the rhythm in the words against his trouser leg.

I watched the faces of the committee members growing bored with the performance. So far, I was relieved: they had seen nothing to suggest the master's incompetence. After a few of the students had recited verses from the Psalter, Reverend Norcross, the Congregational minister, spoke up. "We understand that you've accomplished some impressive work in mathematics, Master Read. May we move on to that subject?"

"Certainly, sir," Amos Read answered respectfully.

When Amos requested my son Charles to move to the front before the examiners, my heart thumped proudly at the master's selection of my second son, and I shifted forward in my seat. I took in Charles's stocky chest and sturdy feet. Unlike his brother John, Charles gave me the impression of someone who could not easily be bowled over.

Quickly Amos rattled off several word problems, and Charles answered each one just as quickly.

Then, in a final flourish, Amos asked, "What will be the price of six dozen eggs at two cents for three eggs?"

My mind was a flurry. I tried to calculate the sum in my

head, but I was immediately confused. I saw the foreheads around me furrowing in calculation, too.

When my second son swiftly answered, "Forty-eight cents," the assembly looked astonished, the examiners applauded, and Charles strode off on his sturdy legs, broadly beaming.

How I struggled to keep my composure! I dipped my head down modestly. Pride was not becoming in a woman, even if that woman was a mother.

Celia Tanner

I confess Charles Common gave an impressive performance. After he sat down, Master Thatcher, the teacher from Troy, cleared his throat. "It is *fur shore* the case, Master Read, that a *tee-chur* often singles out his most talented *stew-dint* to perform. But the progress of the *backkerd stew-dint* needs to be tested as well, *fur shore*. Can you tell us about the *larnin* of a *bacckerd stew-dint* who may have arrived not so finely prepared as one of Reverend Common's *chilrun*?"

I confess I struggled to understand what the master said. I think *backkerd* meant *backward*. I think *larnin* meant *learning*.

Amos looked over the group. "Well," he said, "there's the Irish boy."

I wondered why the master called on Sean. He had been banished to learning among the girls, but Faith had taught him well.

The committee called Sean Hungerford to the front. His sunburned, freckled face glowed with the purplish hue of embarrassment, and Master Thatcher seemed surprised to see such a big lad in a group with such young children.

Amos Read cleared his throat and looked down his nose in Sean's direction. "Mr. Hungerford came to us entirely deficient in any mathematics at all," offered Amos. I caught the slur in Amos's backhanded praise.

I confess I hoped the masters would ask Sean a question he could answer. I looked around at the other girls who had observed Sean's progress over the last few weeks. Sarah Tyler. Vera Cramer. Betsy Fisher. Their faces said they were hoping he'd do well, too.

Reverend Norcross made a suggestion. "Well, what about his multiplication tables, Mr. Read? That would be an amazing accomplishment if one as ignorant as you claim could go from nothing at all to mastering the nines table, for instance."

I felt my heart sink. They were going to ask Sean the nines table! It was exactly what gave him the most trouble!

As Sean began, I crossed my fingers behind my back for luck. Nine times two. Times three. Times four. Times five. Then he halted.

"Nine times six," he repeated. He shuffled onto first one heavy boot and then the other. I could tell he had entirely forgotten the answer.

The committee watched intently as Sean wrinkled his brow.

I thought back to the trick Faith had taught Sean when he struggled with the nines. I hoped he would remember it now. Over and over Faith had helped him practice.

"Let's say you want to multiply nine times three, all right? And let's say you've forgotten the answer. You use the ten fingers of your hand to help you. You number them from left to right. So, what number, then, would be the pinkie finger on your right hand?"

Sean wiggled separate fingers from the pinkie of his left

hand to the pinkie on his right. He was counting. "Well, the pinkie on the right is number ten."

"Right," Faith said, grinning. "I mean *correct*, Sean."

Sean grinned back.

"So, if your problem is nine times three, for instance, you bend back finger number three. Then you hold up both hands with the three finger bent down. Count the number of fingers to the *left* of finger three, Sean."

"Hmmm," he said, studying his giant hands. "Well, that's the pinkie to the left and the finger next to it. Makes two."

"Good. Now count the fingers to the *right* of the three finger."

Sean dipped his head over his hands, counting. "That's seven, Faith."

"Right, Sean! Nine times three is twenty-seven!"

Now, before the masters, I watched Sean's lips move as he talked himself through the problem at hand. I could tell he was having trouble concentrating.

Then I saw him hold his two hands out in front of him. He began to mutter to himself. Then Sean looked straight ahead at the masters, double-checked his calculations, and drew a breath. "Fifty-four," he said. "Nine times six is fifty-four."

The examiners looked astonished; then they gave Amos Read satisfied nods. "Congratulations, Master Read," Reverend Norcross said. "It appears your reputation as a teacher of mathematics is well deserved."

I confess I couldn't believe what the master then said. When I glanced at the other girls, I could tell they couldn't believe it, either.

"Well, it wasn't easy," Amos said, his milk blue eyes blinking from behind his glasses. "I was required to spend a great deal of time with him. After all, that's what a devoted master does, isn't it?"

The committee members smiled.

Ellen Gordon

After Sean Hungerford had been examined, I fixed on Faith Common's face. It was red as fire.

All of a sudden Faith stepped forward, and the words flew from her mouth. "Excuse me, honorable committee members," she said, addressing the assembly, "but Celia Tanner is an outstanding student. She's not wealthy, but if you count ability, she's rich as a banker. If I may say so, that is."

I felt something inside swelling and growing. It was something like the hope you got for an oak tree when you planted a tiny acorn.

Reverend Norcross turned his gray-whiskered chin in Faith's direction. He frowned, and Faith stepped back, awkward now, for she had caught the narrowing eyes of her mother.

"And Master Read's classroom is one of a very few schools," she added, attempting to redeem herself, remembering her mother's approval of Amos Read, "in which a young woman can get a thorough grounding in mathematics. Particularly geometry." I saw that Faith Common could even be brought to praise Amos Read if that praise brought credit on us girls.

"*Mathematics?*" Lionel Loring had almost fallen asleep; he had now roused himself. "Master Read has attempted a thorough grounding in mathematics—for *young women?*" Mr. Loring's face said that he could not imagine a woman's use for mathematics.

Now Mrs. Putnam spoke up. "Excellent, Master Read," she interjected approvingly. "Not every schoolroom is so progressive."

I knew I'd go home and try to capture Mrs. Putnam's likeness before the looking glass. I liked the firm set to her chin and the scolding tone in her voice.

"At the very least," she continued, "a knowledge of mathematics helps a woman figure the price of eggs; at the very most, it keeps her calculating and sharp. How many women are cheated by the grocer, the tax assessor, the stage-coach driver for their lack of ability to make simple change?"

The masters stared at Mrs. Putnam the way the women in my mother's Dorcas Circle often did, but I understood her. Especially about the cheating part. In practicing our sums, we girls often recorded the ways in which Albert Biggs cheated our mothers.

Lionel Loring responded. He was now fully awake. "I would propose that young women would be *unable* to master the kind of logical deduction required by geometry. Logic, *everybody knows,* Amanda, is the province of men."

I saw Faith pulled up short on the reins of "everybody knows."

"Well, then," Faith asserted, "with all due respect, Mr. Loring, why don't we *establish* a young woman's logical abilities? Right now. I'm certain Celia Tanner will oblige us."

"All right, Miss Common," Amos Read said, picking up his ruler and bouncing it off his palm while he gathered his words. "We'll take up your challenge. But I must warn you, masters," he said, addressing the committee, "teaching a girl to master geometry is a bit like teaching a mule to dance."

Now Amos turned and smiled outright at Faith. A chuckle ran through the line of examiners at the table. I could feel my eyeballs burning.

"Step forward, please, Miss Tanner," Amos said, waving Celia to the table before the masters with his ruler.

Celia glanced over at John Common before she approached the examination table. She had never looked more shy, and I read John's nod as an attempt at encouragement.

Celia peered out from under her bonnet into the examiners' faces. She wore a new bonnet that made me sad and happy at the same time. She had made it from pasting old newspapers together and covering the pasteboard with cheap homespun cloth. Her new bonnet drooped limply. The face under the bonnet said it was more unwilling than unable to be questioned.

Now Amos cleared his throat. "What conclusion about lines, Miss Tanner," he asked, "can you draw from a right angle?"

Inwardly, I sighed, relieved. Celia had often overheard Amos's definitions as she sat stitching with us girls by the fire. She knew about lines and angles. She knew that the lines of a right triangle were perpendicular to each other. It would be an easy question for Celia.

"Let's see," Celia began hesitantly. "A line is . . . *a straight distance between points. An angle is . . . two lines with a common end point. A right angle is . . . an angle whose measure is ninety degrees.*"

Good Celia, I thought. Celia had taken a nice logical approach. She had begun with definitions.

The masters leaned forward across the table. Resting their chins in their hands, they looked interested.

"No, no, Miss Tanner," interrupted Amos. He was impatiently swatting his palm with his ruler. The ruler made me nervous. "I didn't ask for *definitions.* I asked for a *conclusion.*"

Celia blushed. "I know, Master Read," she stuttered. "I was gathering my thoughts."

"Well, don't gather for too long, else you may be accused of *wool* gathering." Amos smiled at the examiners, gloating over the pun only he found clever.

Inside, I whispered encouragement to Celia. Stay calm, Celia. Don't let him rush you.

"All right, master," Celia said. "A conclusion. Yes," she said, stumbling over the words. Now I saw that Celia's green eyes were fixed on the tapping ruler. "Could you repeat the question again, please?"

Amos raised his eyebrows in that haughty way he had.

I saw Faith glancing worriedly at the other girls.

Amos repeated the question slowly. As if Celia were hard of hearing. "What conclusion . . . about lines . . . ," asked Amos Read, "can you draw . . . from a right angle?"

"Let's see," Celia said, thrown off stride by the prancing ruler. "A right angle is ninety degrees," she said, thinking aloud.

"No, no, no," Amos said, interrupting. "Not a conclusion about an *angle,* girl. A conclusion about *lines.*"

I caught the condescension in his use of the word *girl,* and so did Celia: she had grabbed her faded blue-and-white apron between her thumb and index finger.

"Well," she began, hesitating, "the lines connect." She was now tightly twisting the cloth of the apron.

"Of *course* they connect, dear," Amos said, exasperated. As if Celia were intentionally trying his patience. "If they hadn't connected, they could not form an angle, isn't that right?"

The masters nodded in response. Reverend Norcross concealed a grin behind his palm.

"But what *conclusion* can you draw, Miss Tanner, about

the connection? The question was about *conclusions.* After all, logical *conclusions* are what geometry is all about."

I was certain Celia knew the answer. The girls overheard the word often enough. *Perpendicular.* The lines that met to form a right angle were *perpendicular.* At recess Celia had once observed that one perpendicular edge of a triangular scrap of wood butted up nicely to a rectangular pole to make the steps on a pair of stilts.

"The lines are straight ones, sir. One horizontal. The other vertical. They meet each other at the angle. The right angle, that is." As she spoke, I noticed that Celia had twisted the cloth of her apron into a tight cone.

Amos now raised his voice in annoyance. "Yes. Go on." Then he began wildly waving his ruler.

"The lines are per . . .," Celia said, keeping her eyes on the ruler. "P-per . . . p-pen . . ." She had begun to stutter. Her limp bonnet trembled.

Now Amos flung the ruler, whacking it across the surface of the examining table. It made a sharp cracking sound. "We haven't got all day," he said. He whacked again.

Suddenly I saw Celia's green eyes sink to the floor. Her lips began to move as if she were inwardly counting. Her eyes stayed fixed on the floorboards and her lips kept moving, and soon I sensed that somehow Celia had floated away. She had entirely forgotten the question.

Reverend Norcross stood up, dismissing Celia. "That will be all, young lady. Thank you very much." The masters bent over their papers, recording marks of assessment.

"Like I said," Amos continued, swaggering in front of the committee. "Teaching a young girl logic is like teaching a mule to dance. It's not easy, and the mule never really learns to enjoy it anyway. It goes against his nature."

The pounding inside my chest was so fierce that it

drowned out the rest of the program. I hardly heard the final
Bible verse, the final hymn and prayer. When they were over,
I saw that Faith had determined to carry out her plan. I had
questioned the propriety of it, and although she had listened
thoughtfully, I knew she would make up her own mind.

Quickly, as the assembly began to disperse, Faith
arranged the girls' copybooks on tables against the walls,
interspersing them among the copybooks of the boys.

I followed her. So did some of the others. Faith would
not be the only girl to seek revenge on Amos Read.

Then Faith stomped out the schoolroom door, and we
other girls stomped out behind her.

I knew there would be trouble.

I, for one, would never be sorry.

John Common

While the rest of the crowd spilled out the door and across
the lawn, heading for the table set with lemonade and cookies, I heard music inside my head, violin music that seemed
composed just for Celia. It was made up of hurtful tones, of
strings scraping against feelings of shame. It was made up of
notes not played smoothly, but plucked: like tiny stinging
pinches at the heart.

The girls gathered together for solace. They comforted
Celia, treating her like a comrade wounded in battle. They
put their arms around her waist, reassuring her. I fetched her
a cold glass of lemonade, and Ellen Gordon pressed the icy
glass to Celia's flushed brow.

After that I stood at a distance from them. Truth to tell, I
was sorry for their humiliation but relieved not to be banished to their company today.

All I could think of was Amos Read, swaggering in front of the committee.

Celia's green eyes misted over.

Celia had been proud of her new bonnet, and when she found me at the brook to show it to me, I had played an airy tune on my flute in celebration.

"Well," my sister said, her words gathered like a fist to throw into the faces of *everybody* who seemed to *know* so much, "I'm so mad I could *spit*."

The girls nodded in agreement. Then they turned to her, seeking advice, and the furious face of my sister lit up with an idea.

"If we're *all* so mad we could spit, ladies," she said, "*why don't we?*"

Gleefully, they followed her lead, pulling slices of lemon out of their glasses, picking out the seeds. As they dived and fished for seeds, lemonade splashed their hems and aprons.

"You need to place the seed right between your front teeth," Faith said. "You have to rear your tongue back like a slingshot and get a blast of air behind it. Then you have to thrust the seed with the tongue and the air. Good and hard."

Henry Stump and Peter Burbage jumped aside as Faith's seed sailed past their feet.

The girls' eyes grew wide as they placed seeds behind their lips, centering them behind front teeth. They spit. *Whoosh.* Again and again. *Ping.* The girls fell onto the ground in fits of laughter, spit seeds landing on their collars or down the sides of their shoes.

From a distance I watched, their high spirits relieving the guilt I felt. I could see a quiet smile forming on the lips under the limp bonnet of Celia.

Now, from the corner of my eye, I saw what Faith and

the girls were too preoccupied to see: the disapproving glances of parents and the frowning faces of the committee members as they marched across the grass. The examiners had a red-faced Amos Read in tow, and they were striding directly toward the refreshment table.

Truth to tell, I knew that somehow my stubborn sister was about to gather a great deal of trouble.

Biddy Bostick

Ha! If you ask me, it was the liveliest dinner table I'd ever hosted, and the boarders didn't even bother to eat.

Folks who never said a word suddenly had the gift of gab.

No! they said, bending forward over their plates, their napkins getting soggy in the gravy. *You don't say!*

They forgot their usual complaints: too little molasses in their coffee or too much pepper on their greens.

Imagine that!

What in the world's come over this younger generation?

Why, in my day, I'd never dare to think *such a thing!*

Which brings me to thinking. From what I could tell, seems like the girls up at the schoolhouse had started doing some, and folks didn't like it. *Ha!* I wasn't alarmed that Faith Common was at the bottom of it. I was downright pleased.

Herman Totweiler, the booby who boarded with me, passed out the information over the dinner table like it was money in the pocket, which it was in a town like Millbrook. Most folks had more gossip than they did ready cash.

Mr. Totweiler had no one in the world for a friend but another booby named Jeremy Thatcher, a *dummkopf* who passed himself off as a schoolmaster in Troy.

Ha! It seems the girls had used their copybooks for a new kind of penmanship practice. Instead of copying verses laid down by their master at the head of their pages, they had copied down questions set out by Faith Common:

> Why is it assumed that a girl's greatest ambition is to roll a French knot?
>
> Why are books put into the hands of boys and needles into the hands of girls?
>
> Why are girls taught to think flattery more appealing than justice?
>
> Why did God make the mind of a girl if it were not to be used?

The boarders didn't even notice that the corn bread was stale or that I'd drowned a few old slabs of it in gravy. *Ha!* Their mouths lay empty and their fingers sat forkless. I'd never heard such a row over a schoolhouse examination. Or felt so much pleasure at the outcome, either.

PART FOUR

Spring–Summer, 1838

Lucy Putnam

I declare, I'd never seen a handsome boy cry before.

We were out behind the slop trough at the back of Biddy Bostick's boardinghouse. It was just the two of us sitting on one big slab of stone.

"Here, Amos, I'll hold your glasses."

While he blubbered, I tried stroking the back of Amos's neck with the creamy white hands he'd always claimed to like, but Amos didn't seem to notice. He just went on and on about how ruined he was and how he'd end up just like his father. A no-account. A ne'er-do-well.

I declare I didn't know what to do. All I could think of was Mama when she took charge of Daddy.

"Now get ahold of yourself, Amos," I said.

I stood up from the rock and fluffed my skirts. He finally looked at me.

"You don't have to take this."

"I don't?" When he blinked, his tears seemed to dry a smidge.

"Of course not, Amos. You just leave things to me. We'll get back at Faith Common. You just watch."

Now Amos stood up and put his arms around my waist. I could feel the scratch of his chin on my cheek.

"Oh, Lucy," he said. "What did I ever do to deserve a woman like you?"

I declare, I had to think about that question for a minute.

But when Amos ran his hands through my hair, I felt a tingle all the way to my toes.

"What will you do, Lucy?" he crooned.

While I tilted my lips up to his, I was thinking. Hard. I

fluttered my eyelids down over my cheeks like a fan. "I don't know just yet, Amos," I whispered, "but I'll figure a way."

I could feel his soft lips brushing mine.

Then all of a sudden I heard Biddy Bostick yelling out her second-story window.

"Scat, Lucy Putnam," she bellowed. "You too, Amos," she said. "Skedaddle!"

Then Biddy reared back, put her hands on her hips, and laughed. I declare the whole boardinghouse shook.

I could feel the anger creeping up my cheeks as Amos hurried me away.

"You just wait, Amos," I said. "You just stick with me. I'll figure a way to get back at them all."

John Common

When I stepped outside into the crisp May morning, tiny bumps pricked the surface of my arms, and the spring breeze tingled the back of my neck. All of a sudden, delicate shades of green were climbing the bare branches of winter.

My own ears heard him before we saw him. They picked up the sound of the cart wheels squeaking, the reins snapping, and the deep baritone of "Hioooow, Onward." And suddenly there he was on the ridge, his long hair flowing loosely across his shoulders, his strong hands lifting his hat and waving it in my direction. Now he was suddenly here, swooping down from the wagon, gathering up first my mother, and then the rest of his family, wrapping them in the voluminous breadth of his cloak.

"Have you kept up with your logic, Charles?" he asked as Charles lifted his knapsack from the back of the wagon.

"And your reading of the Testament, son?" he asked

Wesley, who had begun to wipe down the horse with a blanket.

Then he turned from my brothers and asked, "And what about my firstborn?"

As Faith stepped forward, her head tipped up expectantly; the tail of her red braid lengthened, touching the bow at the waist of her apron.

With his long, strong arms, Father reached across her, and I felt his big hands squeezing the knobs of my shoulders with affection. "What about the progress of my firstborn son?" he asked.

Faith stepped back. The tail of her braid seemed shorter somehow; it lay silently against the line of buttons down the back of her shift.

Father asked his questions of me all in a rush. "How far have you moved through your text? Have you mastered Homer enough that you're ready for Plato, son? How would you rate your command of syntax?"

I was relieved he had not stopped for an answer. I had neither moved through, mastered, nor commanded much of Greek.

Then he turned to Faith.

I saw the apprehension in her dark brown eyes.

Now he asked, "Have you been a dutiful daughter, Faith?"

A pang of discomfort rose on her face.

But Faith changed the subject to one she could deal with more truthfully. "I have greatly improved my sewing, Father," she said.

Faith slipped the black cord from around her neck and displayed her scissors.

"Ahhh, good, child. I'm thankful you have put my gift to good use."

I swallowed hard, wondering when Father would detect my neglect of the gift sent to me.

Thankfully Mother took Father's hand, leading him to the supper table before any more questions could be asked.

Inside, Faith quietly hung Father's cloak on the nail by the door. We caught each other's eyes. They said what we both knew: she had not been a dutiful daughter and I had not progressed in my Greek.

Mother settled her husband, preparing to feed him. Faith brought Father a mug of cider while my brothers interrupted each other, vying for his attention. Even Grandfather seemed excited to have his adversary within sparring distance.

Mother set before him the plain white bread and fresh churned butter that was sweeter than any in the county. "Ahhh," Father said, gazing hungrily at the loaf. "A man's family is like this bread, Emma," he said, beaming at his wife. "Good bread," he said, recalling the Psalter, "*which strengtheneth man's heart.*"

"And Faith has learned what makes this bread so good this year, haven't you, Faith?"

Startled, Faith nodded quickly. "Yes, Father," she offered, observing that Mother had given her an opportunity to redeem herself. "Air in the batter and good fresh yeast."

"Dutiful daughters know those things, John, dear," Mother replied with a peck on Father's cheek.

Mother was trying to smooth the way for Faith. After all, it would be only a matter of time until Father heard what Faith had done.

Father looked around the table at the family he had been away from so long. "Let us take this moment to bow our heads in gratitude, shall we?"

He looked at Mother. At Grandfather. At Charles and Wesley and me. Then he looked at Faith, at the open windows that were my sister's wide brown eyes. "Faith," he said, "will you offer us a prayer?"

Faith was taken aback. She had never been asked to offer a prayer before. Although in the past Father had invited Faith to light a candle or bring the Bible to him for a reading, only my brothers and I had been asked to offer the occasional prayer at table.

Grandfather snorted like a horse before a meager portion of oats. "Unseemly, John Common," he pronounced. "Irreverent. I know about you Methodists. Encouraging public praying, you do. And by women, no less."

I was not sure what, exactly, my grandfather meant. I was aware that my father included women in his services. Often I had seen them walk to the anxious bench at the front of the crowd to confess their sins.

"Yes, Calvin, Methodists encourage women. Their prayers are as welcome before the Lord as any man's." Father thrust his square chin firmly in the direction of his father-in-law. "Go on, Faith. You may begin."

My sister's face told me that something inside her was opening up, expanding. Her father had honored her with his request, and he had now reaffirmed the honor.

I took the scowl that crossed my grandfather's face as a hopeful sign.

Faith bowed her head and folded her hands. She peeked over at Father. His head was bowed. On his lips was a reverent, anticipatory smile.

She took kind Hetty White's prayer over biscuits as her model. "Dear God," she began. "Bless this food and those who eat of it," she prayed. "May we be ever mindful of the great gift that is the nourishment of thy tender love. Amen."

I remembered how tenderly Jacob White looked at his

wife when she prayed those words at her breakfast table over the buttery smell of her steaming biscuits.

Then, like Hetty, Faith seized the freedom to add her own special message. "And bless our father, whom you have so graciously returned to us."

Although my grandfather frowned, I was far more interested in the expression on my father's face. At first his mouth opened briefly. As if he were thinking to correct her prayer. And then it had just as quickly closed. As if he had decided not to.

Faith sighed, pleased and proud.

Lucy Putnam

Why in this world did I have to have a mama who was always getting a bee in her bonnet?

After the examination, Mama declared that Papa would write an editorial on the topic of female education. Mama stood right over his shoulder, dictating changes in most of his words. Instead of "public acknowledgment of the problem," Papa wrote "public support of reform." Instead of "civic importance," Papa wrote "civic urgency." And why did Mama insist on raising even more questions? Hadn't Faith Common convinced the girls to raise enough questions of their own? Being as how Mama wouldn't let up until Papa included them, these questions appeared in Papa's editorial, too:

> If a woman has a gift for developing systems for sewing and cooking and keeping a house, why is she not permitted to use that gift to develop systems for classifying plants or cataloging the constellations?

If a girl's steady eye quickly detects the patterns in a cloth, why can't she use those same eyes to identify the patterns of minerals or crystals?

Why did my mama insist on turning things of concern into matters of alarm? She sounded like Paul Revere galloping across the countryside, warning the citizens of approaching ignorance. Well, I was so mad at her that I threw my mathematics text. It slammed so hard against the wall that the fireplace tongs shook. What was wrong with my mother? Why couldn't she just be like other mothers who simply hoped a little schooling might prevent their children from becoming complete ignoramuses?

Emma Common

Praise God that my husband has been returned to me!

"Emma, dear," John said only the day after he returned, "you have stitched enough plain work for a suite of tailors. Take some time for the fancywork that you love."

In truth, with John so often away, I could scarcely keep up with my plain work. Daily I worked on the homely items required by our household: handkerchiefs and pantaloons, chemises and smocks, towels and sheets, aprons and shawls. Stitches poured from my fingers like rain from clouds. How I longed in secret for a dry spell to devote to my fancywork!

John wondered aloud, "What happened to that fancy quilt you started several years ago? It was something Italian, I think."

The coverlet had lain in an obscure corner of my workbasket, quietly waiting for the day when I had time. But during difficult times, my longing for it returned. When Father's rheumatism launched a new series of pains, when Faith's dallying over her housework tested my patience, when John's awkward attempts to help pushed me behind, not ahead, the image of my coverlet seeped into my consciousness.

Blessed by the time to stitch, I marveled at the design under my fingers. I used a technique called *trapunto,* an Italian embroidery in which a design is raised from its background. Years ago I had traced out the design with nutmeg. It was a tree of life motif, with a sturdy trunk and symmetrical branches and lovely globes of fruit hanging from the limbs. It reminded me of the verse from Proverbs: *Hope deferred maketh the heart sick; but when desire cometh, it is as a tree of life.*

How wonderful it was to have John home! Everyone took lighter steps. With gratitude I watched John turn over the garden, spading in manure and sand. He cleaned the horse's cracked hooves, treating them with a poultice of boiled carrots. He built a brick boiler attached to a bathing tub at the side of the house, establishing privacy with a hedge of boxwood. He hammered up a lattice portico onto which my morning glories could climb. Much as my sons had tried to help, their efforts could not equal those of my strong and experienced husband.

And to my great relief, he handled Faith's transgression with equal strength and experience. "Emma," he said, having listened to my version of Faith's troubles, "transgression is the bread and butter of a pastor's life. Right conduct will follow if Faith heeds God's holy word."

Over my stitching I listened as John counseled our wayward daughter. Only a few days after he arrived home, he sat her before the fire in the evening for a conversation while I stitched quietly on my coverlet.

He asked Faith to bring him the Bible.

He instructed her to open it to a chapter in Proverbs.

He explained that before her lay an important passage, a passage describing the psalmist's definition of a virtuous woman. He said that heeding it would lead toward right conduct and away from transgression. He insisted that she read it aloud and learn it by heart.

As a child, Faith listened spellbound, feeding on the holy words that fell from her father's lips: *A time of war and a time of peace; A time to be born and a time to die; A time to rend and a time to sew.* As she grew older and the words became more difficult, she sometimes interrupted, seeking explanations for the meanings that eluded her: *Handmaiden. Manna. Majesty. Pestilence.* All that was well and good, and John answered her with patience.

But then, as she grew into young girlhood, her brow furrowed as her father read longer sentences and passages: *A soft answer turneth away wrath. All wickedness is but little to the wickedness of a woman. A wise son maketh a glad father.* Then, questions flew from her lips like loose sparks from the fireplace, sputtering dangerously on the hearth.

"Isn't a loud answer, Father, heard more clearly than a soft one?"

"Why should a woman's wickedness be thought greater than that of a man?"

"Why can't a wise daughter make her father as happy as his son?"

Faith's questions were followed by predictable responses. Sniggers from her brothers. Condemnation from her grandfather. Uncomfortable silence from me.

But what I remember most vividly was the reaction from John. His head snapped in Faith's direction like a horse brought up short. His dark eyes narrowed as if trying to bring her into focus. The narrow slits that were my husband's squinting eyes said he could not yet understand this daughter.

Now, with great relief, I listened to Faith repeat the verses from Proverbs John had assigned for memorization. She raised not a single question, not a solitary squeak of protest.

"Very good, Faith," John said when she had successfully memorized the passage. "Excellent, in fact. You learn quickly. Now all that remains is for you to write a letter of apology to each of the masters."

Faith opened her mouth to protest. Then, thinking better of it, she quickly closed it again.

Ellen Gordon

I was flattered that Faith sought my advice about the letters she was required to write. She had only done something like that one other time.

It was at the end of the school year, that shameful time between the masters' visit and the end of school. Trouble had followed on the heels of our tricks. We girls had to bear the disapproving looks on our parents' faces at home. We girls had to bear the torture of being kept separate, forbidden even to play together during recess.

Sean Hungerford had shuffled over to Faith, dragging his big feet and hanging his head.

"Excuse me, Miss Common," he began.

"Faith," she corrected him.

"Well, then, Miss F-F-Faith," he stammered.

"Faith."

The big boy cleared his throat. "You've been generous with your f-f-favors to me," he said, taking a big breath to power what was to come. "I was w-w-wondering if I could ask one more."

He had asked her for a letter of reference. He wanted to find better work to help his mother. In a store. In a laundry. What I remember was the way he smiled when he added, "Any place that might need my c-cyphering."

Faith had asked me to look over the letter. It was written in her firm handwriting, the letters lined up evenly. It was addressed to "To Whom It May Concern." She had used phrases like "hardworking" and "kind." She had praised both the sums he had learned and the patience used in learning them. She had explained about the mother and the brothers and sisters. She had mentioned the palm hats and the white shirts. She had recalled Sean's ability to impose order on the woodpile.

To my mind, it was a fine letter. When Faith gave it to Sean, he had blushed from head to toe. "Thank you," he stuttered, "F-F-Faith."

Now Faith came to me, her frayed copybook in hand. She had a new challenge before her in her letters to the masters. "I want to apologize without feeling ashamed, Ellen," she announced, passing the drafts of her letters to me.

I couldn't see how this was possible. Apologizing required you to keep your head bent. Not feeling ashamed required you to keep it held high. Doing both at once seemed impossible.

"I want to apologize only in words of absolute truth," she continued, screwing up her brow in that intense, focused way she had. "I want to say I'm sorry it *happened,* but I don't want to say I'm sorry I *did* it. Do you understand, Ellen?"

I thought I did. I thought I understood the things she was sorry for. Faith was sorry for how everything turned *out*. But she was *not* sorry for standing up to Amos Read.

As I looked over her letters, I could see that Faith had spent a great deal of time drafting her letters to each of the examiners. Whole paragraphs were scribbled out, and many of the words were deleted, indicating places where she had changed her mind and started over again.

I agreed with her sentiments. "I'm not sorry for what we did, either, Faith."

In the end Amos Read had not been punished at all. Reverend Norcross and Master Thatcher agreed that Amos Read had been too inexperienced to deal with such outright rebellion among children and that the embarrassment of the incident would be punishment enough.

Still, in my view it was Faith who ended up most deeply embarrassed. After her letters to the masters appeared in *The Millbrook Gazette,* everyone in Millbrook had an opinion about Faith Common and the sincerity of her apologies. In the energetic letters to the editor which flew back and forth across the pages of the weekly paper, most citizens believed poor Amos had been tricked by rebellious girls and their revolutionary leader. Only Mrs. Putnam protested the ignorance of our teacher and the insults to his female pupils.

But Faith herself complained little about her public humiliation. What bothered her more was that her father, finally home, spent most of his free time with her brothers.

"I get," Faith complained, "only a quick nod or pat on the top of the head."

I put my arm around my friend's shoulder. I hadn't really expected her to let me leave it there. She was not one to seek comfort or admit to needing it.

She shrugged off my arm, returning to the angry Faith Common that was more familiar. "He can't see *me*!"

I knew what she meant. My mama and daddy couldn't see me, either. They couldn't see the girl who felt more real before the mirror than away from it, the girl who could only remain her parents' daughter by being someone else.

Lucy Putnam

Well, I felt like the cat that caught the canary when I heard about what happened to Faith Common. She and the other girls had it coming. They had humiliated sweet Amos. They deserved what they got. I declare the irreverent questions Faith had made the girls copy into their copybooks were bad enough. But some of the other girls had drawn outrageous pictures and put them on display before the masters, too. Liddie Martin drew a picture of Amos with his feet up on the desk and a fishing pole in the schoolroom water bucket. Sarah Tyler sketched a series of pictures of Amos and me. One showed us bending our heads together over Amos's desk, but Mama didn't believe me when I said the picture was a lie and Sarah was just jealous. Betsy Fisher displayed a limerick she wrote; it described Amos as a donkey with hanging ears and an overbite. Ellen Gordon wrote a play in which I was cast as a scullery maid and Amos a stable boy.

Somehow only Faith was punished, though. She had to write a letter to each of the masters on the examination committee, apologizing for her behavior. The only reason she did it was being as how her father came back to town. If Bishop Common hadn't returned, she would have gotten away with her tricks.

Well, I wasn't one bit sorry for the way things turned out for me, either. Being as how I talked someone I know into getting his hands on those letters of apology so Papa could run them in the *Gazette*, I came away best of all. When

Papa bought me some red satin slippers and a new paisley shawl, he gave me a great big kiss and said he'd never sold so many papers in his life!

Emma Common

Only a week after his return came the marvel of John's preaching under the revival tent. Aware of the power of his ministry and their own need for spiritual revival, the citizens of Millbrook made an immediate request for his services.

Under the tent in the meadow on that fine May morning, he had preached for hours on many subjects, moving easily from text to text. But my dear husband touched my heart most deeply when he was moved to preach from Proverbs, on the text Faith had committed to memory: Proverbs 31:10.

"*Who,*" my handsome husband exhorted the crowd, "*can find a virtuous woman?*"

I felt he was not only speaking directly to the virtuous women of Millbrook, but also directly to me.

Perhaps, I immodestly imagined, my husband was even speaking *of* me as his powerful baritone recited the traits of a virtuous woman.

"*She worketh willingly with her hands,*" he said, his own strong hands uplifted in praise. "*She looketh well to the ways of her household. She eateth not the bread of idleness. She maketh fine linen. She stretcheth out her hand to the poor; she reacheth forth her hands to the needy.*"

Finally I felt my heart lifted heavenward when my John concluded, "*Her price,*" he said, pausing pointedly, his eyes seeking and then connecting with my own, "*is far above rubies.*"

How the blush rose on my cheeks!

Afterward, how happy I was for the many visitors who came to our house, flooding our quarters with praise and requests for more preaching! Stowell Brownell asked for John's services at the Freewill Baptist church in Wilburn. Mayor Girton requested that he give the invocation at the Fourth of July ceremony. And in the glow of John's success, the good citizens of Millbrook flattered my dear husband into a decision: John would resign his bishopric. Immediately. He had missed his family deeply. He had traveled on behalf of his church for years. Now it was time for him to stay home, to build a church among them, among us. He would gladly stay. And my Dorcas sisters, with their characteristic generosity, elected to devote the profits of the fall's Benevolence Fair to the building of John's church. How elated I was!

Finally, I felt the fortune in the fancywork under my fingers. Sometimes I worked on the coverlet late into the evening, so eager were my fingers to stitch on my husband's behalf. I tried to stifle my pride when I saw how lovely trapunto is when illuminated by candlelight. As the evening gathered around me; as the light cast shadows now on one part of the quilt, now on the other; as the point of my needle flashed like a silver star across the glowing shapes of the tree of life spread out across my knees, I recognized the value of my handiwork. My coverlet would command a great price in town, a price to benefit my husband.

When I stitched, secretly admiring my talent, I thought back to that verse in Samuel. *I know thy pride, and the naughtiness of thine heart.* I was ashamed of my naughty pride. But I trusted God to understand that my handiwork was offered up not for myself alone, but for another, more worthy, cause.

Ellen Gordon

Of course, I didn't explain it to Mama this way, but to my mind, Bishop Common's preaching had been the closest thing to a drama this side of a theater. The greening meadow was his stage. The bright May sun was his lighting. The tent under which he preached was as packed as a matinee. The townspeople, dressed for the performance in their bright bonnets and clean collars, spread out across the grass like excited theatergoers. The anxious bench in the front, where the converted gathered to confess their sins, was his—and our—stage.

To my mind, Faith's father was handsome as Edward Bonnet had been in *Manly Courage*. Bishop Common was tall and broad shouldered. Everything about him was square and upright: his firm chin, his straight shoulders, his steadfast stance. Everyone in the audience was captivated by the power of his voice and the conviction in his manner. His preaching was delivered, Vera Cramer said, in a baritone so sweet it might have been music. He spoke his words with a confidence, Sarah Tyler said, that seemed a natural gift. The sincerity of his manner, Betsy Fisher said, was apparent in the way he rolled his eyes heavenward, beseeching the Lord's help in forming his words and in uttering their truths.

"*Dorcas* was the Greek name for Tabitha," Bishop Common began, his strong chin thrust forward. "She was the model of a virtuous woman. She was a Christian woman, full of good works."

As he preached, I imagined how I might act out the various parts. The tired widow, her work piled around her in various stages of completion. The beggar children for whom Dorcas stitched tunics and blankets. The elderly for whom she stitched lap robes and caps.

"And Dorcas, this virtuous woman," Bishop Common said, his powerful gaze scanning the crowd, "never expected money for her work. She never expected thanks. Never did she appear on a public platform to receive praise for her good work. Never did she complain of the difficulties of her hard life. It is no wonder that when she died, Dorcas, that virtuous woman, was mourned by all."

Listening to him preach, I imagined the virtuous Dorcas laid out for burial in an upper room, her unfinished work piled about her. It was not difficult to picture the women of Joppa, crying and weeping, leading Peter into the upper chamber, telling him about the virtues of their friend, pointing out all the coats and garments she had stitched for others.

"After a while, Peter asked them to leave," continued the bishop, building toward his climax. "They did so, and Peter fell on his knees and prayed beside the body of this virtuous woman. Then he stood and said, *Arise!*"

A hush fell over the crowd.

"Ladies and gentlemen, girls and boys, sinners and saved," he cried out, addressing the crowd, "it was then that Dorcas opened her eyes, sat up, and rose from her bed!"

The crowd gasped, holding its collective breath. "And this virtuous woman," he concluded, "this virtuous Dorcas was returned to life, and she remains the only person in the New Testament raised from the dead by one of Jesus' disciples. God be praised!"

After he had finished, I looked around. Many of the girls were weeping, and many of their mothers were wiping tears from their eyes.

The conversions came in waves.

When Sarah Tyler approached the anxious bench, she turned to the crowd, begging them to offer her a special prayer. Bishop Common had quickly led them in one. I was transfixed by a whirling sound like something holy and by the anguished shrieks of Sarah as the blessed spirit of the Lord consumed her.

In fact, I myself, like so many of my friends, became swept up in the power of God's love and approached the bench on the heels of Sarah's example. I rose to my feet on the enthusiasm of hands stretched high; I was drawn forward on the music of the "Amens"; I was moved to speak of my sinfulness and my salvation. Without hesitation and with the experience of many hours of practice before the mirror, I made my confession before the audience, encouraged by their thunderous applause.

After that, when we girls stitched, we often spoke of that important May morning and the newfound faith that united us. When we spoke of our conversions, Faith often took the opportunity to turn our conversation from serious matters to lighthearted ones.

"Girls," she said, winking, "did you see Lucy Putnam's antics at the altar? She can hardly understand the difference between conversion and a fainting fit."

We girls glanced at one another and grinned.

Then Faith stood up, mimicking Lucy. I couldn't have done it better myself if I had practiced for a week.

"First, Lucy dimmed her eyes, girls." Faith narrowed her own eyes into slits no wider than slivered almonds.

"Then her limbs began to shake." Faith set her own arms and hands to trembling.

"And then," joshed Faith, "Lucy's head swooned as if it were too heavy to be supported on its very own neck." The girls followed Faith into a head swoon.

"*But*," Faith added, "not before the eyes rolling back into her head found the figure of Amos Read in the crowd."

Then I rushed forward, swaggering heroically, imitating

Amos Read. As Amos had done that day, I held out my arms, and Faith collapsed into them like a marionette whose strings have been snipped.

Sometimes I wondered if Faith was anxious because she herself had not yet professed her own conversion. After all, Faith was even older than most of the girls who had flocked to the anxious bench to confess their beliefs before her father. After all, she, not they, was the daughter and granddaughter of ministers. After all, she, not they, bore the name of "Faith."

Celia Tanner

Grandma Birdie fell sick again, and I couldn't up and leave her to go to school.

Sometimes I slept beside Grandma Birdie at night, pressing my head to Grandma's chest to listen for the sound of her beating heart. I confess I was afraid.

Sometimes I thought about fear. I played my shame before the masters over in my mind, and I confess I understood something new. It was my own fear that had caused me to stumble over the straight lines of the word *perpendicular.* Now I hoped I wouldn't stumble on my fear again. Fear of having enough bread to live on. Fear that Grandma Birdie might die. Fear of being all alone. Fear that it would be just me and Pop and the noises made by heavy things in his hands. I told myself to stay strong. I confess I tried powerful hard to hold on to the quiet faith Hetty White talked about, the faith that helped you go on when you knew you just couldn't.

Sometimes holding Grandma Birdie's hand into the night helped calm my fears as much as the peony drops helped calm her heart. That and Hetty's words about how God provides.

When Mrs. Putnam appeared on our porch, I was flabbergasted. I hope she didn't think me rude, but I didn't want such an important lady to step over the dirty sill or take a seat on an upended crate or see Pop passed out in the rocker. I explained that Pop was taking a nap, and it would be best to talk out on the porch.

"I've brought you something I think you might profit from, Celia," Mrs. Putnam said. She seemed a tad huffy. "It's a mathematics text given to my Lucy. She hasn't even bothered to touch it. I thought it might interest you."

I looked at the textbook she placed in my hand. The spanking new cover. The tight binding. It looked as if it had never even been opened.

I didn't know what to say. I couldn't remember ever having anything like this before. Surely never something so dear to my heart. "Thank you, ma'am," I said.

"You're quite welcome, dear," Mrs. Putnam replied. "Of course, it's only on loan. I will ask you to return it in the fall when my Lucy goes off to Miss Lyon's school in South Hadley. But I thought you might use it yourself in the meanwhile," she said.

"Yes, ma'am," I said as she left. "Thank you again, ma'am."

I stood on the porch for a long time, watching her go. I confess I treasured the book and the way Mrs. Putnam called me "dear." It felt almost as fine as having Emma Common kiss the top of my head.

Ellen Gordon

Ever since Bishop Common announced he intended to build a church in Millbrook, our fingers were never still. Vera

Cramer, Sarah Tyler, Liddie Martin, Betsy Fisher, and many other girls had begun to stitch together again. And, as we had in the classroom, we stitched under Faith Common's direction. We had been organized into a group that Faith anointed with her special name: The Young Ladies' Missionary Society. Not only was her father building a church in Millbrook, but he was also planning for a young man to serve as a missionary to spread the word of Methodism in distant lands. Our mothers were raising money for the church building; we girls were raising money for the missionary. With our efforts added to the efforts of our mothers, this fall's Benevolence Fair promised to be the most profitable of all.

Thus, in parlors all over Millbrook, stacks of goods created by our fingers began to pile up. Liddie Martin wove dozens of ribbon wreaths. Vera Cramer stitched short poems across the grounds of samplers. Faith herself hammered out birdhouses and stools from scraps of wood, and she stitched scores of needle books.

I made the mistake of asking Faith why she had launched such a frenzy of stitching.

Immediately she grabbed the front of my blouse and began shaking me. "Don't you *see,* Ellen? The only way Father will see me is if I become a 'virtuous woman.' A woman who cooks and washes and helps the poor day and night. A woman just like my mother. A woman who *sews.*"

Under her grip I felt the curls bobbing on my head. I was both frightened and fascinated.

"When Father preached about the virtuous woman, Ellen, he was advising us. To govern by mildness, not force. To prefer flattery to justice. To ignore our own talents. His meaning is no different from the rules in Lucy's book on politeness."

Now, just as suddenly, Faith let go of my blouse. I was wondering how I could explain all the wrinkles to Mama.

"I *detest* sewing, Ellen. How can I ever become a virtuous woman if I hate to sew?"

Faith seemed at that moment a grand heroine to me. I longed to be able to capture before the mirror the way she lifted her head, the way her eyes filled with resignation, the way she determined bravely to meet her fate.

Celia Tanner

I confess I wanted to show John my textbook. I knew he'd be happy for me. After what happened at school, I missed seeing John most of all. But both he and Faith and their mother had been busy with the return of Bishop Common, and when I slipped to the river on occasion, hoping to share some time with him, John was now in the company of his father: the bishop was trying to teach my quiet friend to preach.

Now, when I spied them by the river of late, John seemed different. Thinner and smaller.

I learned that Bishop Common expected a number of things from John. To prepare John for a successful ministry one day. To serve as a missionary for the bishop's own church on funds raised by the Young Ladies' Missionary Society. To experience his first public appearance by giving the invocation at the Fourth of July parade.

Today, as I watched from a distance, Bishop Common urged his son to select a passage to preach on.

Since nothing came to the son's mind, the father chose the text for him. Proverbs 8:11. It was something about wisdom being better than rubies. It wasn't a text I knew. Neither Pop nor Grandma Birdie was ever religious-like.

147

"This ledge with the river below is the perfect place to develop your preaching powers," the bishop said. "You can stand on this outcropping of rock like a pulpit. And the noise of the churning river below provides a splendid opportunity, son. If you can make yourself heard over that noise, you will know what it is to throw your voice over a crowd."

I was worried for John. Like me, John was not one for throwing his own voice.

For a great while, Bishop Common listened as John practiced speaking the text from Proverbs.

Then John's father sat down with him on the rock ledge. "Let's think about what you might preach about this text, son."

John looked at his father blanklike.

"Let's start simply, John," the father said. "Rubies, John," he said. "What are rubies?"

"They're precious stones," said John.

"Good," the father said, relieved. "And what color are rubies?"

"Red. They're a color like fear. Like the fearful music of the mare with her mane on fire. Or the sounds of shame."

Bishop Common looked puzzled. He didn't understand his son the way I did.

Bishop Common frowned. He returned to the text. "What about desire, son? *And all the things that may be* desired *are not to be compared to it.* What does it mean to desire something? What would be something that you, son, might desire?"

John thought for a great while. Then he said, "To be able, Father, to play the sounds in my head."

Now the bishop didn't look just puzzled. He looked alarmed.

"Here, Father," John said. He pulled my pop's fiddle from his sack and raised it to his chin. He gave a long, sad pull on the bow. The sound John coaxed from the violin was exactly like the longing of desire.

Bishop Common listened close, but the frown on his lips told me he was disturbed.

When John stopped playing, he looked square at his father. Bishop Common did not return his gaze. "What about wisdom?" he said. "What does it mean to be wise?"

John hung his head and did not answer. I began to count on John's behalf. One, two, three.

"You've been studying your Greek, I know, son. What is the word for wisdom?"

John hung his head.

"Well, let's refresh your memory, son. It's *sophia*. Do you remember that?"

In John's eyes was reflected the confusion he reported to me when he described his attempts at Greek sentences, Greek words, even the Greek alphabet.

Then Bishop Common rose to his full height. He towered over his son. "Well, I suppose that's enough for one day, son," he said. Then he turned to leave.

"I think I'll stay awhile, Father," John said. "If you don't mind. I think I'll stay and practice my prayer for the invocation on the Fourth of July."

"Good idea, son," his father said, giving his son a sad smile.

I kept real still. So still I could hear the muttering of his father's voice as he tramped out of the forest. "Pity," he mumbled. "Such a pity he's a boy." His words ripped at my heart like an apron caught on a nail. Soon the sound of his heavy boots was swallowed up by the forest.

Amanda Putnam

Millbrook was straining at the seams on the Fourth of July. Jacob and Hetty White hosted a breakfast for the abolitionists from Worcester. The temperance society had come over from Troy. Even tiny Wilburn sent over a reporter to cover the parade for the county.

I had to stand on tiptoe to see the Fourth of July parade units. Frankly, I was irritated. The boning in my bodice poked into my ribs, making me feel like a trussed chicken. First passed the Presbyterian Ladies' Charitable Association; then the Wheelwrights' Cooperative; after that the Masonic Lodge, the Carpenters' Association, the Christian Female Reform Society. Marchers from all over Millbrook stepped in unison carrying flags, sounding bugles, waving to spectators.

Frankly, I was furious at Ted Putnam. And at his daughter, too. Lucy had begged to ride in the parade. If she wanted to ride with the temperance unit or even the prayer circle, I would have agreed. But I refused to have a daughter of mine parading nothing more than her beauty before the entire town on wagons featuring little more than pretty empty-headed girls. But that husband of mine refused to back me up.

I caught a glimpse of Lucy's wagon from behind the throng lining Exchange Street. The July sun beat down on the pretty misses in their wagons, smiling in spite of the beads of sweat forming like mustaches on their upper lips, seemingly indifferent to the skirts that weighted them down and the petticoats that buoyed them up.

First came Amy Callendar, ringing cowbells, representing the dairy farmers.

Next came Veronica Tyler, surrounded by barrels of

nails, circles of rope, and kettles of soap. She represented the Merchants' Association.

After that came Olive Sanders, representing the Flour Millers' Association. Olive looked like she'd turned a flower-pot upside down on her head. Every flower in God's creation bloomed atop her bonnet. Frankly, I believe Olive had not grasped that she was representing *flour*, not *flowers*.

And then came my Lucy's wagon. When I saw Lucy's soft white waving hands, I stifled the memory of the hours she had spent whitening them with lemon juice and softening them by sleeping in kid gloves. But I could not suppress the bile rising in my stomach when I realized my own daughter, my very flesh and blood, representing Millbrook's apple growers, was dressed entirely in red from head to toe.

Around me the spectators conversed stupidly.

Ignorance, ignorance, ignorance. Frankly, I should never have attended the Fourth of July parade. This year I had scant civic pride. No one had heeded my calls for better schooling for girls, and instead of using the profits from the upcoming Benevolence Fair for Mary Lyon's dormitory beds or slates for the primary school, my Dorcas Circle would use them to help John Common build a church.

Frankly, there was nothing for me to do but speak my mind. "Well, ladies," I said, "I believe that another church is just what we *don't* need in Millbrook."

"But even you must admit, Amanda," said Marguerite Gordon, smiling benevolently on her converted daughter Ellen, "that Bishop Common preaches on topics directed to us women personally. He understands our needs, and he reflects that understanding in his prayers.

"And at First Presbyterian," said Marguerite, "John Common prayed for Evelyn Bruce."

I sniffed. We all knew that Evelyn Bruce had recently lost her job at the mill. She had set her children to making tassels or matchsticks or umbrellas, whatever piecework they could find. Our Dorcas Circle had taken food to the family every Sunday so they could have at least one good meal a week.

Frankly, I could hold my tongue no longer. "Perhaps John Common is aware of these needs because of Emma herself." I knew Emma was often the first to learn about the troubles of those in Millbrook. Frankly, I did not like to praise Emma Common too freely. Although her charity to individuals was without peer, she never supported the causes of groups like the abolitionists or the moral reformers. Her concern was the condition of the trees, not the forest.

Emma blushed and changed the subject. "Now, Amanda, nothing we do can equal the power of prayer uttered through the lips of a gifted pastor."

The other women nodded agreement.

Frankly, I was incensed. Not a single friend of mine could summon up the view that their own attentions were a kind of ministry. Was it prayer that had provided Anna Landis with firewood every winter? Was it prayer that had furnished clean mattresses for the Hungerford children? Was it prayer that had finally accomplished the purchase of the new fire pumper and bell for Millbrook itself? I had to bite my tongue. Hard.

After the horses from Gordon's Livery trotted by, draped in red, white, and blue and pawing the ground, the parade ended. A few children danced in the street behind the animals while the crowd dispersed to the lemonade barrels and the shade under the awnings of merchants.

It was almost noon. The community ceremony was about to begin, and the townspeople wandered toward the platform in front of the Central Bank of Millbrook. It was an impressive building with Greek columns and marble steps, and I wondered what burst of civic pride had managed to inspire it. On the platform sat the mayor, the selectmen, Bishop Common and his son John, and other dignitaries who shielded their eyes against the blazing sun.

At the edge of the crowd I saw two rough strangers on horseback, dusty from a long ride, and I hoped they would be impressed by the civic accomplishments of Millbrook. I glimpsed Ted, positioned by the edge of the platform where he could hear and see clearly. Frankly, I would willingly have gone home had not my accurate eyes been required to appraise the day's events. After all, it was an important event. It was just a little over one year to the day after the terrible fire, and Millbrook could now finally bless and dedicate the new fire pumper and bell. Frankly, it was essential that I stay: Ted's reporting for the *Gazette* was so often muddled.

First Bishop Common stepped to the podium to give the invocation. Frankly, I must admit that he cut an impressive figure. Long black hair flowed to his broad shoulders. Jet black eyes winked in the sunlight. Standing on the platform before the bank, John Common's presence reminded me that, in Millbrook, a spiritual gift like his was as powerful as money. As the bishop scanned the crowd, a hush fell over the citizens. Then, to the crowd's surprise—and, frankly, my own—Bishop Common, vibrant against the bright flags and bunting, announced his pale substitute for the invocation, his own son: John Common, Jr.

The boy's face was white as the flour my Lucy used to dust her cheeks. His presence contrasted starkly with his father's. The one thrust his head forward with confidence, clearly hearing the word of the Lord; the other cocked his head to the side, still listening for inspiration. The one projected his voice with force into the crowd; the other whispered as if to himself alone. I caught only a few words from the lips of the frightened boy. "Hands to the needy." "Price . . . *mumble, mumble* . . . far above rubies." "Deliverance from fire." "Heeding God's holy word . . . *mumble, mumble* . . . more important than speaking it."

I surveyed the praying crowd. I saw Emma Common huddled with our Dorcas sisters near the platform. I saw Faith Common nearby, surrounded by a number of girls. After the son's mumbled invocation, Bishop Common introduced Mayor Girton.

The band played "Yankee Doodle" as Mayor Girton bounded to the platform. Swinging his arms like a conductor, leading the crowd in clapping and singing, Mayor Girton amused the spectators.

Suddenly the new pumper and bell were rolled up a ramp onto the platform by Millbrook's four volunteer firemen. They were dressed in their new red flannel shirts and black pants held up by fancy suspenders, and Mayor Girton led the crowd in wild cheering at their appearance, ringing the new fire bell in celebration.

Mayor Girton passed folded American flags to the selectmen who had traveled all the way to Seneca Falls, New York, to purchase the water pumper and bell. He was offering clear ringing words as praise: "deeply grateful," "exemplary service," "public trust." Frankly, he sounded as if he were running for reelection.

The brass insignias on the firemen's leather helmets glinted in the July sun as they waved their flags. The crowd broke into cheers and whistles. The band struck up "Yankee Doodle" again, and Mayor Girton applauded the firemen, the selectmen, and the pumper and bell once more.

And then the band, still playing, marched off the platform. Mayor Girton and Bishop Common and the fire-fighters and the selectmen bounded off behind them.

I was thunderstruck. Was that to be the end of the ceremony? Was no word to be said on behalf of the subscription campaign or the hard work that had made all this possible?

John Common

My brothers and Faith and I had volunteered to clean up after the parade. Swatches of bunting and stray flags, dropped by forgetful children, were strewn about.

My sister fumed, kicking at the litter up and down the street, swooping down and yanking up stray bits of paper as if they were chickens in a yard, grabbed by the neck in anticipation of supper.

Alvin Hobbes, a friendly lemonade vendor who was pushing his barrel home, waved as he passed. I waved back, but Faith set her teeth against him and refused to wave. I suspected that was because Mr. Hobbes was also one of Millbrook's volunteer firemen. He was wearing his new uniform. He was carrying a flag.

When I rose for the invocation, my knees knocked as Father introduced me. I had written the invocation myself. It was filled with praise to God as well as praise for Mother and the good work of the women in Millbrook. As I spoke the words of the invocation, I tried to enunciate, to project my words over the crowd as Father had taught me.

But my heart sank at the end of my prayer. Truth to tell, it seemed as if the townsfolk were not sure if I had finished. They lifted their heads one by one, bobbing up and down like corks in a stream.

After the ceremony I broke away from the dignitaries to

seek out Mother. She was standing amid her circle of friends as the crowd dispersed. They were quietly congratulating one another, pressing their hands together, dipping their bonneted heads in mutual appreciation. As I moved to congratulate the women for their work, Mother finally turned to me.

Her bonnet shaded her face. Only her chin and mouth were visible. Unwillingly, I believe, she faced me. From under the brim of her bonnet, Mother's gray eyes emerged. They were filmed over like thin ice across a muddy puddle. The ice looked fragile, as if it would crumble into slush under a sudden footstep.

Mother's cheeks were red.

Was it the red July heat?

Was it her red shame at my weak performance?

Or was it, perhaps, a red anger that I had seen only on my sister's cheeks, never on my mother's?

Still, Mother had kind words about my invocation. "I am proud of you, son." When she said, "I appreciate all those kind words you spoke about us women, dear," her cheek twitched.

Later, at home, Father seemed irritable. Perhaps he was tired from all that parading up and down Exchange Street. Perhaps it was all that heat. And yet secretly I wondered: Was Father irritated because he was ashamed of me?

As Mother and Faith prepared dinner, I noticed a distinct change in Faith's behavior. I witnessed a sudden devotion to Mother, an anticipation of her every need. Faith fetched the water from the well without being asked. She lifted the heavy kettle onto the hearth before it was required. She reached for the ladle before Mother needed it. She poured out Grandfather's molasses and my brothers' cider before Mother had time to.

Father must have noticed Faith's exceptional behavior,

for when we gathered before our dinner, he singled her out, embracing her warmly and then stroking her hair. When he asked her to offer the prayer, I gulped air. Father was rejecting me.

Before she bowed her head, Faith reached over and took Mother's hand, holding it firmly for an instant. Then she folded her own hands together before her wooden bowl.

"Dear God," Faith began. She spoke especially clearly, and I envied her ability. *"Father and Mother of us all."*

Faith's invocation recalled those I had heard over breakfast biscuits at Hetty White's table. It was an invocation that may have suited Quakers, but it was not one likely to be welcome in our Methodist home.

"Bless this food and those who eat of it," she continued, rushing ahead as if anticipating objection. "May we be ever mindful of the great gift that is the nourishment of thy tender love."

Out of the corner of my eye, I saw her tilt her head in Mother's direction as she added, like Hetty, her own words to her prayer. "And may we be ever mindful of the great gift that is the nourishment of our *mother's* own tender love as well. Amen."

When she had finished, we lifted our heads in unison. Then Faith reached over and squeezed Mother's hand again.

"Who taught you that invocation, daughter?" The baritone was deep and sonorous. Like the vibrations of a French horn.

I had expected the sour expression on my grandfather's face. But I had not expected the expression I now read on my father's. Not the pursed lips. Not the knitted brow.

"Well, Father," she began, "I wasn't actually taught it. I just learned it. I learned it by listening. To Hetty White. When Hetty prayed."

I knew I could never have produced responses as quick or as forthright as my sister.

"Freethinkers," my grandfather scoffed. "The Whites and your Methodists are nothing but freethinkers, they are. Religious radicals, the both of you."

"That's enough, Calvin," John Common said. "Methodists are not freethinkers. We are not as radical as Quakers."

Now he turned to his firstborn and only daughter. "But we invoke only one God," he said sternly. "Our *Father*."

The sharp taste of salt rose in my mouth, and I swallowed hard. In a family such as ours, even prayer could be a source of trouble.

Lucy Putnam

Sweet Amos and I knew it would be easy to sneak out that night. Mama would be busy writing an editorial about Mayor Girton's snubbing of the women of Millbrook, and Papa would be joining the men at the bonfire.

I liked the way the darkness draped us like a shawl. I liked the way Amos admired my red dress. I liked the way the satin swished as he turned me to kiss him. Best of all, I liked the shivers of pleasure I felt in his arms.

I declare the cemetery out behind the Whites' house was a fine place to meet. We could hide under cover of the woods and rest our backs against headstones cool against our necks. I'd never before realized that kissing could raise such a sweat.

Jacob White

It was turning dark, so I wondered why the lad hadn't gone to the fire. The menfolk lit a bonfire every Fourth of July outside of town, on the high ridge the lad himself had named Half-A-Loaf Mountain. His face had a worried look about it, but he sat silently in the parlor.

I had come to understand something about quiet folks over the years. They're the ones who say the least and stand over the coffin the longest.

"Did you see the parade today, Jacob?" John asked. He kept his eyes cast down the way his mother often did.

I nodded. "Wouldn't have missed it for the world."

"Did you stay around for the ceremony afterward?" He tapped his toe as he spoke.

"Yup. Surely did."

"And did you happen to hear the invocation, Jacob?" He stopped tapping and sat perfectly still.

"That I did, lad. Didn't thee see me at the back of the crowd? I was waving to thee after thee had finished."

Finally he raised the awning over his eyes and looked at me. "What did you think, Jacob?"

When the lad traveled somewhere, he took the longest route.

"I was too far off to hear it all. I was standing in the back of my wagon. I was a far piece from the platform."

I could read the look in his eyes without his saying a word. It said that any preacher worth his Psalter would be heard at the back of a crowd.

"But I could hear enough of it, lad, to admire what thee was trying to say."

His troubled eyes glistened faintly. "You could?"

"Sure. Thy voice didn't always reach me, but thy message did. Thee was the only one to recognize the hard work of thy mother and her friends."

Now the lad shuttered his eyes again, disappearing behind them, and I was reminded of the young boy I had come to know over the years.

"Even thy father, lad, wasn't skilled the first time he got up before a crowd."

A doubtful look crossed the boy's face, and the buckets of his eyes filled with water.

Suddenly I realized that Rufus Thomas had been listening from the doorway.

Quietly he stepped forward and laid an arm across the lad's shoulder. "I've watched you over the years," Rufus said softly, "trying to wear your father's shoes."

The water lifted to the very brim of the bucket and shuddered there.

Rufus took a deep breath and said, "The only shoes you ever have to fill, John Common, are your own."

While the water sloshed over the sides of the buckets, I kept quiet.

Now Rufus looked over at me. "I put out the quilt, Mr. Jacob," he said. "Got a call for a delivery. Wish me good luck and good night."

I nodded, trusting Rufus not to luck, but to the Lord.

Then Rufus slipped away.

"I can't explain it, Jacob," the lad heaved.

"Shhh, lad," I said, stroking his hair. It felt like stroking a puppy, all soft and warm. "Sometimes when folks are most troubled, no words can come. But I'm sure of one thing, lad," I continued. "Thee's going to be all right."

John stayed still. He said not a word. But I knew he was thinking. "How do you know, Jacob?"

"Thee understands where to find the inner light."

"I'm not sure what you mean," he said. "The inner light?"

"The place where God lives," I said.

"Will the inner light help me learn to be a preacher?"

"Thee has to trust, lad. Trust that God will teach thee what thee needs to learn. In time."

"How *much* time?"

"Anything that's worthwhile takes time, lad. Maybe thee wasn't ready yet."

He nodded his head.

The lad still looked troubled.

Suddenly I remembered Rufus. He'd been the first to notice that, around the farm, the lad preferred the chores that raised a sound: the singing of the scythe, the clanging of the horseshoes, the rhythmic whooshing of the flail against the threshing floor.

"Here, son," I said, pointing to the sack resting beside him on the floor. "Why doesn't thee just *play* me what's on thy mind?"

The lad gave me first a puzzled look and then a pleased one. He untied the drawstring on the sack at his feet and pulled out his violin. The melancholy sounds that he coaxed from the instrument spoke more clearly than words.

Emma Common

How could there be so much reverence and irreverence in one small family? Hadn't one of the letters to the Corinthians claimed that *God was not the author of confusion, but of peace*?

After the meal the menfolk left to gather on the hills outside of town to light the bonfire.

I anticipated where Faith would be: in the attic, writing in her copybook. How agitated she made me! I felt the need to thank her and criticize her, to embrace her and shake her all at once. But as I climbed the stairs to stand at her shoulder, I had not anticipated her question to me. "Mother," she said quietly, putting down her pen, "do you ever feel invisible?"

I felt as I always did when Amanda Putnam challenged me.

But Faith ignored my confusion: she barreled straight on ahead. "Well, I do, Mother. Girls are made to feel invisible all the time. With the exception of John, my brothers acknowledge me only when I can be of use to them."

I thought back to the dedication ceremony.

"And Father's the worst of all," Faith said.

I hope Faith hadn't observed my agitation. When she mentioned John, my heart churned like the clothes in the tub when I beat them with the dolly stick.

"Father pats my head when I bring him a slice of cake, but that only reminds him to tell my brothers about the pancakes and johnnycakes and hoecakes in the West."

On the heels of her words, I turned rapidly away and stared out the window. I could make out the figures of the men in my family marching across the horizon and the bonfire on the hill flickering in the distance.

Now Faith returned to her copybook and reached into some pages behind the back cover. Folded inside were the quilted squares she had stitched beside the fire with the other girls in the classroom. She pulled them forth and presented them to me. "Do you know why we girls began to stitch these blocks?"

"Why, to improve your sewing, of course, dear."

"No, Mother." Faith shook her head. Even in the dim light of the attic, I recognized the fierceness creeping over my daughter's features. "We stitched these as a trick."

In the face of my confusion, Faith continued. "The idea for it came to me from John, actually. In teaching John Greek, I discovered what I liked best about *The Iliad* and *The Odyssey*. It was the clever trickery I found in both books that delighted me."

I was entirely confounded now.

"So I played a trick on Amos, Mother."

"A trick?"

"Not just me. The other girls, too," she explained.

Then she laid out her blocks one by one.

"See the trapezoid shapes in the wings of those geese, Mother?" she asked, tracing the trapezoidal lines with her fingers on the block called Flying Geese.

I nodded.

"And do you see the equilateral triangle and the square in this pattern called Log Cabin?"

I, now fully aware, was astonished.

"Mother," she explained, "we were learning *in spite of* Amos Read."

Quickly I began to rummage through Faith's quilted squares, asking her to name the shapes behind the forms of wagons and fence posts and wheels and haystacks. Hexagons. Ellipses. Octagons. Trapezoids.

Now that Faith was certain I understood, she needled me once more with her question. "Have *you* ever felt invisible, Mother? As if you were hidden in full view, too?"

I felt a kind of understanding rising inside me like dawn: A woman participated in the world only if she helped others. Quietly. Without expectation of gratitude. "Yes, Faith," I said shyly. "Perhaps I have."

PART FIVE

Summer–Fall, 1838

Lucy Putnam

What in the world had possessed my mama?

"There's never been such a grand time for newspapering, Edward Putnam," she'd say, shaking my papa's shoulders so hard his spectacles slipped down his nose. "One day people will look back on 1838 and recall how newspapers, husband, changed the world!"

Then Mama paced around the room, muttering. "Look, Ted," she'd say. "We're helping to reform the schools! Imagine that! After that flap over the examination with the masters, Horace Mann himself wrote for a copy of my editorial."

Papa cleared his throat. "Correction, Amanda," he said, "that was *my* editorial."

Mama raised her eyebrow and ignored him. "Then there's Biddy Bostick stomping up to town to protest her tax assessment. Think of it, Ted! Perhaps one day this little paper can claim to have launched a woman's right to vote!"

Finally Papa gathered his wits. "Common sense would tell you, Amanda, that the interest in Biddy Bostick would have more to do with the town's hatred of our local tax assessor than with your nonsense about a woman's voting!"

Mama did not even look at Papa. She kept on talking. "And with just a little more work, Ted, I think my comments about Biddy are ready to go to press."

"Amanda," Papa huffed. "*I'm* the editor of the newspaper, if you don't mind. And I'll say when it's time to put the newspaper to bed."

Mama picked up a pencil and starting taking notes. She was off in a new direction. "And about those bounty hunters. It's bad enough for them to show up looking for two escaped slaves. But then they demand that the magistrate ask for Rufus Thomas's freedom papers. The nerve of their suggesting that they might be forgeries! It's an indignity, Ted. Simply an *indignity*."

I'd never seen such carrying on. I thought Mama'd finally cracked her china.

"Think of it! After I get through with my editorial about it, Edward, I can write to Jane that *The Millbrook Gazette* has affected the course of the entire abolition movement!"

Why did I have to have a mama without one bit of sense? Why couldn't she see that selling papers wasn't about changing the world but about changing life for the Putnams? After the masters' examination, the 105 extra papers Papa sold bought me the new kid gloves I wore to bed each night to keep my hands white and soft for Amos Read.

The only good thing about the sparks that flew between Papa and Mama was that my parents paid less attention to me and Amos. From atop the soft bed of pine needles out behind the Whites' farm, we'd begun to wonder about the comings and goings we'd seen there. Every once in a while we'd hear whisperings or shadowy figures crouched in the darkness.

I liked it when Amos leaned close and whispered about running away and getting married. I liked it when he held my hands in his and said he'd never felt anything so soft and tender.

When Amos said things like that, I just dropped my eyelids and said that Our Maker must have sent them to me. As a gift just for him.

Naturally, I didn't add that the gift fell to earth by way of *The Millbrook Gazette*.

Biddy Bostick

If you ask me, some things just stink and it's no use even holdin' your nose. In Millbrook it's the stink of lye soap jellin' in tubs and cowhides hangin' in the tanyard. If you ask me, justice in Millbrook plain stinks, too. *Ha!* If you're a woman or an imbecile, the law treats one just like the other. A woman can work for pennies a day makin' artificial flowers or bindin' shoes, and then they can slap her with a tax assessment without her say-so.

Which brings me to taxes. When Ralph Underhill sent mine, he said I owed extra on account of that hole on the roof and the sagging front-porch step. Didn't even bother to notice that the hole's right over the eaves of the porch where the rain runs off and don't hurt nobody. And if you ask me, the saggin' front step is a tribute to my business. Wouldn't sag if there wasn't so many folks willin' to trade with Biddy Bostick. *Ha!*

I was hopping mad. Told Ralph Underhill what I thought of his property assessment. Stank like a tub of lye soap, I said. Waved his paper right in his face. *Ha!* Got even madder when I saw that young Irishman in the office signin' up to vote. That boy couldn't even spell his own name, but Ralph Underhill said his *X* would satisfy.

Which brings me to satisfaction. It's as hard to come by in Millbrook as money. Drew a crowd when I stomped my foot and said that I ain't payin'. That a single woman's got no right of protest. No vote or nothin'. Taxation without representation, I told him. Same thing we fought King George for.

It didn't do no good. Only satisfaction I got was stoppin' some folks dead in their tracks to listen and watchin' the rest of 'em drop their jaws. *Ha!* Stomped home mad as a hornet, so mad I finally got rid of that loafer Ephraim Hall. He'd been boardin' for two weeks and hadn't paid a red cent. Heaved that ne'er-do-well out on the sidewalk my own self. Wriggled off both his boots to keep for collateral. Only good laugh I've had all week was watching that cheater flyin' down Exchange Street in his socks.

Which brings me to flyin'. At the supper table gossip was flyin' like chicken feathers. Wasn't about me, though. Was about Rufus Thomas. Miss Edna Simple blabbed all about it over her third helping of lima beans. Some bounty hunters showed up before the magistrate. From Virginia, they was. Had one order for two escaped slaves. Both women. Had another order for Rufus Thomas. Said Rufus had to produce his freedom papers. Said they was a forgery. Said there's a ring in Philadelphia that produces fake ones. Said they was fixin' to prove it.

Like I said, some things just stink and no amount of perfume's going to sweeten 'em up. In Millbrook we've got mor'n the stink of slops steamin' in the public street. If you ask me, ain't no justice for women and imbeciles. Free blacks, neither. *Ha!*

Calvin Mercer

Stunned I was when Rufus Thomas told me what he'd said to the magistrate. Now I knew how Job felt when he watched his fields on fire.

"You shouldn't have done that, Rufus," I said. "Not without asking me."

I'd thought back over the conversation many times since, I had. I was sure I had done the right thing.

"I told them up to the magistrate's office, Mr. Calvin, that you'd stand up for me. You and Miss Emma. *Vouchsafe* was the word they used. 'Have you anyone to "vouchsafe" your character, Rufus Thomas?' the magistrate asked."

Studied Rufus Thomas's face, I did. His eyes rolled like hatching eggs.

"Had to ask the magistrate what it meant, Mr. Calvin. *Vouchsafe* meant 'stand up,' the magistrate said."

At the time I didn't know why Rufus Thomas thought I could help. I still didn't.

"I knew you and Miss Emma would stand up for me. Lord knows, Mr. Calvin, you've seen me take out my freedom papers often enough. They've got a gold seal and everything."

Rufus was right about that, he was. I'd seen the papers. The seal winked like a pharaoh's gold.

"They'll believe you, Mr. Calvin," Rufus went on. "You've been a preacher. Folks always believe preachers. And Miss Emma, too. Nobody'd doubt her, either."

I studied Rufus Thomas through my good eye. Rufus's forehead rained sweat. Watched as he pulled an old rag from his pocket, I did. As he swabbed his face with it, I recognized that cloth. It took me back to that day in the barn with the pruning hook and my clumsy grandson and the fiery pain in my eye.

Informed Rufus of his error, I did. "You shouldn't have done that, Rufus," I said. "Not without asking me."

Rufus hung his head.

Turned to him, I did then. "Do you know what you're asking of me, Rufus Thomas?" I said.

"Yes, sir, Mr. Calvin," he said. "Asking you to stand up for me."

"No, Rufus," I said. I felt like I had whenever one of my parishioners asked a stupid question about a Bible verse, asking me to explain something that should have been as obvious as the sores and boils on the body of Job. "No, you're asking me to go against the Bible," I said. "Don't you know what the Bible says about masters and servants, Rufus?"

"No, sir," he said. "Can't say that I do. Besides, I ain't no servant. I'm as free as the next man who's his own master."

"Ephesians 6:5," I snapped. "Read it."

Confused I was by the look around his mouth. Something at the corner of his lips began to twitch.

"Don't have no Bible, Mr. Calvin," he said. "Can't read noways. Will you kindly read it to me?"

Emma Common

When Rufus came to ask for help, it was a Monday. The wicker basket at my feet was heaped with wet clothes. I had been hanging garments on the line: Father's thick stockings, John's white shirt, Faith's pantalets, the boys' knickers and trousers. How precious were these items to me! I had been singing while I worked. Even wash day seemed pleasant with my husband returned to me!

Rufus's head hung down as he spoke. "Can I ask you for some help, Miss Emma?"

"Of course, Rufus. Of course you can," I mumbled, taking a clothespin from my mouth and dropping it into my apron pocket.

He lifted his eyes slightly. "Thank you," he said. "I told the magistrate you and Mr. Calvin would vouchsafe my character, Miss Emma. I was wrong about Mr. Calvin. Mr. Calvin said I shouldn't offer him up without asking. I was wondering how you might feel about standing up for me, Miss Emma."

"Wait, Rufus," I said, dropping Faith's wet jumper into the wicker basket. It made a quiet sucking sound as it joined the other articles. "What's this about?"

"My freedom papers, Miss Emma. I don't have them no more."

I wasn't understanding. "Did you lose them, Rufus?"

"No, miss. Had them taken from me."

"Taken? Do you mean stolen?"

Rufus nodded.

"Some men, Miss Emma. Stole 'em right off my body and took them to the magistrate."

"What men?"

As he spoke, his mouth twitched like Dolly's tail as she flicked at flies.

"The men that rode into town. Slave catchers. Said they'd heard my freedom papers was fake."

"Whatever gave them that idea?"

"Something about a forgery ring. Claimed I got fake freedom papers from Philadelphia."

Confused, I turned absently to the clothes on the line. I noticed that the bleaching soda had failed to remove that stubborn stain on my husband's white shirt.

"I promise, Miss Emma." I saw the agitation in Rufus's round black eyes. "I've been to Boston and Manchester and Worcester and such. But I ain't never been to Philadelphia."

Rufus's body tilted like a twig. His short right leg made him look weaker than I knew him to be. I wanted to prop him up, to make everything about him square the way I did when I smoothed a bedspread with a broom handle. "So how can I help you, Rufus?"

His eyes had finally lifted, and a look of relief flooded his face. "You can vouchsafe me, Miss Emma. Tell the magistrate Rufus Thomas is an honest and upright man."

"That I will, Rufus," I said, knowing his bent body had never prevented Rufus Thomas from being upright. "There's no doubt about that."

I thought back to the first time I met Rufus. He had helped haul Faith down from the apple tree. I had been grateful for his help then and since. Absently I remembered that our first meeting had come on a Monday, too.

A breeze kicked up, rustling the nightshirts and petticoats, stirring something inside of me. "Even better than
that, Rufus," I said, "I'll get John to intercede, too. Everyone
respects my husband. Don't you worry. John will help you
make it all right."

John Common

Father had been out late into the evening gathering support
for his church from contributors in Wilburn. Mother was
stitching her coverlet by the fire when he arrived. I had
stayed up later than usual, and my eyes were closing over the
pages of my Greek textbook.

I'd been aware of their voices only as background
sounds: like the chirping of insects on a summer evening.
But when the sounds suddenly shifted into a higher pitch, I
began to listen.

They were talking about Rufus Thomas, and when I
looked over at my mother, her face was unfurling a hot red
flush. "But, John," I heard her say, "Methodists oppose slavery on principle, don't they? Hetty told me that good
Methodists had permitted her friends the Grimkes to speak
when Congregationalists forbade it."

My father's baritone became a bass. "Most Methodists,
Emma," Father said, "resist slavery on principle. But there is
not universal agreement. The most troubling issue is that the
controversy is threatening the church itself. There are rumors that the church will soon divide in two. One north,
another south."

My mother ducked her head. Her coverlet was draped
across her lap, and from where I sat, the tree branches on its
surface looked like brown throbbing veins. When she finally

responded, she kept her eyes cast down. "What would be so terrible about that, John? If the principle is wrong, wouldn't justice be served by separation?"

My father looked disturbed. I recognized that look. It was the same look he gave me when I practiced preaching with him beside the river.

"After all we've done to build the church, Emma?" he said. "After all our struggles to free it from the strictures of Calvinism?"

Mother studied her quilt while Father continued.

"Methodists are about *connection,* Emma. Not separation." His voice was a chord of anger and disbelief.

"But doesn't justice require separation from things that are wrong?" she asked firmly. "And doesn't justice often provoke controversy?"

"Controversy," he replied equally firmly, "is not the province of women." The timbre in his voice declared the conversation over.

Now Mother looked up. "But what about Rufus, dear? This isn't really about the larger issue of slavery. Or the state of the church. It's about standing up for a kind friend."

I thought about the kind friend my parents were discussing.

Father raised his brows. "Such generous hearts you women have," he said. "It's what makes you so beloved, my dear. And so naive."

Father pulled his watch from his pocket. "Rufus knows how much we appreciate all he's done, Emma," he said. "The magistrate is familiar with Rufus Thomas. He knows his character. Let justice do its work, dear."

Mother did not look entirely convinced. "Still, I think your intercession would help, John."

Now Father flipped open the face of his watch to read the

time. He looked tired. He reached down and took the coverlet from her lap. He folded it neatly, setting it at a safe distance from the fire. "Think about it, dearest," he said, offering her his hand. "You wouldn't want me to support activities that threatened to divide the *church,* would you, Emma?"

Now, rising, preparing to retire, Mother said, "Of course not, John."

Amanda Putnam

Frankly, I was campaigning. I wanted my friends to write letters in support of Rufus Thomas, and at our last Dorcas meeting, I did not hesitate to say so. "Ladies," I had urged them, "there is power in numbers. The magistrate reads the *Gazette.* He will not be able to resist the sentiments of an entire town."

My Lucy's face squinted like someone in need of spectacles. "Mama, you've already written five letters yourself! Can't you see that people find a topic tiresome when you force them to think about it so much?"

My Dorcas sisters nodded in unison, their beaks picking at stitches like parrots at seeds.

"Well, then," I said, impatient to counter the rudeness of my own flesh and blood, "we'll file a petition with the legislature."

Miranda Callendar looked up from the petticoat hem she'd been repairing. "Who has time to collect them, Amanda?" she asked. "And what good do they do?"

All the women nodded again. I'd never before seen such a limp-brained assembly of women in one place.

"Well, then," I insisted, fastening on another stratagem, "we'll get to our representative in the legislature. And our

Henry Tindale is a man with a great deal of influence. I'll make it my business to speak to him myself."

Esther Grimes knit her brow. "How could he be bothered about one set of freedom papers in a little village like Millbrook?"

Then Marguerite Gordon put down her skein of embroidery floss. "If you want to get the attention of Millbrook, Amanda, you should get John Common to preach about it."

All eyes turned at once to Emma Common. I had to admit that Marguerite might have made a bit of sense.

"John chooses his own subjects, Marguerite, dear," Emma said, a crimson flood washing over her face. "I'm afraid he's not open to persuasion."

Emma looked up from her lap. "Why don't we ask Hetty White," she offered quietly, "to persuade her friend Sarah Grimke to intercede?"

Suddenly all eyes lifted from their needles. They looked first at Emma and then at Hetty.

Hetty put down her knitting. "I thank thee for that suggestion, Emma, dear," she responded, "but I already have."

In the quiet I heard only the soft spin of the thread unraveling from the reel boxes.

"Sarah is checking on the status of Rufus's papers through her Quaker circles in Philadelphia," Hetty added. Her knobby knuckles rested beside her knitting needles. "And she'll arrive here tomorrow afternoon by stage. I've invited all of thee to take tea with us after that. And the next morning she'll speak with the magistrate."

I was indignant. "Well," I said, relieved and irritated at once, "why didn't you say so, Hetty?"

"Mama," a voice wailed, "you didn't give her a chance!"

Imagine that! Wherever had such an impudent child learned such impertinence?

Ellen Gordon

I'd been away in Philadelphia for most of the month of August, and I hadn't been eager to return to Millbrook. I'd seen six plays with Aunt Thelma and came home with a trunk stuffed with new fashions and fabrics and the knowledge that the broad neckline had fallen out of style along with plump leg-of-mutton sleeves. On the train ride from Philadelphia to Boston, I'd watched some rude girls sucking lemons in the back of the car, and I took it as a sign. To my mind, Millbrook, unlike Philadelphia, would be as dull as dishwater.

I'd been right. Instead of afternoons at the matinee, I'd spent afternoons darning the holes in my father's socks. Instead of shopping for tulle and mousseline, I'd picked over calico remnants in Albert Biggs's store. Instead of the sound of rousing applause concluding a theater finale, I'd been part of the chattering committee welcoming Sarah Grimke's quiet arrival at the stagecoach depot.

Still, I was curious. Like her sister Angelina, there was drama surrounding this simple woman in simple dress. She carried no parasol or reticule; she avoided bustles and flounces. Yet she attracted admiration. I struggled to understand it.

"Oh, dear," said Rebecca Kinder, batting at the dust on Sarah Grimke's dove gray skirt, "such a dirty business is traveling, dear."

"My, but you must be hungry," said Miss Esther Grimes. "I know there's not a decent place to sup between here and Worcester."

Now, as Miss Grimke spotted her friend Hetty White, they squeezed hands and kissed each other's cheeks.

"Dear Friend," said Hetty, "I have missed thee so."

"And I have missed thee just as much, dear," said Sarah Grimke. "Sister sends her love, for she's busy with work in Philadelphia." I wondered about what the Grimke sisters did in Philadelphia. I doubted it had anything to do with matinees.

In honor of her friend, Hetty had held the Dorcas Circle meeting at her home. Hetty wanted everyone to get to know Miss Grimke. I could not have predicted that a Dorcas meeting would turn out to be more exciting than anything I'd seen in Philadelphia.

Hetty White

My old hands shook over the tea things. 'Twant certain whether it was because of my excitement about Sarah's visit, my worry about Rufus Thomas, or my fretting over Sarah's plea before the magistrate tomorrow morning.

I tried to turn out a wholesome table for my Dorcas sisters and my tired and hungry friend. I'd set my pine table with fresh baked bread and fresh churned butter. Sweet Emma had brought her famous apple cake.

Sarah passed around copies of freedom papers she had brought from Philadelphia. She had deemed the samples authentic, and the ladies nodded over them, impressed by the neat calligraphy.

I knew Sarah possessed an accurate eye for authenticity, but we both understood that she made her assessments for reasons only she and I were privy to. We knew Rufus's papers were genuine, but the abolitionists in Philadelphia often studied such genuine freedom papers in order to copy them; then they supplied escaping slaves with these authentic-seeming freedom papers, hoping to buy them time until they could reach the safety of Canada.

My women friends were full of questions.

"Don't you and your sister tire of traveling, Miss Grimke?" asked Marguerite Gordon.

'Twas aware of the weariness of Sarah and Angelina. 'Twas aware of the five to six engagements a week in as many towns. 'Twas aware of the boiled cabbages that passed for supper, the thin mattresses that passed for lodging, the constant colds they passed back and forth between each other.

"Doesn't the opposition to your speaking frighten you?" asked Miranda Callendar.

I knew about the armed crowds and angry threats.

"Aren't you embarrassed by all the jeering that accompanies you?"

"That is true, Mrs. Kinder," replied Sarah. "Angelina and I endure all manner of rude behavior. But it only makes us more determined."

"Aren't you afraid of bringing division into your church?"

I looked over at Emma, the woman who had been like a daughter to me. 'Twas a shame Emma felt so divided herself. Just recently, over tea, she had shared her distress about Rufus Thomas and her husband's fear that the issue of abolition would divide his church.

"Quakers are not divided on this subject, Emma," Sarah said. "We think of every person as a 'Friend.' King or subject, male or female, freedman or slave, we address all with equal respect as 'thee' or 'thou.' Naturally, we uniformly oppose slavery, dear."

Emma had stuck her needle in her pincushion to listen. Her elbow was resting on the arm of her chair, and her chin was resting in the palm of her hand.

Amanda Putnam

Frankly, it was the most successful Dorcas meeting we'd had in months.

Miss Grimke was entirely accurate in her appraisals. She mentioned that slaves in the South were forbidden to learn to read or write.

"Exactly so, my dear," I agreed. "My editorial in July complained of just that."

"And they cannot travel without their master's permission."

"Entirely correct," I said.

"Their masters can separate families one from another and sell them away at will."

"The very worst situation of all," I said. "I took it up in the issue of July twenty-ninth."

Frankly, though, I hadn't recognized the subtlety of Sarah Grimke's intellect.

"How can a person consider himself free," Miss Grimke said, "if he must always carry around a paper to prove it?"

Frankly, I had not considered that point before. I had written—August fourteenth, to be exact—that free blacks were treated unfairly. After all, they had to sit belowdecks on a steamer and couldn't ride inside a stagecoach with the other passengers.

"It seems to me," continued Miss Grimke, "that this requirement implies that a free black is to be always under suspicion unless he produces the evidence to prove otherwise."

I watched Faith Common writing in her copybook. It was a discerning point. I was making mental notes, too.

Imagine that! Something new for me to consider. I would have to remember that finespun phrasing and those subtle arguments for my next editorial.

Ellen Gordon

Faith concentrated on her copybook as Miss Grimke talked. She wrote rapidly, trying to keep up with Miss Grimke's words.

Miss Grimke recited the disabilities of the slave. "A slave is . . . *unable to make a will, unable to vote, unable to own property, unable to handle money, unable to use the courts for remedy.*"

From where I sat, it looked as if Faith were arranging those words into columns in her book. I was curious about Faith's copybook. I had seen her writing in it many times. When Amos was the teacher at the primary school, she assigned us girls questions for penmanship practice from the pages of that book. When she wrote her apologies to the masters, she penned her letters from that copybook. When she wrote her letter of reference for Sean Hungerford, she let me review her work. But Faith had never shared what she had written there of her own private thoughts.

I had grown sleepy listening to so much heavy conversation. I drifted off, dreaming of the light patter of quarreling lovers, the birdlike laughter of flighty heroines I had remembered from Philadelphia.

It was then that I heard the hoofbeats. At first I believed the sounds to be coming from my dream. Auntie Thelma said two empty coconut shells pounding against wood made the stage sound of hoofbeats. But then the sound grew closer and louder. I heard hoofs clattering in the yard. I heard chickens squawking and flapping in their coops.

The two men did not knock. They burst through the door.

The women shrieked. My mama jumped out of her chair, tipping over her workbasket. Thimbles and needle cases and thread winders flew across the floor. The tall man brushed by the women, scattering pins and sewing implements everywhere.

The short man stomped right on through the middle of the room and headed out the back door.

The tall man headed upstairs. As his dirty boots tromped across Hetty's clean stair steps, Amanda Putnam grabbed him by the shirttail. "You can't go up there. This is a private home."

The man turned swiftly around, ripping his shirttail from her fingers.

He moved close to her, placing his menacing hands on her small shoulders. "Watch me, madam," he said. Then he tipped his dusty hat to her and mounted the stairs. I'd never expected to see a woman like Amanda Putnam tremble.

I studied the looks on the women's faces. They seemed frozen in a tableau like I'd seen on stages with my aunt. Amanda Putnam's face registered an alarm bordering on outrage. Emma Common's face bore concern for her frightened friends; her hands had reached out to hold the hands of my mama and Rebecca Kinder. Hetty White and Sarah Grimke had bent their gray heads together and circled their arms around each other's waists; the concern on their faces was tinged with faith, with a steadfastness that all would be well. Betsy Fisher's and Sarah Tyler's faces shone with outright terror; they clutched at their skirts like Celia Tanner before the masters.

We stood in silence while the clamor of overturning mattresses and slamming doors went on upstairs. When Hetty heard the sounds of shattering porcelain, she winced, "Oh, dear. That's my dear mother's china washbasin!"

Sarah patted Hetty's hands. "Be still, Friend. They'll be gone soon. Jacob will mend the basin."

Only Faith Common was not still. Faith had grabbed

the butter dish from the tea table. She smeared butter across the stairs to the upstairs bedroom.

Now the short man stumbled in from the back, a white chicken feather caught in his greasy black forelock. "Hey, Sam," he shouted to the man upstairs. "Nothin' much out back. I searched the fields and out by the woodpile. Went under the porch where a slave could crouch. Even searched through the chicken coop. Everybody knows a slave will hide anywheres. Even in a henhouse."

Now the short man called up the stairs. "Find anything up there, Sam?"

The tall man bounded down the steps. "Nope. Must have escaped before we got here." Suddenly the tall man's feet slid out from under him, and he toppled backward, slamming his head against the newel post.

Furious as a rabid dog, he had just begun to lunge at Hetty White when Jacob burst through the door, young John Common behind him.

As he marched across the room to confront the men, Jacob lightly touched Hetty's shoulder. Then Jacob straightened his spine and his white beard bristled. He towered over both men, even the tall one. "Just one moment, strangers, you can't burst in here like this."

The tall man sneered rudely. "I guess we just did, though, didn't we, mister?" he said, rubbing at the lump forming on his right temple. Then he pulled an official-looking paper from his pocket. The gold seal on the paper winked.

"On orders from Virginia," the short man said, thumping the paper with his thumb. "A master's entitled to possess his own property now, ain't he, mister?"

Now Hetty bustled over to stand beside her husband. "What property?" she asked. "And why Virginia? We've never been to Virginia."

The man moved closer to her, and Hetty huddled against her husband's side. "You know very well what property, Mrs. White. Slaves. Stolen property. Escaped from their master in Virginia. He's offering a five-hundred-dollar bounty for the return of each one. We know they're hiding somewhere. Likely here. Hiding stolen property's the same thing as stealing itself."

Quickly Faith stepped forward. "Why, that's absurd. Hetty and Jacob don't steal. They don't even charge for their own labor most of the time. Anybody in town could tell you. They're not thieves."

The short man turned to Faith. I could see the stubble of his whiskers on the lower half of his face and imagine the stink of tobacco on his breath. "We know what they say about Quakers, missy," he said roughly. "First place to look is for the Quakers. Where there's a Quaker, there's likely a stolen slave and a stationmaster on the Underground Railroad."

I was confused. I did not understand the man's words. *Stationmaster. Underground Railroad.* The closest railroad to Millbrook ran from Worcester to Boston. I didn't think either Hetty or Jacob had ever traveled on it.

Then Jacob threw his broad shoulders back and stepped even closer to the men. He thrust his face into theirs. *"There are no slaves here,"* he said firmly.

I felt relief. I knew Jacob spoke the truth. Quakers didn't lie.

"Well, then, we'll just see about that, mister," the short man said, turning toward the parlor to riffle through the things there.

"Yes, we will," Jacob said, blocking the short man's path.

The tall man was rubbing his head. A huge knot had formed on his right temple. It was swelling by the minute.

"I told thee," said Jacob. "There. Are. No. Slaves. Here."

He said the words slowly, one at a time. It was the way Miss Sprinkle pronounced words when she tried to teach Henry Stump to read.

Then the short man turned to the Whites and shook his fists in their faces. "Just be sure we've given you plenty of warning, mister. A slave is property. It ain't yours to hide. Hiding property, Mr. White, that's stealing. And we've got jails for folks who steal."

"Let's go," the tall man said. "We're wasting time here."

Before he followed, the short man stepped across the room through the group of trembling women. The heels of his boots left clods of dirt across Hetty's clean floor. Then he reached for a biscuit from the tea table and took a bite, sending the tin plate clattering across the floor. As he stomped through the door after the tall man, the chicken feather in his hair floated gently to the ground.

John Common

Mother's Dorcas sisters stayed behind to help Hetty and Jacob clean up the room. They rewound scattered threads into reel boxes; they ran the sewing magnet across the floor, scouring for pins; they returned stray books to the bookcase; they washed up the tea things and put them away.

When everyone left, Faith and I stayed behind to comfort Jacob and Hetty and Sarah. Miss Grimke bent her head over Faith's copybook, nodding with Faith over the comments my sister had scribbled there.

I examined the pieces of Hetty's mother's washbasin. "I think I can fix it, Hetty," I said. I held one large piece in each hand. "It's not shattered." The basin had been broken neatly in two; one giant crack separated the pink flowers on its surface from their leaves and stems. "It's a neat break, Hetty, and a clear one. A neat break like that's an easy mend."

Sarah was seated at Hetty's writing table. "I'll send off this note to Angelina. She may not be able to expect me as planned. It will depend on what happens here. Would you mind taking it up to the post rider in town, dear?" she asked, handing the letter to Faith.

Faith had just put the letter in her apron pocket when it happened.

I heard a sneeze. So must have Faith. The two of us looked at the Whites: they both looked startled.

"Did either of you sneeze just now?" Faith asked.

Both Hetty and Jacob lifted their gaze and blinked at each other, confused.

I had just bent my head back to the basin when I heard it again. Another sneeze. It was unmistakable. It sounded like it was coming from behind the bookcase. Neither Jacob nor Hetty could deny it this time.

It was then that Jacob and Hetty looked squarely at each other. Jacob took the two halves of the basin from me and set them on a nearby table. "We're among friends, Hetty, dear," he said.

She nodded. "Yes, husband," she replied, "we truly are."

Jacob moved to the bookcase and gave it a heavy push. Slowly the bookcase swiveled on a turntable to reveal its back side, and I saw three forms in shadow. Two were female: one young, the other older. Their mottled skin was damp with sweat, and they were clutching a third person in terror.

And as the back side of the bookcase swirled into full view, I saw that the third person leaned to the left to steady himself, the toes on the foot of his short right leg pointed for balance. When the dark face scurried across the faces in the room for sign of friend or foe, its eyes finally alighted on me.

And as I looked into the kind eyes of Rufus Thomas, I saw something there. Something I had never seen on his face before. But something I recognized. Something familiar that I struggled to name.

"Oh, Mr. Jacob, sir," Rufus whispered. "I apologize for Ruby, truly I do, sir. But it's so dusty back there."

The young girl he called Ruby covered her nose and face with the skirt of her apron. Peering from under the cloth, her eyes were red and tired.

"Are you all right?" Jacob directed his question to all three. "Did the men scare you too badly?"

"I won't lie, Mr. Jacob," Rufus said. "There was shaking going on behind this bookcase here. I made Jewel and Ruby put their fists in their mouths. I bit down hard on this rag here."

The older woman Rufus called Jewel nodded her head in agreement. The young girl he called Ruby was still trembling.

Then Rufus shook out the checkered rag, swabbed his forehead with it, and folded it up. The sight of it startled me. It was the same rag Rufus had pulled from his pocket that afternoon in the barn when Grandfather had lost his eye. On that day, Rufus had wadded it up, offering it to Grandfather, urging him to bite down hard. Grandfather had agreed.

"But bein' scardt is something they've both been through many times before this," Rufus said. Then Rufus acknowledged me. "And young John here knows what it is to be in hiding. To be so scared you run away."

I gulped. I hadn't realized Rufus Thomas had seen the fear in me.

Then, taking the women's hands, Hetty moved them from the darkness into the light. I took in the black skin that glistened as if smeared with salve. I saw the patches of skin on their throats and hands that looked at first like patches of leaves throwing dappled shadows. Then I realized what the patches were. Some were pink and tender; others were yellow and white; still others were crusted and brown. As Hetty moved them to chairs by the tea table, I caught a bitter whiff of arnica. It was clear both women had been badly burned.

"Here," Hetty said, urging them to sit. "Please. Sit and rest. I've made some fresh tea. Hot tea always soothes the spirits."

The women's eyes darted around the room from one face to another, landing on Hetty's face like frightened birds on a limb. But they did what she asked and sat. Their hands were shaking so badly they could scarcely hold their cups. I saw that Jewel, the older woman, sipped only from the right corner of her mouth. When she turned her profile to me, I could see that the left side of her face from her cheekbone to her temple was drawn up tight; the cheek below hung loose and swollen. Truth to tell, it looked like Mother's string purse when she stuffed it to the brim and then pulled tight.

Jacob White

I had just loaded the box into the back of the wagon from its place by the woodpile when the ladies met me in front of the house. My Hetty's dear hands held a basket of fried chicken.

I was trying to adopt a casual manner. Helping Emma and the wee one and Sarah and my Hetty up into the wagon, I said, "May I give thee ladies a lift to town?" Nervous about this trip to the magistrate's office, they returned only stiff smiles to me.

The lad climbed up beside me; he did not yet know that I would need him for something other than a visit with the magistrate.

A crowd had gathered when we arrived in town. I helped the women down from the wagon, and then I looked over at the boy.

"Ladies," I said, "I'm going to need to borrow the lad this morning."

Their eyes frowned. They had been counting on my presence with them before the magistrate.

I said that a friend was suddenly in danger of dying and that a box might be needed over by Springfield, halfway to South Hadley.

"Why are you taking John?" asked Faith. She had snapped her head around so fast that her braid now dangled across her chest.

I had known she wouldn't like it. She was the one I usually asked to accompany me, and now I was asking her brother.

"I need thee here with the ladies," I said. "Thee can help with the questions and answers. Thee can help them stiffen their spines. Thee's good at things like that."

She eyed me suspiciously.

"Who died, Jacob?"

"Didn't say anyone died." I could feel a burr of irritation rising in my throat. "Said someone was in *danger* of it." That wasn't a lie. That was the very truth.

A pout had settled across her young face. "Who?"

"A friend."

"What friend?"

Hetty attempted to usher the wee one off, but Faith would have none of it. Instead, she shook off Hetty's hand and turned around, standing on tiptoe to stick her nose right next to mine.

"Why did you lie to those two bounty hunters, Jacob?"

"Lie?"

"You said there were no slaves in your home. And there were. They were hidden right behind the bookcase. I thought a Quaker never lied."

"It wasn't a lie," said Hetty, stepping forward now, tipping her gray head in Faith's direction.

Faith looked puzzled. "I know a lie when I hear it," she insisted.

Now I gathered one arm around Hetty and the other arm around Sarah Grimke. "Quakers don't believe in slaves," I said. "We believe every person is free. Free to heed his or her own inner light. We believe there is no such thing as slavery."

Now Sarah spoke. "Quakers believe what the Bible says in Galatians. That God makes no distinctions between *Jew and Greek, slave or free, male or female.*"

Hetty added, "So, Friend, when we say there are no slaves around, we truly believe there are not. Jacob was speaking a Quaker truth. Quakers everywhere understand what those words mean. Quakers do not believe a slave can exist anywhere."

"Not even behind the bookcase in his own house," I said.

By the by, as we had planned, my Hetty managed to hurry the pouting wee one away, and I was grateful. I was grateful, too, for the basket of chicken Hetty had left with me. It would be a long day.

I took a different route to Springfield, a rough path called the Springfield Trail. As the wagon lurched over the winding road, the lad said, "You know what I think we should call the Springfield Trail, Jacob?"

"No, what, lad?"

"I think we should call it the Silas Enders Trail."

I wasn't following him.

Then the lad grinned at me. "Silas Enders never spits straight."

John Common

Jacob drove boldly, snapping the reins with confidence, heading straight through the center of town. Past the lapping sounds of horses at their troughs and the sweeping sounds of women at their brooms. Past the canvas storefront awnings that snapped in the wind and the sleeping bodies of drunkards that snored in the doorways. Past the rustling sounds of women's petticoats and the thudding sounds of men's boots on their way to the magistrate's office. Past the people in town who waved in greeting, the arcs of their hands rippling the damp September air like conductors' wands.

As I rode through the middle of town beside Jacob, I was still surprised that he had asked me to accompany him. But I wasn't sorry. I knew a controversy was likely to take place in the magistrate's office. I had come to look out for Mother, just as Mother had come to look out for Hetty. But I much preferred riding out into the countryside with Jacob White.

The ride gave me time to think. Had it been only yesterday that I had learned about the fugitives from behind Jacob's bookcase?

Jewel was Rufus's older sister, and Ruby, her daughter, was his niece. Jewel and Rufus had been separated from each other as young adults, not much older than Faith and I. First Jewel was sold away to a new master in Virginia. Then Rufus gained his freedom when his master died, freeing all his slaves by will. Rufus had been trying ever since to bring his sister north to freedom. He had not even known that she had a daughter and he a niece.

With the help of some friendly Quakers, Jewel and Ruby had escaped first to Maryland and then to Pennsylvania where some friends of the Grimke sisters had directed them north, in the direction of the Whites' farm. When they finally arrived in Millbrook, they understood that bounty hunters were close on their trail. But they could not travel any longer. The last meal they remembered after arriving in Millbrook early one June morning was two half-eaten ears of corn from a slop trough behind Mr. Gordon's livery. After that was the terrible fire, and after that they had taken up life behind a bookcase, their burns nursed by Hetty and Jacob and Rufus for over a year.

The winding trail was muddy from the sudden showers of yesterday. Today's skies were filled with the clouds that made up September's uncertain weather.

I looked over at Jacob; his brow was a trail of tiny bird tracks. Had it been only yesterday that we learned about the secret life of Jacob and Hetty White? A *railroad* was a route from the slavery of the South to the freedom of Canada. This railroad operated secretly: *underground.* A silent network of *pilots* gave directions for the journey, and *conductors,* inviting danger to themselves, helped lead the slaves north. *Cargo,* or *passengers,* were the runaway slaves themselves; they rested from their travels and the danger of bounty hunters in *stations,* or *depots,* safe houses operated by *stationmasters.* And *stationmasters* were people like Jacob and Hetty White.

I looked up at the sky. I studied the blanket of clouds and the sun that was struggling to break its way through them. It was the way I had felt after Jewel and Ruby's revelations: struggling to break through to some kind of understanding. Now I pondered the sky with its gray-and-white clouds. First they seemed one thing: like gray puffs of dust that Mother swept from the floor. Then they seemed like another thing: white drifts of cotton batting that she stuffed into quilts.

It was Jacob who broke the silence. We had just passed a thick stand of red maples when he said, "I need thy help, son." I could barely hear him over the clopping of the horse's hooves.

I looked over at Jacob. He looked tired. I could almost see the years of dust and wood shavings gathered in the lines of his face. "Ruby and Jewel can't stay at our home much longer, son."

I noticed that Jacob hadn't called me *lad*. He called me *son*.

"The bounty hunters will be back. And it's not safe for any of them to try to escape right now. And Rufus's not likely to get far on that bad foot of his."

I wasn't understanding what that had to do with me.

"They need a safe place to hide, son," Jacob continued. "Temporarily, I mean. Until things have quieted down. I was counting on thy help."

"Me? But why me?" My tongue tripped over my words the way my fingers tripped over the strings of the violin when I was first learning to play. "Why not Mother? Or Faith?" In my mind, my sister Faith would be most likely to help. She was bold. She could be counted on to step up to trouble.

Jacob shook his head. "Helping might be difficult for thy mother, even if she wanted to. Helping Jewel and Ruby out might cause trouble between her and thy father."

I nodded. I could see what he was saying.

"But Faith?" I asked.

"Thy sister's spirited, son. Noisy, too. She's too likely to call attention to herself. The help I need requires somebody like thee, lad. Somebody with a quiet courage."

Like the clouds above me still wrestling with the sun, I felt both the pride of being asked and the fear of answering. But I wasn't sure what Jacob meant. How could courage be *quiet*?

I thought about what he'd said for a long time.

Finally, Jacob turned the horse up a rutted path. "We're here," he announced.

At the end of the path was a tiny cottage surrounded by a large well-tended farm. A quilt hung on the white fence post by the door—just as at Hetty's.

A tall strong man who wore a beard like Jacob's appeared on the porch. He was followed by a woman in a plain gray dress with a plain white cap like Hetty's. "Simon Welton and his family's been friends of Hetty and mine for years," Jacob said.

Three or four sons and two or three daughters peered out doors and windows, watching their parents.

"Greetings, Friends," said Jacob.

Jacob introduced us all around, and then Simon Welton's strapping sons hauled the coffin from the back of the wagon, setting it on sawhorses in the parlor.

May Welton set about serving platters heaped with pork and corn and acorn squash.

Truth to tell, I was hungry and thirsty. But before I could sink my teeth into an ear of corn, Simon Welton lifted the coffin lid. When a young black man in a pair of tattered overalls stepped out of the coffin, Simon's daughters heaped up a plateful of food for him and then hurried him down to the cellar.

I felt my head reeling as I sipped May Welton's lemonade. Jacob and Simon and his family fell to their dinner as if what I just witnessed had been something they did every day.

Jacob White

On the ride back home, I gave the lad the reins, letting him drive for the first time. As we talked, I sensed that the lad hadn't understood.

"Didn't you say a friend was *dying*?" he asked. "Didn't you say that a friend needed a coffin delivered?"

"No, son," I answered, seeing that the boy believed I had not told the truth. I remembered the explanation I had given to his sister. "Friend's only in *danger* of dying. And I didn't say anything about delivering a coffin. I said only that a coffin *might be needed*. The coffin back there," I said, pointing to the box in the back of the wagon, "doesn't seem to be needed anymore."

I knew the lad had a great deal to think about. I knew he was confused. I tried to explain the purpose of our trip. That I hoped the lad would be coming with a delivery himself one day. That I hoped for him to learn the route. That I hoped he would be ready to make the trip when the town was distracted with other things like the missionary contest or the Benevolence Fair.

"What would I deliver?" the lad asked.

"*Passengers*," I said. "From a *depot*. Three of them."

I watched his head nod. He was counting. Jewel. Ruby. Rufus.

"And how would I deliver them?"

When I nodded to the pine box in the back of the wagon, the lad's eyes grew big as soap bubbles. They looked ready to burst. I'd seen that look many times, and I knew he was afraid.

John Common

Jacob handed me the reins on the ride back to Millbrook. "Thee must drive this time, son. I need a rest." Jacob pressed on his back and shifted in his seat. "I can feel every bump and throttle from this winding trail on the tail of my spine."

Somehow the reins felt right in my hands. Although I had never driven Jacob's wagon before, I felt proud. Driving the wagon had been something my sister sometimes did.

"One of the reasons I brought thee, lad, was to teach thee to drive. If thee's going to help, thee can't raise any suspicion. The folks in town need to get used to John Common riding all over the countryside making deliveries for me."

I gulped. "What if I *don't* help, Jacob? What will happen to Rufus then?" I was frightened for Rufus.

"Can't say."

"But what do you *think* will happen?"

"Rufus will do the only things any of us ever does, son. Trust in the hearts of friends, and our own quiet faith."

I struggled to understand what Jacob had said.

"Son," Jacob said, "seeing the fear on Rufus's face when I turned the bookcase around yesterday reminded me of thee."

"Me?"

"Yes. Thee was only a boy then. Thee had run off. Something thy grandfather said or did had frightened thee."

I remembered. Truth to tell, the incident was as vivid as yesterday. I was only a small child, and Mother had laid the supper table with ham and corn and cider. I, too small to see over the top of the table, longed to be *seen*. Quickly slipping from my chair, I ran to the family Bible. If I could pull the heavy volume from its stand and hoist it onto my seat, then I would be tall enough to be visible.

I can still remember the brown leather in my hands, its surface lightly veined and soft as summer leaves. I can still remember the rustle of parchment pages and the swish of tissue as I lifted it up. I can still remember its perfume trailing like incense behind me as I crossed to the supper table, staggering under my load.

Suddenly I felt the slap of my grandfather's voice. "Irreverent child!" he seethed. "How dare you denigrate God's holy word in this way!" I can still remember his words: I was a splinter in my family's eye, a stone in its heart, a rasp in its very breath.

I had first buried my head in Mother's skirts, but when Grandfather began to shake his cane in my direction, I ran off into the fields and hid under a basket. I wished to remain invisible; to hide; to crouch in the darkness; to desire never to be *seen*.

Now Jacob observed, "Both thee and Rufus had the same look of fear on thy faces. I could see it in thine eyes. It had something to do with the shame of having to hide."

I nodded. Truth to tell, I was always, somehow, in hiding. Hiding had become my deepest habit. When I hid, I could remain invisible: like a candle under a bushel.

I thought back to that night long ago. The winking stars. The frosty grass. "I would have hidden under that bushel all night if you and Hetty hadn't found me."

Jacob wrinkled his brows. "Me and Hetty?"

"Sure. You and Hetty found me and carried me home, Jacob, remember? You wrapped me in a blanket." I could still remember how warm it felt to be held in that blanket with Jacob's arms around me.

"Hmmm," said Jacob. "May have carried thee home, son. Didn't find thee."

"You didn't? Well, then, who did?"

I tried to concentrate on the signposts in the landscape as I waited for Jacob's answer.

"Why, Rufus, of course."

I was astonished at this revelation.

"Rufus insisted that we keep up the search that night. Said it was a terrible thing for someone to be separated from his family. Said he could trust himself to find a boy with a sense of rhythm."

"Rhythm?"

Now Jacob clapped his hands together. *Ta-da-DUM-da-DUM. Ta-da-DUM-da-DUM.*

I traveled far back in my memory. Back to the sounds I heard from under the basket. I could still recall the rhythm I heard then. *Ta-da-DUM-da-DUM. Ta-da-DUM-da-DUM.*

"That's how Rufus found thee, son." He clapped again. *Ta-da-DUM-da-DUM. Ta-da-DUM-da-DUM.* "Rufus knew he could lure thee with sounds."

I now noticed how the reins in my hand bounced up and down in time with the switching of the horse's haunches and the nodding of his head. And I began to hear the soothing sounds behind the regular clop-clop-clopping of hoofbeats. From where I sat, the jingling of the bells on the harness and the whirring of the wheels of the wagon mingled with all the other sounds, coming together, melding like chords. They made a kind of music.

Ellen Gordon

The welcoming committee was now the farewell committee.

At the depot, Sarah Grimke said calmly, "My business here may be unfinished," she said, "but I trust all of thee to help carry it on."

I wondered how Miss Grimke could remain so calm. Was she merely playing a role? The magistrate had been at least partly convinced that Rufus Thomas's freedom papers were real, but then Rufus had come up missing, and the magistrate withheld his judgment.

Sarah Grimke tied her cap strings neatly, preparing to

leave. "Ah, friends," she said, "the difficulty of saying good-bye is eased by the pleasure of having been among you. Thank you for your generosity."

She had turned to leave when Faith said, "Wait! Miss Grimke!" Faith fished for something in her pocket. "I have something for you," Faith said. "So you won't forget me."

"Oh, my, Faith. How thoughtful of thee, dear," Miss Grimke said, turning to Faith. I was still confused by Miss Grimke's demeanor. Wasn't there something odd about a woman with fierce opinions in such modest clothing? Wouldn't flamboyant dress have represented her better?

Faith brought the cloth from her pocket and unfolded it. Then she pressed it into Sarah Grimke's hand.

Miss Grimke turned the article over and over, examining it. It was a simple pocket, something commonplace, something ordinary, something all women wore tied under their skirts and around their waists to keep useful items close at hand.

"I know it's not fine work with the needle, Miss Grimke," Faith said. "I'm not fond of stitching." Standing beside Faith, I could see that the seams were less loose and ragged than they had once been.

Sarah Grimke smiled. "Well that makes *two* of us," she said. Then she added, "But the fact that it was not easily stitched makes the gift that much more valuable."

Now Emma Common spoke for the first time. "Twice blessed, I'd say," she offered.

Now Miss Grimke paused and looked over at Hetty White. She hesitated. Her eyes moved from Hetty's face to Emma's and then to Faith's. Now she said, "But I'm afraid I can't take it, dear."

Miss Grimke read the confusion in Faith's darting brown eyes. "It's made of cotton, isn't it?" she asked.

Faith nodded her head.

"I never touch anything made by the hands of slaves, Faith. Cotton cloth is one of the most visible products of slavery," Sarah Grimke said, passing the pocket back to her. "It's an article of faith with me. A vow. I simply refuse to touch the products of slavery," she said, "no matter how lovingly they may have been produced."

A frown crossed Emma Common's face. To my mind, Miss Grimke's refusal was rude.

Later, before the mirror, I tried to mimic the expressions I had witnessed. Faith's confusion. Emma's frown. But especially Miss Grimke's expressions. The calm eyes. The restful mouth. The unlined brow. Above all, her peaceful composure. The way she had not apologized or pleaded for understanding. The way she firmly stated her position and took no offense if others opposed her.

As the driver helped her into the stagecoach, Miss Grimke turned to Faith. "Keep up the work in thy copybook," she said. Then, winking, she added, "I don't need a gift to help me remember thee, dear."

Miss Grimke then settled herself in the stagecoach and peered out the window, addressing Mrs. Common. "The world never forgets the gift that is a spirited young woman," she said.

Mrs. Common blinked; her mouth flinched.

Then Sarah Grimke waved and was gone.

I wondered: Was there drama to be found even in a place like Millbrook?

Biddy Bostick

If you ask me, the world runs on gossip. Gossip at the tavern. Gossip at the milliner's. Gossip at the harness shop. *Ha!* The gossip was all about Rufus Thomas. He hadn't showed up at the magistrate's office to explain about his freedom papers. Those slave catchers came stomping on up to the magistrate saying that now the five-hundred-dollar bounty for the escaped slaves applied to Rufus, too. All over town floated the rumors that Rufus Thomas had killed hisself. Some thought by leaping into the river. Others thought by hanging from a rafter somewheres. I knew that weren't true. I didn't usually know the names of the cargo that passed through my root cellar over the years, but I knew the name this time. Besides, folks that killed theirselves had no hope, and as long as the magistrate hadn't ruled on his freedom papers, Rufus still had some.

Which brings me to hope. Hope laid an egg right on my own front stoop. *Ha!* Maybe Ralph Underhill hadn't heard what I said about my taxes, but some women in town had heard me loud and clear. They'd begun bringing more things to sell on my front stoop. Violet Haskins's knitted pocketbooks. Alma Greencastle's feather fans. It was mostly spinsters and widows, the women who didn't have the umbrella of a husband against a rainy day. Like Miss Esther Grimes, for one. Her brothers escaped with the family fortune, dropping it down a silver mine in Nevada, leaving her without a penny.

Ha! Like I said, it was gossip that turned the wheels of Millbrook. Folks was whisperin' about things they thought was secret. *Oh, my! Didja hear?* They jabbered about underground railroads and safe houses and pilots. But from my porch, I could see that their trains was a bit slow in pullin' from the station, if you ask me. From Biddy Bostick's front stoop, us women knew about safe houses firsthand. Men had their banks and insurance contracts, their wills and trusts. Those things was networks of connections right out in the open. But from my stoop, women had a few connections, too. A railroad of a different stripe, you might say. It was right out in the open, too. *Ha!* Just didn't nobody see it.

PART SIX

Fall,
1838

Ellen Gordon

The Benevolence Fair was fast approaching. Sometimes we girls worked on our projects for the missionary fund right alongside our mothers, while they worked on projects for Bishop Common's church.

But, to my mind, the most beautiful offering of all was Mrs. Common's coverlet. On it, a network of fruits and branches blossomed. Mrs. Common had stitched each dangling apple in a different way; all were similar round red globes, yet each was outlined in a different stitch. Like the characters I longed to play on the stage one day, every apple was distinctive, each one unique.

"Such artistry, Emma!" exclaimed my mother's friends.

"You should put it in the window of Albert Biggs's store," offered Rebecca Kinder. "It should fetch a marvelous price, Emma."

Mrs. Common lifted her chin, casting her dove gray eyes first on the trunk, then on the branches and fruits of her creation. "Do you think so? Well," she began, "perhaps."

"There's no 'perhaps' about it, Emma," insisted Miss Grimes. "You could purchase an entire row of pews for John's church on its profits."

"Well." Mrs. Common hesitated. "I cannot imagine a worthier cause."

Suddenly Amanda Putnam spoke up in her strong-willed, sure-of-herself way. Often Mrs. Putnam reminded me of Faith Common. "But how do you know Mr. Biggs will put a fair price on it, ladies? Frankly, he's nothing but a simple cheat."

"Oh, Amanda, you suspect anyone who doesn't think like you to be a cheat or a liar or worse," harrumphed Rebecca Kinder.

"I know what I see with my own eyes, ladies. Rebecca, what did you pay for that lace trim on your collar there?"

Mrs. Kinder looked at the collar in her lap. She was stitching a row of lace trim to its hem. "I believe it was three cents a yard, Amanda. Why?"

"Exactly, Rebecca." Mrs. Putnam's voice carried a slapping sound: a card player laying down a winning hand. "That Albert Biggs tried to charge me six cents a yard for the very same lace. Thinks because Ted earns a finer living than most of the folks hereabouts that he can charge me more than you."

The ladies rolled their eyes, dismissing Mrs. Putnam. They were tired of Amanda Putnam and her complaints against the world.

Then Mrs. Common turned her kind face to Mrs. Putnam. "Well, you have no proof, Amanda," she responded, whispering cautiously. "And it's not Christian to think ill of others, to bear false witness against our neighbors."

Mrs. Putnam was incensed. "Frankly, I may not have a minister for a husband, Emma, but that doesn't make me any less a Christian than anyone in Millbrook! And if God hadn't wanted me to have the proof of my own eyesight, why was I given the power to *see*?"

Celia Tanner

Grandma Birdie had turned worse. When I put my head to her chest, I didn't hear the whirring like a hummingbird's wings anymore. I heard a *tock* like a clock winding down. Grandma's heart was tired. Like you get after you've carried something heavy for a long time, your muscles all trembly-like.

I confess it helped when the other girls came to visit. I had missed them. When Emma Common sat by Birdie's bedside, Faith sat beside me, and we worked together with straw. I plaited brooms to sell on Biddy Bostick's front porch while Faith plaited hats for sale at the Benevolence Fair. Once Ellen Gordon appeared with bouquets of ribbon streamers, and together we pinned them to Faith's hat brims. The rainbow colors floating through our fingers helped me hope that Grandma Birdie might just get well. I reckon sitting side by side with another girl kept the lonely feelings away for a spell.

More often I kept the loneliness away by studying my mathematics text. As I sat beside Grandma Birdie, sometimes I'd make up word problems, like the book suggested. But they often ended up being about Grandma: *If one-eighth ounce of peony drops is dissolved in one-third ounce of cherry syrup, how much medicine makes up the whole?* And the simplest-sounding problem ended up being the most complicated: *Take one girl and her grandma and her pop. Subtract one grandma. What do you have left?*

Grandma was restless. The peony drops didn't work much anymore. She thrashed around like a fish on a line, but when she finally slept, she was asleep for hours at a time. That's when I'd escape to the woods. I'd watch John from a distance. I'd sit on a bed of pine needles quietlike, practicing problems in my mathematics book. I didn't talk to him about Grandma Birdie. John needed steady practice without interruption now. I knew from the girls' talk that Bishop Common had invited some missionary candidates to preach; he hoped to choose one of them to send on a mission across the ocean. John's father expected him to be one of the candidates.

There wasn't any music coming from John of late. Mostly he just tried to memorize words and call them into the forest. My heart felt sorry as I listened to him. It was something like the way I felt when I sat beside Grandma Birdie, wishing she would get better as I thought up mathematics problems. Sometimes I found myself making up problems for John, just like I did for Grandma Birdie. *What would happen, John, if you took twice as long to say 'light a candle' and half as long for the other words around it? What if you divided the words* candle *and* bushel *in half, pronouncing each half distinctly instead of mumbling them all together?*

One time I put my book down and stepped from behind some trees. I couldn't stand to keep hiding when John needed my help.

"Celia!" he said. At first he looked startled. Then embarrassed.

"The words need to be said at different paces, John. So your audience can understand what they mean."

John looked at me. I had never seen him scowl before.

"I reckon some of your words need to be stretched out, John; others need to be tightened up. Some words need to be soft; others need to be hard. Some of them need to be said fast and some slow."

John looked surprised. I don't think he realized how poorly he sounded.

"You don't want your words to be like the way Henry Stump reads, do you, John?" I asked, bold as a boulder. Henry Stump read the words one at a time, at the same tempo and pitch. Over and over *thief* was said the same way as *and*. "Remember that time Miss Sprinkle fell asleep on her desk listening to Henry read?"

I confess I don't know where all my gumption around John Common had come from of late, but around him I forgot to keep my head down.

What I said next came to me suddenlike. "Well, John," I

said, "think of your preaching like mathematics. A kind of musical mathematics."

I think he liked the way I explained it. Half the volume. Twice the volume. A slow beat over there. A beat three times that speed over there.

"You mean, Celia, that I'll need to take two full beats to say the word *candle*? Something like that?"

I nodded.

"And I need to turn up the volume on that phrase, *giveth light unto all that are in the house*?"

"I think so, John. And then turn *down* the volume on the words around it so that the words about the shining light stand out."

After that, John's speaking improved. It wasn't yet good. But it was better. The look on John's face told me he could never be the preacher his father was.

"John," I added, remembering what Hetty White had always told me, "you've got to have faith. A quiet faith. That God will provide."

I confess I had talked enough for one day. There were things I didn't tell John, things he would find out in his own time. I didn't tell him about my fear of being alone in the world. I didn't tell him that Albert Biggs had put a price of only a dollar on his mother's coverlet. And I didn't tell him what I had heard in town: that one of the missionary candidates would be Amos Read.

Lucy Putnam

Well, I shouldn't have been one bit surprised at the way Faith Common treated sweet Amos at the picnic before the preaching. They said she'd decided to improve her behavior after her father got home. But being as how she was as rude as ever a girl could be, I saw she hadn't changed one bit.

Faith took her turn behind the serving table, spooning out potato salad and cabbage slaw like the other girls. But when Amos approached her station, holding out his empty plate, she asked, "Would you like your ham *perpendicular* to your potato salad, Amos? Or would a thirty-degree angle suit you just as well?"

I pushed Amos aside and slammed the serving spoon into the pot of baked beans, pleased as punch when I saw the beans and brown sugar splattering all over the front of Faith's clean white apron.

Then I whisked Amos away to the dessert station, so he wouldn't have to answer her saucy old self. Distracted, Amos looked over the cakes melting icing in the heat and pointed to a thick slice of airy white cake. "I'll take that angel food over there, Miss Lucy," he said.

I rushed to serve him the biggest slice on the plate. But I thought I'd faint after that. Being as how Amos said, "Like a pretty girl, angel food is a godly treat. It's even mentioned in Psalms."

I felt the same way I did when Amos whispered in my ear in the woods behind the Whites' woodpile or when he said he'd stow me away on the steamer to the South Seas after he'd won the missionary contest. I didn't dare tell him what I was thinking: How would we ever be able to book passage on a ship if we hadn't a single penny between us in this world?

Calvin Mercer

Spied Alberta Tanner in the middle of the green, I did. Looked small and hunched in the wheelchair. The summer breeze rustled her hair. Even with the gray in it, it still looked pretty.

Looked like she could take on some weight, she did, so I brought her a plate of food. I remembered that she always liked custard.

"Here's something to sustain you, Birdie," I said, placing the plate on her knees. "Knew you liked custard."

Her birdlike eyes darted from under their lids, glancing suspiciously at the plate of food and then landing even more suspiciously on me.

"Well, that's kind of you, Calvin," she said. "Very kind."

When she looked at me close up, my heart pounded. I saw how pale she was, how tired. I studied the deep creases in her face. One elbow rested on the arm of the wheelchair, and the sagging flesh of her face was draped over her fist the way Emma's children draped their clothes over the newel post.

I stared at her lap. Watched the custard melting in the sun, I did. "I hope you get to feeling better, Alberta," I said.

"Have to," she declared, looking up from her plate. "There's no 'hope' about it. Can't leave sweet Celia alone, now, can I?"

I don't know why I said it, but it just popped out. "Why don't you let me take you to church one Sunday, Birdie? It might perk you up to get out more."

Her eyes peeked over at me like I was a suspicious crust of bread. "Are you trying to convert me again after all these years, Calvin?"

I pulled up short on the reins of her boldness, I did. I *had* tried to convert her after my Anna died. But Alberta was wild for Ben Tanner, who left her with a child and then skipped town. I might even have married Birdie after Ben ran off. If she'd baptized her son. Or joined the church.

"Well, Calvin," she said, "I might consider it if I could find one where they behaved like Christians instead of heathens."

"*Heathens,* Birdie?" To my mind, the heathens were *outside* the church, not *in.*

"Take Rufus Thomas, for instance. Not a single Christian in town besides the Whites and Amanda Putnam has taken up for him." I could see the color returning to her ashen cheeks as she spoke. "He's helped every farmer in Millbrook with haying at one time or another. Yet few will give him a sheaf of kindness in his time of trouble. What kind of religion is that?"

"But it's against the law—God's *and* man's—to escape from a master."

"Not every law is right, Calvin," she said. "Besides, how do you know he's escaped? Didn't Rufus have freedom papers?"

"Yes, but they're forgeries."

"How do you know? Has that been proved?"

"Well, doesn't have to be. Rufus ran off, right enough. That's proof of guilt, if you ask me."

Birdie turned to me, she did, with that fiery look she often got. "I wouldn't give a cent for what passes for Christian proof from you, Calvin Mercer."

I don't know what it was about Alberta Tanner. She could take the air right out of a man.

"Maybe running off just means Rufus could read the pages of justice in the Bibles of Millbrook's Christians," Alberta said smartly.

Now Alberta slumped back into her chair. Exhausted by the effort of speaking, she was. I was grieved to see the spirit go out of a woman, however irritating that woman might be.

She shivered, even though it was a September day as warm as any blanket.

"Here, Birdie," I said, "you need that lap robe from the back of your chair?"

She nodded. "Thank you, Calvin. Never thought I'd be the kind of woman to take cold in September."

She poked at the custard on her plate as I reached for the blanket to spread across her legs. She had eaten only a bite or two.

Then she passed the plate to me, she did. "It was *caramel* custard that I always liked, Calvin. This is *coconut*. But I thank you all the same."

John Common

Seated on the platform between Amos Read and Leonard Tompkins from Troy, I recalled the way Amos Read had behaved at the picnic. He hadn't changed at all. He flattered his way into extra helpings. When admirers swarmed around him like ants around Mrs. Callendar's raspberry jam cake, he acted like he had already won the preaching contest.

"Good luck, son," chirped Mrs. Kinder on the arm of her husband. "We always knew that Duncan Read's grandson would do Millbrook proud."

"Yes, Master Read," echoed Robert Kinder. "Your grandfather Duncan was the salt of the earth."

Amos smiled condescendingly. "Salt of the earth," he mused. "That's Matthew 5:13."

Truth to tell, I was glad to discover that my sister was still fond of challenging him.

"How do you know, Amos," she asked, wiping a thread of raspberry jam from the corner of her mouth with the back of her hand, "that the natives in a foreign land *want* to have Christianity brought to them?"

"It's something you just *know,* Faith," Amos said. "Everybody who's been converted, in fact, knows it, too. It's something you understand once you've been converted yourself." The jab in his voice stabbed at Faith's unconverted state. Then he passed her a napkin. "Jelly," he said, pointing out the red jam dribbling down her chin.

Now I looked out into the audience, at the girls arrayed in neat rows like the tulips that lined Mrs. Gordon's walk. I searched the crowd for Celia, but caught only the faces of Betsy Fisher and Sarah Tyler. Then I spied my sister sitting beside Ellen Gordon. Faith gave me a grin and a wave.

When my father introduced us, he praised the work of those who brought Christian light to heathen darkness. I trembled as I listened for Father to reveal the order of speakers. I dreaded going first. I felt relieved when he announced that Amos would be first; after that, me; and then Leonard.

I watched Amos stride to the pulpit, his forehead pressed forward, his chin down, his Bible tucked under his arm. I shuddered, imagining a far-off country with beaches and palms and a broad-shouldered young man striding across the sand, bringing the word of God to the waiting natives.

Emma Common

How tall young Amos Read looked from his place at the pulpit!

"I take my words of praise not from myself alone but from First Timothy," he said, finding the passage in his Bible. "Timothy had girls and women just like those here in Millbrook in mind when he advised them to *adorn themselves with modest apparel.* It is my great joy today to bear witness to your modest and becoming demeanor, young ladies, a demeanor that fulfills the commands of Scripture."

How right he was to admire their fresh aprons, their clean faces, their hearts open to the word of God!

"And Proverbs—like Timothy—also admonishes young women to adorn themselves with good works. You have all been treated to the eloquence of Bishop Common on the subject of the good works of virtuous women, so I will only suggest today that these young women arrayed before us are exactly what the Proverb had in mind." I felt a fluttering inside when he nodded in the direction of my John.

"In their stitching on behalf of this good missionary cause, as the Proverb says, *they worketh willingly with their hands.* In the handicrafts they have turned out, as the Proverb says, *they eateth not the bread of idleness.* In their devotion to fathers and brothers, as the Proverb says, *they looketh well to the ways of their household.* In the coins that they drop into their mite boxes, their actions testify to God's grace working through them, and there is no doubt that these young women before us today will one day become as virtuous as their mothers."

How heartening it was to hear the word of God falling from the lips of the young!

Ellen Gordon

Faith poked me in the ribs and whispered loudly in my ear, "What would Timothy have thought of the feathers and ribbons in Lucy's hair today?"

I looked across the tent at Lucy Putnam. She was stealing glances at Amos from the front row. To my mind, she looked ridiculous. "Faith," I exclaimed. "Look at those enormous sleeves! She must have stuffed them with pillows!"

I clapped my hands over my mouth to keep from giggling, explaining to Faith that Lucy's vanity had fallen for my trickery.

I had told Lucy that enormous leg-of-mutton sleeves—the plumper the better—were still the style in Philadelphia.

Then we both turned our attention to Amos Read.

"And *what else* does Scripture tell us about virtue in women and their daughters?" Amos asked. "How *else* can young women be taught to grow in virtue?"

I couldn't believe what I was hearing. Was *he* going to explain to *us* about *virtue*?

"For one thing, Scripture tells us that a fair woman possesses *discretion*. In fact, without discretion, a woman is no more than a *jewel in a pig's snout,* as the Proverb says."

I looked at Faith. Her eyes had snapped to attention. She had shifted forward in her seat. The other girls and I had shifted forward, too.

"And Scripture is clear about other aspects of discretion, too," Amos was saying. "A woman of discretion," he continued, "will not seek to teach, nor to *usurp authority over the man.*"

As he lectured us, Amos appeared to swell and expand: like dough in the presence of yeast. "She will avoid learning geometry and Greek and calculus and astronomy."

I was taken back to the schoolroom and my banishment to the fire with my needle. I could feel something hot simmering in my veins.

"She will avoid the public platform and the vanity of its attentions, for she will know that these indulgences inspire a pride that leads girls away from their duties."

Now the simmering began to bubble.

"Instead," Amos rolled on, relentless, "she is to be in silence. If she is to learn, as Timothy says, she is to *learn in silence with all subjection.*"

Now Amos paused for dramatic effect. Like Harry Churchill, the actor who played Brutus in the Philadelphia production of *Julius Caesar.* Could I believe what I had just heard?

"In fact, as Corinthians tells us," the traitor continued, "a woman of discretion is commanded to be under obedience. If she wishes to learn, she is to ask her husband or her brothers at home."

I looked down the aisle of girls seated beside me. I caught the frown on Betsy Fisher's face, the agitated glances that flew between Sarah Tyler and Liddie Martin. Could it be true, I wondered, that Amos was seeking revenge against Faith and the rest of us through his *preaching*?

"Yes, a young woman of discretion practices silence. Silence at school. Silence at home. Silence in the streets. Silence in the shops."

Here Amos paused and looked intently from face to face in the crowd. I studied the traits of his arrogance: the tilted nose, the smirking mouth, the chin held at a sharp, silencing angle. How could I have ever thought him handsome?

"Silence even in the church," he declared. "As Paul's letter to the Corinthians commanded," Amos said, poking with his index finger at the passage in Scripture, "women are to keep silence in the churches. Even there, it is not permitted unto them to speak."

Faith reached for my hand, and I gripped hers tightly. Up and down the row we girls reached for one another's hands. I was nervous and excited all at once. Somehow I felt myself preparing for something: a grand entrance or a finale. I wasn't sure which.

Faith rose. And then, together, we followed her.

John Common

I fixed on the girls who had risen: my sister and Ellen Gordon and Betsy Fisher and even little Vera Cramer. In the gasping silence my ears picked up the sounds: the whispering of their curls as they tossed their heads, the swishing of their skirts as they lifted them with their fingers, the padding of their feet as they moved into the aisle and out of the tent. Following my sister, they held their heads high: I admired their lack of discretion.

I looked across the tent and saw Celia. She was standing beside her grandmother's wheelchair. But I could see only her bonnet, not her face. Her head was cast down, hidden under the bonnet brim. She looked as Amos Read had made her feel: shamefaced and sober and silent.

Before Amos gave up the pulpit, he turned and looked at me. His eyes said that he would defeat me before this audience, before my own father.

Amos was right: my preaching was a disaster.

In my confusion I struggled to hold on to the advice Celia had given me. About speaking at twice the volume or half. About adding to the pace or subtracting from it.

Truth to tell, I was certain I had failed. I could tell by the way Celia was twisting the fabric of her apron, wringing it into a knot. The same way she had done before the masters in the schoolroom.

Emma Common

When we returned from the preaching on the green, my father began the harangue. Waving his cane at my husband and me, he bellowed that *our daughter* was the perfect model for *lack* of discretion, the very example Scripture sought to condemn.

I was horrified that my John appeared to agree with Father. "You have been a rude, irreverent girl," my husband cried. "You have behaved like a mote in the very eye of your family!"

I was appalled. I had never heard John raise his voice to any of his children. I had never heard him use words so severe.

But Faith shouted back, eye to eye with him: "If I am a mote, then, Father, recall your own Scripture! It says to worry, Father, about the beam in your own eye before you concern yourself with the mote of another!"

Now my father pounded his cane on the floor. "A pig's snout. A very jewel in a pig's snout, John Common, is this daughter of yours!"

Faith continued to pace in front of her father, warming to her own words. "What if I, Father, were a native woman on the shores of Burma, and I saw a young man striding across the sand toward me? What if that young man insisted that I keep silent. At home. In the streets. Even in the churches he established?"

How unprepared I was for the upwelling of emotion that surged in me! I focused on my daughter's questions.

"Would I be expected," continued Faith, "to obey the things that young man knew without his having to *prove* them? Would Amos Read demand silent subjection from the women of Burma, too? And can we, Father," she said, seizing the Greek text from the tabletop, "assume that Amos Read understands the words that he speaks?"

Faith slapped the cover of the text with her hand. "When Amos Read commands that women are not to *speak* in church, can we trust that he has gone back to the original Greek? That he is certain the Scripture doesn't mean 'babble' or 'chatter' or 'whisper' or 'gossip'?"

My John looked stricken, confused. He had not realized how thoughtfully his daughter—if not his son—had considered the Greek of the New Testament.

"Why did Amos Read choose the verses he did, Father? Why? He could have chosen many others. He could have preached that *a virtuous woman is a crown to her husband.* He could have preached on the words that encouraged your sons and your daughters to prophesy. He could have preached on the verse that says there is *neither Jew nor Greek, neither slave nor free, neither male nor female.* Couldn't Amos have preached on that?"

I glanced over at my son John. He had been standing quietly by, apart from us, awkward and silent. He kept his head down the way I kept mine over my sewing. How dejected he had looked on the pulpit today! How weakly he had performed! No wonder my John decided to postpone his decision about sending a missionary!

John Common

When I slipped out of bed, dawn had not yet broken.

For three days now I had slept fully dressed, afraid the sounds of my dressing would disturb the sister and brothers who lay snoring beside me on their pallets in the loft.

I slipped out from under the coverlet, tiptoeing across the floor, avoiding the board that creaked. I could not afford to be heard. I could not afford to be found out.

My fingers found the pitcher, and they dived easily into the water. Although I could feel the snap of the September air, the surface of the water had not yet begun to film with frost. I splashed my cheeks and rubbed my eyes with my fingertips.

I descended the short stairway. I wiggled my stockinged feet into the boots by the door.

Then I stepped over the sill.

It was dark outside. And chilly.

I thought back to the confrontation after Amos Read's preaching. The rapping of my grandfather's cane drowned out much of what was said, but I did remember Faith's words: *There is neither Jew nor Greek, neither slave nor free, neither male nor female.* Those were the words Sarah Grimke had declared when Jacob explained there were no slaves in his house.

But I had never seen my mother behave as she did then. While my grandfather banged his cane, describing ours as the very family cursed by Scripture, recommending the rod of punishment for my sister, my mother stepped up to him.

"Scripture, Father," she declared, "says that ours is a God *ready to pardon, gracious and merciful.*" Mother's eyes were tethered to my grandfather's like loose buttons on long threads. Her words yanked them tight. "Why should Faith be punished for her irreverence if Amos Read is to be forgiven his?"

Then she turned away from my grandfather and to my father. "My daughter and her friends, husband—like my own Dorcas sisters—had put down their ribbon wreaths and dried apple dolls, their lemon cakes and measuring tapes to listen to Amos Read. Before they departed for this event, they had stuffed last-minute pennies into mite boxes for his missionary effort."

Watching Mother's face, I was reminded of the effort she had made on behalf of the subscription campaign.

"An arrogant young man has behaved like a schooner under sail, unaware of the source of his wind. *Why,* John," she pleaded, "should *our daughter* be punished for *Amos Read's* failure to appreciate the efforts on which *his* success depends? Was she to sit silently by and listen to him discredit the goodwill of the girls on which his opportunity arises?"

My astonished father looked at my mother straight on.

She looked straight back. "With all due respect, John," she said to her husband, "didn't Amos's preaching run counter to everything that Methodists stand for? Wasn't he preaching *separation and division,* not *connection and union?*"

It was then that I had made my decision. I wasn't anything like my sister. And perhaps it didn't matter. If she could achieve things noisily, perhaps I could achieve things quietly.

I shuddered as I picked up the iron lantern. I reached for a rush to use for a taper. I clamped the rush in the lip of the lantern, then fumbled for a match. I struck the match against the side of the house, lighting the tip of the rush that flared weakly against the darkness.

Picking up the handle of the lantern, I headed for the barn, grateful the path was familiar. I knew how many paces it took to reach the hole in the earth, the hole that my brothers had failed to cover up after they had dug for treasure. I was careful not to trip and let the sound of a sudden stumble give me away. I knew to avoid the roots of the giant maple that had heaved out of the ground after last winter's hard freeze.

Then suddenly I froze, frightened by a sound. A sudden snuffling. I looked back over my shoulder, relieved that it was only one of the pigs, snorting in the trough.

Finally I reached the woodpile. That meant I had almost reached the barn.

Suddenly I heard a scratching. Then a snapping twig. A shiver of fear pricked like nettles up the back of my neck. I held the lantern higher. It cast its light on a shadow darting into the woods. I sighed, relieved. What I had seen was only a chipmunk, rising from its bunkhouse in the woodpile.

Now I reached the barn.

I lifted the heavy latch. I pulled the door open only wide enough to slip through. Around me the sharp smells of animals were muted by the sweet smells of hay. I heard the groaning of Dolly, lowing to be milked.

"Are you there?" I called into the darkness.

I heard the shuffling sounds from the hayloft that meant they were.

As I climbed the ladder to the loft, I recalled my quiet burglary of the last few days: the crusts of bread left at our table and hidden under a napkin; the apple saved from my own dinner to be divided among three others; the handful of walnuts gathered from beneath the old tree; the raw turnips fetched from the dark cellar that would later gnaw at hunger.

I recalled the way three pairs of black hands had reached out to me from behind the hay, stuffing food into their mouths, snorting and gnashing like hungry animals. I recalled their gratitude for the warmth of dog-eared shawls and moth-ridden stockings pilfered from my mother's mending pile. I recalled how difficult the two women had found it to trust me and how Rufus's assurance of my goodwill buoyed my spirits. I recalled the secrets they had begun to tell: how Ruby had once been whipped by her master for failing to keep her dress clean; how Jewel had once been imprisoned for stealing a slice of bread from the master's table and how Ruby had slipped strings of meat to her mother through the chinks in the cracks of the prison cabin; how both had barely survived the trek north by eating wild berries and fruit, by snatching flesh from hog hides floating in soap barrels.

Now Rufus said, "For you, John." Then he passed me the walnut shells.

I puzzled over them. The walnuts inside were gone.

"First I carved out the nut meats, of course," he said. "And then fed 'em to Jewel and Ruby."

I winced, wondering how they had survived on an apple for one meal and a handful of walnuts for another.

Now Rufus pulled out his checkered rag and placed the walnut shells on it. "Used my penknife to carve out the shells," he said. "Then used the end of a corncob to rout the inside smooth. Used the juice from the apple core to oil it all up," he said proudly.

He spit on the rag, showing me how he had polished the inside of the walnut shell.

Now, as I studied the walnut halves, I saw two holes in the tops of the shells and a long, limp string hooking them together.

"Well, I thank you, Rufus," I said. "But what's it for?"

Rufus grinned. "For your music, boy. Like always."

As I watched him placing one half of a shell around his thumb and the other half around his middle finger, I thought back to all the gifts he had given me over the years: the sticks and drums and whistles that made me feel less clumsy, that I never stumbled over.

"Oh," I said, listening to the rhythmic clicking of the shells, "finger cymbals! But you didn't have to do this, Rufus."

Then Rufus looped the shells around my own fingers and listened as I began to click out a rhythm.

"You ain't got to help me and my family out, either," Rufus said, reaching for Jewel's fingers with one hand and caressing Ruby's head with the other. "You're doing something harder than running a furrow or heaving an ax, boy. You wouldn't mind a man providing a fearless soul with a bit of music to soothe it, would you, boy?"

Looking into Rufus's patient face, I was startled by the word he had used: *fearless.*

Suddenly the memory came flooding back, the memory

of when Rufus had given me my first real instrument: the silver flute.

It had come after that terrible time in the barn.

In my clumsiness I had pruned both the limbs *and* the buds from the lilac trees. Rufus had overheard my grandfather's fury.

"Clumsy boy," Grandfather had shouted, his white hair flying from his scalp in icy peaks. "With a wicked disregard for God's creation."

Trembling, I could hardly attend to his instructions: I was to trim only the woody stalks, the ones grown thicker than a broom handle. Confused, I could barely concentrate on his explanation.

Even after Grandfather had stomped off to the barn, I could scarcely focus on what Rufus had said to me then. Something comforting. Something about lilacs. Something about how you couldn't hardly kill them. Even if you tried.

After that, Grandfather had shouted to me from the barn. I was to return the pruning hook to its place on the wall. Immediately. "Hurry up!" he growled. "Are you as slow as you are clumsy, boy?"

I ran to the barn, tripping over my own feet, fighting back the tears stinging my eyes.

In the barn Grandfather had a place for every one of his tools. The pruning hook hung just between the three-pronged fork and the square-footed shovel.

It had been like that time with the Bible. The place on the wall, like the tabletop, had seemed so high. And the barn was always dark, even if it was broad daylight outside.

Shaking, I had reached for a crate to stand on. Trembling, I set it next to the wall.

"Hurry up, boy," my grandfather barked, leaning toward me menacingly.

I climbed up on the crate and reached for the wall, the hook in my hand.

"We've not got all day," Grandfather seethed, stamping his foot.

Somehow my knees began to buckle. After that, somehow the crate began to wobble. And suddenly the pruning hook had slipped from my hand and into my grandfather's scowling face.

It was the sound I remembered. First, bellowing. Then, gnashing moans.

I didn't wait to hear any more. I ran out of the barn, my feet flying.

Smack into Rufus Thomas.

After it was over, after Rufus stuffed his rag into Grandfather's mouth to stanch the screams, after Dr. Mandell had appeared and seared the eye against infection with a hot brand, Rufus had brought me the flute.

"I was running away, Rufus," I said, biting my trembling lip, trying to make the sounds of Grandfather's cries and the sizzling of the hot brand disappear. "And you told Grandfather I was running for the doctor!"

"Well, it *was* you who fetched Doc Mandell, wasn't it?"

"Yes, but . . ."

Rufus's face grew serious. He pointed to his short leg and the stubbed foot at the end of it shaped like a trowel. He frowned. "You don't think I could have fetched Doc any faster on these here legs, do you, boy?"

I thought about what Rufus said. I had run faster than I had ever thought possible, grateful to see Dr. Mandell's whiskered chin poking out his office door.

"But it was my fault, Rufus. It was like Grandfather said. If I hadn't been so clumsy, it never would have happened."

"Maybe so," Rufus said, pursing his lips. "Maybe not.

There's at least two sides to every story," he said. "Maybe your grandfather was too impatient with a young boy. Hadn't he shouted at you about the lilacs? Didn't he stamp his foot for you to hurry up? Who made the crate you was standin' on shake—*you*? Or *him*?"

I nodded, trying to think on what I had heard.

"Listen, boy," Rufus said, his face somber as a church. "Somebody else's truth don't have to be yours."

I considered what Rufus said.

"Maybe if your grandfather had been more patient with a willing boy, he might still have another eye."

After that, Rufus had handed me the flute.

"Got this from Alma Ferris, John," he said, holding up the silver stick, polishing it with the red-checkered rag he always kept in his pocket.

"Alma said it was thanks for the roof I patched for them," Rufus continued. "She said all the music had gone out of her life now that Abe had passed."

I remembered how proudly Abe Ferris had marched in every Founders' Day and Fourth of July parade in Millbrook, his flute at the corner of his mouth like a silver stalk of hay.

"Thought the music that stepped out of one life might like to step into another," Rufus said.

He gave the flute another flick of his rag and passed it to me. The flute was dented on one flank, but otherwise it was perfect and shining.

Now, in the barn, I listened to the clattering of the finger cymbals and thought about all the ways in which Rufus Thomas had been patient with a clumsy boy. Teaching him how to spread the hay in the field for curing, how to load the dried hay onto the hayrick, how to store it in the mow. After every challenge Rufus had slipped me a small, encouraging gift. Drumsticks or bells or rasps or drums.

Even now, wrapped in secrecy in the cloak of our barn, depending on a fearful boy for help, Rufus behaved as he'd always done.

"Everybody's got different ways of feeling free," he whispered, listening to the quiet rhythms I tapped out. "Yours is your music. Mine is," he said, pausing to glance at Jewel and Ruby, "a place far from here. Maybe someplace as far away as Canada."

I stared into Rufus's round black eyes. I caught a light flickering there like a candle inside a lantern. The light felt like hope.

"I reckon that's what friends do, John," Rufus said. "Help each other get a tad more free."

Suddenly, Ruby sneezed.

Rufus passed her the checkered cloth.

"Bless you, child," said her mother.

"Likely no worse place for a girl with the hay fever than a barn like this," Rufus whispered as the girl swabbed her face with the cloth. "You all right, Ruby?" he asked.

The girl nodded and wiped her nose, but her eyes were still red and weeping.

After I left the barn, I peered up into the night sky. The cool September air pricked my cheeks. The stars I knew so well winked like fireflies on a deep blue meadow. Lifting the bucket at the well, dropping it down the stone tunnel, hauling it to the surface again, I considered how innocent had been my childhood missteps: my awkwardness with scythes and shovels, my running away out of fear and shame. Moving back to the house, the water sloshing against the sides of the heavy bucket, I considered that my actions now were different. They were intentional, deliberate. I could not allow myself to be found out.

I set the brimming pail by the door and shivered. The

night had now begun to pale and fade: like the tattered squares of the quilt that often hung from Jacob and Hetty White's fence. I returned to the woodpile and filled my arms with logs and kindling. Inside the house I set the logs and kindling by the hearth. I picked up a stick, poking at the fire with it until it caught a red glow; then I set it to burn in the middle of the hearth. Adding other thin sticks to the pile, I watched the fire begin to burn brightly. Only then did I put my hands close to the hearth to warm them. Finally I sighed, relieved. I had survived, undetected, another morning mission to the barn.

Ellen Gordon

We girls were plain mad. We had started with Amos Read and his insults at school, but soon we had worked up to his insults from the pulpit. But as we sat together, talking over the handicrafts we were making for the Benevolence Fair, our anger had attached itself to many things. Especially Albert Biggs.

I remembered the ladies' conversation at the last Dorcas meeting.

"Well, I believe I have proof, ladies," insisted Mrs. Putnam. To my mind, Mrs. Putnam was like Faith: she needed everything proved. "In Boston last week I visited a fine tailoring shop with my sister Jane. I am certain I saw one of Phoebe Hungerford's neat white shirts on display there. At a price three times what Albert Biggs sells them for here."

"What are you suggesting, Amanda?" Somehow Mrs. Common was suddenly interested in the conversation.

"I'm *saying,* Emma," huffed Mrs. Putnam, an irritated burr in her voice, "that Albert Biggs ships some of Phoebe's shirts to Boston and makes a handy profit off them."

Now the other ladies began to question Mrs. Putnam.

"Did the shirts have nicely notched collars?"

Mrs. Putnam nodded.

"Neatly tucked bodices?"

Mrs. Putnam nodded again.

"Were the shirts a gleaming white?" asked Mrs. Common, her interest sparked. "As if not a speck of dirt had ever crossed their surfaces?"

Mrs. Putnam nodded. "None whiter."

Later, we girls had been tying ribbons to the brims of hats with Celia Tanner. I tried as often as I could to get the girls to work with Celia, for the company lifted Celia's spirits.

"I'm tired of having to bargain with Albert Biggs for every scrap of muslin," complained Betsy Fisher.

I agreed with Betsy. "Yes," I said. "He could likely afford to *give* it away."

"He made me agree to sweep his sidewalk for a week before he reduced his price on some leftover calico," Sarah Tyler said.

"And Marian Loring had to bring a half dozen of her mother's infant caps for his window," offered Liddie Martin, "before he'd agree to the price I asked for this ribbon."

"But the worst part," said Faith, slamming down her scissors, "is that he is cheating my own mother!"

Now the girls tilted their heads in Faith's direction.

"Naturally, he's put my mother's coverlet in the middle of his window," Faith said. "After all, it was the most beautiful thing in the entire general store."

The girls nodded. They put down their herb packets and baby bibs and embroidered pockets.

"But he's priced it, girls," Faith said, shaking her red braid in disbelief, "at only a dollar!"

The girls shook their heads. Everyone in Millbrook was aware of the value of Mrs. Common's handiwork.

"I wish we could turn the tables on that old cheater!" said Faith.

Celia was tying some of the blue ribbon Liddie had purchased around bouquets of dried lavender. Suddenly a light like dawn passed over her face.

"My," Celia said, jumping up from the circle, "I wonder why I hadn't thought of it before! Maybe I'd been just too worried about Birdie to think of much else."

Celia ran to a corner of the grimy room and started rooting through an old box. "Here they are!" she said, holding up a handful of our schoolroom sum books.

We girls passed them around eagerly, bending our heads together, giggling over what was written there in our own handwriting. *If three and one-half yards of ribbon in Mr. Biggs's store is sold for sixteen cents, why was Edna Barrow given only two yards for twenty cents? If gingham goes for one dollar a yard, why was Mrs. Callendar charged twenty-five cents for only one-eighth?*

I recognized a gleam in Faith's eye. It felt good to be under the spell of Faith Common's cleverness once again.

Biddy Bostick

Ha! If you ask me, the young is quicker than the old, and Faith Common and her friends figured Albert Biggs for a cheat before Emma Common ever caught on. The low price he fixed to Emma's coverlet was an insult and a robbery, so when Faith and the other girls demanded Emma Common's coverlet back from him and Albert Biggs refused, the girls were ready. They knew that stinking thief could cheat quicker than a mosquito bites. *Ha!*

They had proof of Albert Biggs's swindling from Celia

Tanner. It seems Celia kept the sum books from last winter's school. Faith had got the girls to practice their mathematics with problems they made up from watching Albert Biggs cheat their mothers. Like if two yards of calico's twenty cents a yard, why did he charge Kate Loring sixty cents? Or if one yard of grosgrain ribbon's six cents a yard, why did Albert Biggs charge Miranda Callendar ten cents for a yard and a half? *Ha!* It was wrote down on paper, every last cheating transaction.

John Common

Suddenly I heard a sound. After that, a sharp sliver of light pierced the darkness of the barn. Then a musket blast shattered the quiet.

I scrambled down from the loft, my heart throbbing, and I ran straight into the ramrod body of my angry grandfather.

"What were you doing up there?"

"Nothing, Grandfather," I said. Silently I cursed my stupidity. I should have limited my gifts of food only to the early morning hours. But I could not bear to stare into the round starving eyes of Jewel and Ruby or listen to the hunger rumbling in Rufus's belly. Now and again I crept into the loft with extra food.

"Nothing?" My grandfather bent his gnarled frame close to me. He stuck his cold blue eye next to mine. For the first time in years I allowed my eyes to alight on the empty cavern where one eye had been lost to the pruning hook. The lid itself was puckered like threaded stitches yanked tight. The socket looked gray and wounded: like a bruise that hadn't healed.

"Nothing, Grandfather," I repeated, trying to gather my wits. "I had only come in to practice my flute."

He eyed me suspiciously with his one good eye. "Lazy child," he muttered. "With the crops to get in and the hay to be bundled. One more good rain and it'll rot in the fields."

Then he lowered the barrel of the musket and glowered.

Fortunately, my family now flew into the barn from all directions. They had heard the musket blast. Their appearance gave me time to collect my thoughts.

"There are thieves about, John Common," Grandfather roared, addressing my father as if Father had been encouraging the thieves to roam about the countryside.

"Haven't you noticed, daughter?" Grandfather asked Mother. "Food's gone from our own table. There's never any breakfast scraps, and the fruit disappears from the bowl twice as fast as normal."

Mother stepped up to Father. "Yes, John," she said. "I've had a few things come missing from my mending pile. That old gray scarf. Some stockings. A pair of mittens."

"Well, let this be a warning to everyone," Grandfather shouted to the rafters as if to God Himself. "Next time, I won't stop shooting!" Then he flailed his musket in warning, turning on his heels and stomping out of the barn.

Later, Faith had marched up to me in the fields. Wesley and I had been bundling hay. Wesley bundled twice as fast as I did.

Faith tugged on my sleeve and pulled me aside. "What were you doing in the barn, John?"

It was hard to lie into those eyes.

"If you were in the barn to practice your flute," she said, her head cocked, her long red braid an exclamation point, "why wasn't it in your hands or your pocket?"

I shifted from one foot to the other, studying her clever face.

She had me there.

Ellen Gordon

I had never expected Faith Common to hold open her copybook and ask me to read what she'd written.

"Go on, Ellen," she insisted.

I saw that Faith had fashioned two columns down the page. The column on the left she titled "Condition of the Slave." The other column, on the right, she titled "Condition of the Woman."

"Read down the first column, Ellen," she ordered.

As I read, I saw that she had taken down Sarah Grimke's words. They were words Miss Grimke had spoken when she had taken tea with the Dorcas Circle at Hetty White's. They were words about the disabilities of the slave.

In her strong, plain handwriting, Faith had written: *slave is property of master; slave may not possess money; slave cannot vote, make a will, or own property in his own name; slave has no remedies at law; slave is forbidden to learn to read or write.*

"Now read the second column, Ellen," she said.

I saw that the words on the right column had been neatly arranged to contrast with the words on the left. They balanced like items of equal weight on a scale: *a married woman is property of her husband; a married woman's money belongs to her husband; a married woman cannot vote or make a will or own property in her own name; a woman has few remedies at law; a woman has fewer opportunities to learn than a man.*

Somehow Faith Common always managed to stay one jump ahead of me. Now that she had shared her copybook with me, she seemed uninterested in my response. Instead, she unfolded a dirty rag and held it to my face.

"What do you think this is, Ellen?" she asked.

"Well, it's just a dirty old rag, Faith," I said. "Isn't it?" I thought it must have been a trick question.

"Look again, Ellen," she said, stretching the cloth to its fullest length and snapping out the wrinkles.

I looked. I hadn't understood why she was making such a production out of a wrinkled old rag.

"Tell me what you see, Ellen," she insisted.

"Same thing as I saw before, Faith," I replied, growing irritated. "Same old dirt. Same old size. Same old red-checkered pattern. What's so special about *that*?"

"What do you think it's made of, Ellen?"

I shrugged. "I don't know." At this point, I didn't much care, either.

"Well, *guess*," she ordered.

Faith Common could be as bossy as a rooster. "All right," I huffed. "Cotton. It's likely made of *cotton*. What's so special about that? Lots of things are made of cotton."

Now Faith was nodding, agreeing with something in her own head that didn't have anything to do with me.

"And do you remember what Miss Grimke said about cotton?"

I tried to remember. "I think she declared that she didn't care much about stitching on it."

Faith turned away from me, disgusted. I suppose I hadn't remembered what she wanted me to remember.

"So where'd you find this special dirty old red-checkered wrinkled cotton rag anyway, Faith?" I asked.

She eyed me suspiciously. As if I hadn't treated her dirty old rag with reverence.

"Found it in my own barn, Ellen. Heard some sneezing going on in there and then I snuck inside and found this floating from the loft onto the ground."

John Common

I shuddered as I listened to Jacob's escape plan. It would take place on the evening of the Benevolence Fair. After supper when it got dark. While the ladies were holding the auction. I would escape with Rufus and Jewel and Ruby, Jacob said, at the height of the auction. When folks were distracted by the fierce bidding.

I tried to concentrate. I wanted to get it straight. First the fair. Then the supper. After that the auction. It was difficult. I was more scared than I had been when I memorized Bible passages for Father: hoping I would get it right.

"On the morning of the fair," Jacob said, bending his white beard to me and whispering in my ear, "Hetty and I will drive up to thy house in our wagon, the three coffins in the back. We'll bring some of Hetty's fried chicken and biscuits with us. And then we'll engage everyone inside in a round of visiting. That's when thee'll get to work."

While they were talking, I was supposed to slip away into the barn, bring the fugitives down from the loft, and stow them in the coffins.

I listened carefully, trying to keep the plans straight in my head.

Then, when everybody had finished chatting and Jacob had seen me slip back inside, Jacob and Hetty would offer to give everyone a ride up to the fair. Then we'd drop everyone at the green in town, and I'd drive back to Jacob's alone with the wagon. Rufus and Ruby and Jewel could then slip out of the coffins and wait behind the bookcase until evening.

Later, once the auction started, I'd slip back to the Whites', help the slaves into the coffins, and then head out the Springfield Trail to the Weltons'.

While I listened to Jacob, I tried to memorize this part of the plan like I tried to memorize the Greek alphabet. First the drive to our house. Then Hetty's chicken. Then down from the loft. After that the return to the bookcase until evening.

It was hard to remember all of it, but I concentrated harder than I ever had in my life. One thing I was sure I'd never forget was what Jacob said after he'd shared the plan with me.

"I know I'm asking a lot of thee," Jacob said, his big hand reaching out to shake mine like I'd seen men do when they sealed bank loans or building contracts. "I appreciate all thy help, John."

I could still feel my own hand warm in his and swelling to fill his grasp, and I remembered that Jacob had not called me *lad* or *son.* He had called me *John.*

Biddy Bostick

Ha! I was up to the general store when those young 'uns waved those sum books in Albert Biggs's face. He said nobody'd believe the scribblings of children, and then that swindler smiled so wide you could see the tobacco stains between his teeth like fence rows.

Ha! That got their goat. Faith and her friends pledged then and there to stop stitching. Said they'd never buy another thing from Albert Biggs's store and never pick up a needle again. It was just like that time I stomped up to the tax assessor's office. The girls said there'd be no more stitchin' on behalf of the missionary student and no more stitchin' on behalf of Faith's father's church. I couldn't find one thing wrong with that logic. Why should they wear down their fingers working for somebody else with stuff they bought from a cheater?

Ellen Gordon

When we gathered in the evenings, the girls of Millbrook howled, roared, sniggered, and laughed at the consternation of brothers, uncles, fathers, and cousins. I had more expressions to practice before the mirror than ever!

Liddie Martin reported that her father's feed sacks went unrepaired. Betsy Fisher announced that her brother's suspenders went unlengthened. Sarah Tyler reported that her grandfather's socks went undarned.

We were treated to jeers from the boys all over town. Their hee-hawing was a source of their own merriment. As Faith and the other girls and I strolled in front of the saddlery or the bank or the stagecoach depot, either Dick Hardcastle or Ethan Loring or Henry Stump stepped out from the crowd of boys to block our path.

Their jokes grew tiresome. As they pulled on their suspenders or winked broadly to their cronies, they mocked us with questions: "Would you little ladies be fixin' to trade your petticoats for a fellow's trousers next? Are you plannin' on givin' up your lace collars for a silk waistcoat? Or your tea for a swill of brandy?"

As the crowd of boys whistled and hooted, doubling over with laughter, we girls lifted our skirts, stepped around them, and held our heads high.

Emma Common

I knew that Scripture reminds us to think no evil of others. But I couldn't doubt the proof from Amanda Putnam. Her sister

Jane had sent Amanda a shirt purchased for a hefty price in Boston. Even without the "PH" monogram on the tail, I would have recognized Phoebe Hungerford's stitches instantly.

I rose early in order to approach Mr. Biggs before he opened his shop. I would get my coverlet back myself.

I didn't need any more proof of the merchant's cheating. Faith and her friends had given Albert Biggs the schoolchildren's sum books, filled with exercises that confirmed his thievery. How strengthened I felt by the loyalty of my daughter and her friends! On my behalf the girls of Millbrook had stopped their sewing.

They took their scissors from around their necks and their sewing pockets from around their waists.

They folded their patterns and scraps and tucked them away.

In their laps they placed books and pamphlets, handbills and newspapers, gathering the train of their own thoughts instead of a train of stitches.

But Albert Biggs had not budged.

How determined I was to have my coverlet earn what it was worth!

In the distance I saw the stooped figure of a woman approaching Albert Biggs's store from the west end of town as I approached from the east. She was carrying a package wrapped in brown paper.

As she stood at the steps to Albert Biggs's store, I recognized the round-shouldered figure of Phoebe Hungerford. As the pink rays of the morning fell across her hand, she reached for the shop door, and I realized for the first time that she must, every morning, have appeared this early at Albert Biggs's store to deposit her shirts and receive the coins that would feed her children that day. *She riseth also while it is yet dark, and giveth meat to her household. She looketh well to the ways of her household.*

Across my mind unraveled images of Phoebe and her children, their backs humped, their eyes red, their eyelids drooping over linen or palm leaves, matchsticks or umbrellas, their candles worn down to stumps. I heard the rats scurrying behind the walls as the Hungerford daughters pulled out basting threads. I remembered the blue ends of bread and the moldy crusts of cheese I saw when I brought them aid from the Dorcas Circle. At night, when they were cold and when Lucas Hungerford was still drinking in the tavern, they often covered themselves with their work in progress as blankets. Sometimes I had seen Phoebe Hungerford at the grocer's, trading pocket handkerchiefs for food, holding her apron open for yesterday's scraps as she faced the need for sustenance to continue her stitching. *Her candle goeth not out by night. She eateth not the bread of idleness.*

As I reached the threshold of Mr. Biggs's store, I stepped inside the shop, smelling the rye seed heaped in hampers and the melons ripening in bushel baskets, seeing the barrels of nails next to the tubs of butter fresh churned by widows and sold for a pittance. A large open box sat on the front counter.

Phoebe's back was to me, but I saw Albert Biggs's huge hands ripping open her brown paper parcel and exposing about half a dozen new shirts. I knew the quality of the handiwork they displayed; the skilled coordination of hand to eye they represented had grown from practice but was born of necessity. *She maketh fine linen, and selleth it; and delivereth her goods unto the merchant.*

Albert Biggs scrutinized each shirt, his eyebrows lifted over each collar and every buttonhole. He counted the buttons on all six shirts. Suddenly he frowned, recounting buttons again.

"I can't pay you for this one," he said, shoving it back across the counter at her. "A button's missing."

The back of Phoebe's neck blushed red. "I'm sorry, sir. I'll add it and bring it round later."

"No need, Mrs. Hungerford. I won't bother with inferior goods," he said, dismissing her.

"But it took Maud an entire day, sir, to stitch that shirt. A button's a simple repair."

He was counting up the coins to pay her what he owed for the five remaining shirts. "Then it'll be a lesson to her."

Phoebe tried to straighten her shoulders to face Mr. Biggs. "The girl's nearly b-b-blind with exhaustion," she stuttered. "It's understandable that she might miss a button now and again."

"I sell only flawless goods in this shop, Mrs. Hungerford. You know that. It's your responsibility as my supplier to make certain I get what my customers want."

His large cold hands lifted the other shirts into the open box on the counter. I thought I caught an address on the outside of the box that read: Boston.

Phoebe Hungerford brushed by me on the way out, her face red, her head bent with the humility of shame.

Who can find a virtuous woman?

"I've come, Mr. Biggs," I announced, stepping obstinately to the counter, "to retrieve my coverlet. I understand that you've priced it at only a dollar. That's far too low, sir. I'd like to have it back."

"I hate to disappoint a fine customer like you, Mrs. Common," he said, turning his rheumy eyes on me. "But you can't."

"Why not?"

"It's already sold. Fine work sells quickly," he said, trying to appease me with praise.

"Well, then," I insisted. "I'd like you to buy it back. From whoever bought it. The coverlet took me many hours of careful labor. It's worth more than a dollar. In fact, I'd not only like you to buy it back, I *insist* on it!"

"You *insist*?" A smirk crawled up his lips.

But I was firm. My neck felt an iron sinew, my brow brass. I had learned a great deal from my stubborn daughter. "Yes. If you don't bring it back, you'll have cause to regret it."

"Is that a *threat,* Mrs. Common?" Now the smirk turned surly.

How vile he was! Albert Biggs was as vile as the bottles of calomel and ipecac arranged along his pharmacy shelf. He was like Amos Read at the pulpit. Or Mayor Girton on the Independence Day platform. Our goodwill had been his great gift. Mr. Biggs could not afford to humiliate us, to judge us as insufficient without consequence.

"Yes, Mr. Biggs," I said firmly. "Yes, I believe it is a threat." Then I, Emma Common, a minister's wife, turned and marched—very visibly—out of the store.

Calvin Mercer

I'd learned that Birdie Tanner was doing poorly.

Emma sat with her often, she did. And Faith sometimes visited with the other girls. My grandson—the clumsy one—had been visiting with Celia when he could, too. I suppose even a clumsy boy could do more than a son passed out in a chair after a night of carousing. Frank Tanner was more trouble than he was worth. Always had been.

I hadn't expected what I saw. Alberta was scrawny as chicken feet. Pale as dough, she was. She didn't breathe so much as she gulped air.

Stood by her bedside a long while, I did. Didn't know what to say. Finally I cleared my throat. "Feels like Job's curse, doesn't it, Alberta?"

She didn't say anything. I thought I saw her cheeks twitch, though.

"First Ben Tanner running off and you raising Frank

alone. Then Frank's drinking. Then Abby Tanner's disappearing with that patent-medicine salesman and leaving Celia without a mother and now you being sick and all."

Stopped talking, I did. Felt I'd begun to run on. Like when I gave a sermon and the congregation started pulling out their pocket watches.

Now Birdie struggled to raise up from the bed. "Take me out on the porch, Calvin," she said. It wasn't a request. It was an order.

Awkward, I felt, with Alberta Tanner in my arms. Sad, too, when I finally got her onto the porch. Alberta and I sat on the same porch where I used to come courting years ago.

We watched as Celia and my grandson John put the garden to bed out by the fields. Celia was picking what looked like the last of the tomatoes and the summer squash and putting them in a basket. That lazy grandson of mine was leaning on a hoe, whistling a tune and watching the girl.

It was all I could do to keep from rising up and yelling at that boy to get to work. "Looks like Job's cursed us both, Alberta," I said. "First my Anna dying. Then the Methodists taking over. After that my son-in-law heading west, leaving everything to me. And then my eye and that clumsy son of Emma's over there," I said, pointing to the boy, "and then the rheumatism catching up to me and all."

Alberta didn't seem to be listening.

She turned to me and said, "Bring me a handful of dirt, Calvin."

Looked at her funny, I did.

"You heard me," she said.

I pushed myself up from the chair and hobbled over to the garden. I could hardly bend over, but since it was Alberta, I reached down and let my gnarled old fingers bring up some dark black dirt. Then I hobbled back to the porch, I did. I don't know what made me do whatever that stubborn woman wanted.

"Put it in my hands, Calvin," she said, putting her palms together and holding them open like a basket.

Did what she told me. Scattered the dirt into her open hands, I did.

With difficulty Alberta brought her hands to her face. Then she stuck her nose into the damp black dirt and inhaled. The smell seemed to revive her for a spell.

"I've got nothing to complain of, Calvin," she said. "I can still smell the promise in the wet earth. Feel the presence of friends like Hetty and Emma. Find comfort in Celia's lively mind and good heart. Can still appreciate a damp rag on a fevered forehead and the taste of Emma's apple cake."

Poked her nose back into the dirt, she did. I couldn't see what was so special about it.

Then she lifted her face to me and snarled, "You're not anything like Job, Calvin."

Brought me up short with that one, she did. I might not have been cursed with boils and sores, but I knew the curse of loss, blindness, disappointment, and infirmity.

"Job may have suffered, Calvin," Alberta said, "but he never cursed God. He never lost his faith."

She let the dirt slip through her fingers onto the porch. "Take me back in now, Calvin," she said.

Picked her up then and there, I did. Carried her back to her bedroom. Alberta was light as a baby chick. When I laid her on the bed I felt her thin hands. Cold as a winter stream, they were.

"Your hands are so cold, Alberta," I said. Something about them frightened me.

Amanda Putnam

Frankly, I had never expected the likes of Emma Common to launch a protest on her own behalf. But the women of our Dorcas Circle joined forces with her and our daughters. Not only did we refuse to trade with Albert Biggs until he returned Emma Common's coverlet, but we also refused to sew for our families until the merchant had done so. Biddy Bostick offered to let us set up a shop for our goods on her porch steps, and we pocketed the money ourselves. Soon the front of Biddy's boardinghouse was sporting lace fichus and crocheted shawls like the window of Albert Biggs's store. I wrote to Mary Lyon that we women in Millbrook had launched our own great campaign and that I would finally be able to hold up my head around my sister in Boston.

Now when we met, we women and our daughters gathered to share our experiences, and, frankly, a great deal of amusement.

Alice Girton, the mayor's wife, reported that her husband was furious. He had a button missing from his waistband.

"You can't expect Samuel Girton, the *mayor,* to go out with his trousers 'round his ankles, can you, Alice?"

Alice had only smiled demurely and continued reading.

Alvin Hobbes, one of Millbrook's firemen, would be attending a dinner in Bradbury honoring the firemen in the county.

"I'll need that shirt finished by Thursday, Malinda," he said.

"Then get out the needle and thread, Alvin," Malinda reported, grinning. "Time's a-wasting."

Marguerite Gordon reported on her husband's frustration. "Margie," he whined, "the next thing you know you'll be expecting me to fill up the dustbin or round up the children's shoes."

"Yes, Henry," Marguerite had replied, "and someday, dear, *I* may pop a button and ask *you* to sew it up!"

Frankly, I had never expected my women friends to engage in such lively discussions.

"Don't you see, ladies," I said, "that women, defined only in relation to other persons, somehow cease to be persons themselves?"

"Hmmm, I'm not so sure," offered Miranda Callendar, considering my question. "Take my raspberry jam cake, for instance," she said, leaning forward. "The butter, sugar, eggs, and flour surely profit from their relationship together. Don't they, in fact, become something finer as a result, Amanda?"

I folded the latest copy of the *Gazette,* the one with my editorial about Albert Biggs's shoddy business practices. "But, tell me, Miranda," I replied, "don't they lose *themselves* in the process of baking?"

Sometimes our meetings turned riotous. I reported on an advertisement an anonymous man slipped into *The Millbrook Gazette* as a way of mocking our efforts. It read:

Wanted: A good woman who will cook, clean, mind the babies, and rub the knots from my muscles at night. *Must be willing to sew.*

Biddy reported on the dinner conversation at her boardinghouse. "*Ha!* The men are worried." She guffawed, rubbing her strong red hands. "If you ask me, they're afraid. That booby Herman Totweiler groused that if we first stopped sewing, we might next try to adopt some of their sacred male privileges."

"And what are *those*?" asked Esther Grimes, frowning.

"Smoking cigars," Rebecca Kinder quipped.

"Swilling brandy," Miranda Callendar mocked.

"Swearing," Kate Loring jeered.

"What did you say, Biddy?" Emma Common asked. "How did you respond?"

Biddy waved her beefy red arms with a flourish. "I said, *'Shut up and pass the chicken!'*"

Frankly, I laughed so hard I popped my stays.

Emma Common

How elated I was! Albert Biggs had relented and given me back my quilted coverlet. He had likely grown tired of the empty coffers that an empty store produced. How overjoyed were my women friends and their daughters! Many of us continued to trade our goods on the steps of Biddy Bostick's boardinghouse; others of us reentered Albert Biggs's general store with caution. All of us were much more careful with our calculations and our coins.

Calvin Mercer

Seen the wagon pull up, I did. Hetty and Jacob stepped down, and I saw Hetty carrying a basket of her chicken inside. Smelled it all the way upstairs.

While they ate and talked downstairs, I saw my grandson slip away. The clumsy one. Acting strange, he'd been. Going out to the barn all hours of the day and night, he did. He'd been even more clumsy about his chores. Like he had something else on his mind.

I'd hobbled upstairs to get a view of the barn, I had. You

could see the barn best from the loft window. Grabbed my musket on the way.

Saw that clumsy boy slip the lids off three coffins before going into the barn. Made me suspicious, it did. And then I saw two women. Africans, they were. One looked to be a girl. Then the two women each lay down in a coffin.

And then I saw a man. Another African. I laid the stock of the musket against the window frame to steady my hand. Then aimed, I did. When the African placed the lids back on two of the coffins, I saw that he moved with a limp, one leg shorter than the other. I don't know why, but I put down the musket. Just watched, I did. Watched until everyone came out to leave for the fair. Just stood and watched them go, I did.

Lucy Putnam

I declare I hadn't expected to see what I did. Amos and I never slipped out midmorning, but we'd decided to risk it this time. After all, Mama and near everyone in Millbrook would be up at the green for the fair.

Amos had just finished running his index finger down the crook of my neck when we'd heard the wagon wheels pull up. I declare we couldn't figure why John Common would be delivering three coffins to the back of the Whites' house right when the fair was about to begin.

At first we couldn't figure out what John was doing. After he'd lifted the lids on the coffins, what I saw gave me the willies! Three figures—not a one of them dead—climbed out of the coffins. Then they scurried into the house.

Amos scratched his head and said he hadn't a clue what that was about.

I felt my eyelid lift, and said I did.

John Common

Truth to tell, the Benevolence Fair seemed such a success I began to hope the plan would work. The green was a network of tables like the tree branches of my mother's coverlet. The tables overflowed with the fruits of the labors of Millbrook's women and girls: currant jellies and knitted lap robes, jars of pickles and blackberry cobblers. Marguerite Gordon brought her sugared crullers and Kate Loring her infant caps. Mother baked three of her apple cakes. Faith and her friends piled their tables with pockets and potholders; ribboned hats and dried herbs; batches of gingerbread and sugar cookies; and pledges to run errands, tend babies, sweep porches.

After supper, when it grew dark, folks settled into chairs and blankets on the lawn to watch the auction. When I saw that Mother's coverlet would mark the high point in the bidding, I slipped quietly away, heading to the Whites' farm and the loaded wagon that waited there. I looked up into the night sky and took the circle around the moon as a good sign. If rain was on its way, it might cover our tracks.

The path was dark and the moonlight illuminated only a few yards ahead, but I had almost reached the Whites' farm when I heard the hoofbeats. I recognized the sound from a distance. It sounded like rabbit tails thumping in the brush. I knew one thing: hoofbeats meant danger. I ducked into the bushes lining the path as the hoofbeats thundered closer, and then the ominous drumbeats flew past me, heading in the direction of Jacob and Hetty's farm.

I ran, arriving just in time to see that the tall skinny man had balled Jacob's shirtfront into a fist and was pulling hard. "What can you tell us about the cargo in that wagon?"

he said, jerking Jacob in the direction of his wagon, its bed loaded with three coffins.

"Them coffins look like something to hide slaves in, Sam," the short fat man said.

When the moonlight fell on their faces, I recognized the tall man and the short man as the bounty hunters who had broken into Hetty's tea party looking for Jewel and Ruby.

"No, sir," Jacob insisted, steadying his voice. "A coffin's no hiding place for slaves. There's no cargo hiding in there."

The tall man sneered. "Well, I heard it on good authority—the newspaper editor's daughter herself—that some slaves had been slipped out of those coffins early today. Promised her five hundred dollars for each one we found."

"Let's check it out, Sam," the short man said.

The horses whinnied, sending plumes of smoke across the cool damp night.

Now the tall thin man reached for something in his knapsack. The something glinted against the moonlight. Now I recognized the source of that glint. It had come from a blade. The blade at the tip of an ax.

The tall thin man leaped up into the back of the wagon, the ax held high.

Now the fat man climbed up into the wagon, too.

"No!" I shouted, making my presence known. "There are no slaves there!"

The fat man sneered at me and pointed to the tall man's ax. "Well, then we'll just see for ourselves, won't we, boy?"

"Please!" I cried. "Jacob wouldn't lie!" I knew that if they destroyed the coffins, Rufus and Ruby and Jewel would not have a way to escape.

Jacob moved next to me and put his hand on my shoulder.

"Well, I thank you kindly for that character reference,

boy," Sam said with a surly grin. "But we aim to find out how truthful he is our own selves."

Then the fat man, a greasy forelock hanging over his eyes, said, "If there ain't no slaves, then there can't be no objection to our busting things up a bit, can there?"

Now Sam raised the ax blade high and began to strike at the coffins. One blow. Two. Now three. After a dozen or so swipes, the tall man passed the ax to the fat man, and he took a turn with it.

When the ringing ax blows stopped, and the bounty hunters, fierce in their disappointment, growled at Jacob, the blood began to flow again in my veins. The slave catchers jumped from the wagon and onto their horses, whipping them into a fury, doubling back from where they had come, determined to scour the trail from which escaping slaves had fled. Behind them they left splinters of wood where coffins had once been and dust rising from the ground like fog.

Hetty had been watching from the doorway; her pale face looked frightened.

"Bring in the quilt, Jacob, dear," she said. "'Tis not going to be a safe house for a long time now." I could hear the tremor in her voice.

Then Hetty turned to me. "Can thee tell Biddy Bostick to close the door to her root cellar until she hears from Jacob or me? I expect she won't be receiving any cargo for a while now."

I nodded. Truth to tell, I had learned a lot about things in Millbrook. About the things that were in plain view. George Gordon's slop trough. The door to Biddy Bostick's root cellar. Hetty White's quilt. In plain view. Yet hidden.

After that, in the days that followed, nothing else I heard seemed to matter. It didn't seem to matter that the dancing on the green lasted until the wee hours in a merriment seldom seen in Millbrook. It didn't seem to matter that Mother's quilt fetched a hundred dollars from an anonymous donor. It didn't seem to matter that this was enough money to begin work on my father's church. It didn't seem to matter that the Benevolence Fair was so successful that the Dorcas Circle would be able to buy slates and globes for the primary school. All that mattered to me was that, after everything, Rufus Thomas was still not a tad more free.

Celia Tanner

I confess I was powerful frightened. For two days I had been dipping a rag in cold water, swabbing Grandma Birdie's forehead. She'd been feverish-like. And restless as a rabid dog. I confess it: she had finally rambled like one gone out of her head. "Where is Frank, Celia?" Grandma murmured. "Where is my son, Frank Tanner?"

Grandma Birdie was floating in and out of her mind. She was worn out. Weary. I reached into my specimen box, but there were no more potions. I returned again and again to the woods, searching for heartsease. I wanted something to soothe her mind and body, but heartsease had been as powerful hard to find as the lap of my own mama. Finally, I ran to the Whites' farm, and Hetty rocked me like a baby, stroking my hair like you do a kitty: from the crown all the way down to the tip of the tail. When I finally said the truth out loud, that there was no salve for some hurts, Hetty whispered that when things felt that way, you just let God take over.

Hetty and Jacob said they'd sit by me and Grandma Birdie as long as we needed it, and they were true as their word. When I thought about being alone in the world with only my pop and the sounds of banging pot lids and flying skillets, it helped to look over and see the kind faces of Hetty and Jacob bent over Birdie's pillow or holding my hand.

But then Grandma began to ramble in a language I couldn't recognize. And then I reckon I got wild with worry. The teacup I'd been trying to get Grandma to sip from began to shake in my hand and then the cup slid around in the saucer and then they both somehow slipped from my fingers, and the shattered fragments tinkled across the floor like chimes. When that happened, Jacob White said he was riding over to the Commons' farm straight off. To fetch my friend.

When John arrived, I saw that when he held his head high, forgetting to duck his chin, he could fill up a doorway. I tried to identify the feelings that fluttered inside me. Surprise. Relief. Plain thankfulness.

John Common

When Jacob hoisted me onto his saddle to deliver me to the Tanners' farm, Father reached for his Bible and pledged to follow behind.

When I appeared in the doorway, Celia's eyes were wild with fear. Truth to tell, as they studied me, she seemed to steady some, and I felt grateful to have come.

At Grandma Birdie's bedside, I marveled at Celia's courage. It was the quiet kind Jacob and Hetty talked about, not the noisy kind. Celia pressed her cheek to her grandma's ear and whispered tenderly into it. She held her fingers to her grandmother's wrist, feeling for the fading pulse and then stroking her arm. But Grandma Birdie was feverish and unsettled. She muttered gibberish, and in between the muttering I sometimes caught words I understood. "Your *father,*

Celia," she repeated. A thread of spittle leaked from the corner of her mouth. Celia dabbed at her grandmother's lips with a linen towel. "My son *Frank*," Grandma Birdie stumbled. "*Bring* him to me, Celia. I want him to tell me he's going to be all right. I want him to tell me *himself*."

Celia's anxious eyes registered this impossibility, for even I knew that Frank Tanner was unaware of his mother's plight: I had seen him on my way into the house. He was passed out in his rocker, an empty bottle at his feet.

As the light in the room dwindled, I glanced over at Jacob standing reverently in the corner. His hands were folded, his head bent in prayer. Truth to tell, I had never bothered to think that he often stood like this at the beds of the dying, offering his respectful presence as comfort.

I looked over at Grandma Birdie tossing and turning, wrapping herself in her sheets like a shroud. "I . . . cannot . . . *go*, Celia," she cried, "until I'm settled . . . about *Frank*."

Suddenly I was seized with something. Something certain. Something like the uncommon faith Hetty White had once spoken of.

I bent to the floor, reaching for the sack. I pulled Frank Tanner's fiddle from it. Placing the fiddle at my shoulder, I felt certain that an answer had finally come.

As I began to play, I felt the strings of the violin vibrating in my body, in the very air of the room. As I pulled on the bow, the strains of the music floated over Grandma Birdie's anxious eyes and brow and heart. "Ahhh, Frank," she murmured, "there's nothing for pleasure . . . ," she said, sighing, "like the tune a son coaxes . . . for his own mother."

Then her eyelids fluttered and closed slowly over her troubles.

Truth to tell, as it always had for me, the music gathered everything up: the silence, the light, the mystery of silence and speaking, of being born and dying. Music seemed at that moment like something visible and invisible. Like God.

While I played, I felt the fiddle as a light at my shoulder, no longer hidden under a basket, but flickering in plain view. I had not seen my father quietly standing outside the door.

Afterward, Father placed his hand on my shoulder and declared, "That was as fitting, son, as any prayer." The look in his eyes said his son was a passage he had finally begun to parse.

Afterward I watched as Jacob and Hetty White folded Celia into their arms.

Hetty White

After years of watching my Jacob, I'd come to understand a house of grief. 'Tis a truth that a house of grief has a stunned quality, an element of surprise. As if something had suddenly gone awry. 'Twas either a door left swinging on hinges or an overturned stool or a steaming chicken left to turn cold. 'Twas as if its occupants had been interrupted in the middle of a daily task to which they would never return. Now, after Birdie Tanner's passing, no one had bothered to sweep the broken cup and saucer from the floor. I reached for the broom to do it myself, but then thought 'twas a job better left for Celia. 'Twas a sign of healing to pick up a daily routine again.

One thing there's nary a doubt about: a grieving family is glad to see the undertaker, and in my Jacob, Celia Tanner had a fine one.

Jacob White

Over the years, sad to say, I'd learned something about loss. When I first took up undertaking, I'd thought the worst part was *before*. Then for a spell I had thought the worst part was *during*. Now I had learned that the worst part about a death was *after. After* was the worst part. And the most important.

I had got quiet and gone down to the place inside where God lives.

By and by, I felt the light come, and I said, "I think it might be a comfort, Celia," looking into her swollen red eyes, "if you and your friends—John and Faith and me, of course—made your grandma's coffin. Together."

Celia Tanner

I confess I hadn't reckoned on so many folks caring about Grandma Birdie. Mrs. Putnam brought a beef roast that I reckon I'd never tasted in my life and a mushroom sauce that turned plenty into bounty. The table was heaped with potato salads and apple muffins. I confess Miranda Callendar's raspberry jam cake tried to make it seem like a holiday, but I knew what it was instead: the most powerful sad time in my life.

I hadn't reckoned on so many folks caring about me, neither. After Grandma died, Hetty slept with me every night and baked me biscuits every morning. Biddy Bostick brought money over every day, and I suspected she added to what our brooms and eggs and honey brought. I hadn't expected the coverlet. Folks said it fetched a hundred dollars at the fair, but Biddy Bostick said she had bought it just for me. When she said I deserved to keep warm under something fine, I had to bite my lip. I didn't want a strong woman like Biddy to see me bawl like a baby.

It helped for John and Faith and me to build Grandma's coffin in Jacob's shop. I confess it was like Hetty always said: God provides.

I'd measure the length and width of the boards, and then Faith would mark them and John would saw. After that, we'd all sand the wood, and I confess I found it soothing to run my hand over the same spot over and over, watching the grain appear, feeling it sand smooth. Jacob just stood in the background, whittling.

I confess the best part about it was the silence. In the spaces between the measuring and marking and sawing, John and Faith and I worked side by side without talking. Sometimes one of the silences was twice as long as another; sometimes another silence was just a fraction of the quiet space from before. I reckon it seemed as if silence could *speak*. I confess it was something John had learned, and that Faith was coming to: sometimes there was as much speaking in the spaces *between* the words as in the words themselves. When I looked over at Jacob, his kind face bent to his work, I saw that Jacob had like to known it all along.

When we were ready to hammer the boards together, Faith passed me the nails and John handed me the hammer.

I reckon I don't know what came over me, but when I told the both of them to square the boards, to hold them *per-pen-dic-u-lar,* we all three busted out laughing. I liked to think that Grandma Birdie was somewhere: laughing, too.

Emma Common

How shocked I had been at the conduct of my father! Celia's grandmother had been laid out in the Whites' parlor in a simple coffin three dear young people had built themselves. I couldn't believe that Birdie's last request was for Father to conduct her service, but when I saw the way he had slicked back his wild white hair and put on a Sunday shirt, and when I saw the way he stared at Alberta Tanner's still body in the coffin, I knew it must be true.

Then I saw Celia whispering something in his ear. Father's eyes brightened, and he nodded. Then I watched, astonished, as Celia unfolded my coverlet and placed it gently across Birdie Tanner's sleeping body. My eyes began to sting as I studied the tree and the branches and the apples I had stitched for countless hours. I bit my shaking lip and blessed God for the gift of the needle He had so kindly bestowed on me. I watched my father run his hands over the coverlet, smoothing out the wrinkles.

When he seemed satisfied, I caught Celia's whisper: "Grandma deserves to keep warm under something fine, don't you reckon?"

I heard his reply: "Never liked it when Birdie Tanner took cold."

It was as if my father had returned to ministering for one last time. I learned that he and Celia had even conferred about Alberta's service.

There would be no prayers or readings.

Just silence.

In the tiny cemetery behind Jacob and Hetty's house, the mourners stood respectfully. In the quiet I had time for my own thoughts. After Amos Read's preaching for the missionary contest, Faith had followed my John around with her questions, nipping at his heels like a puppy. "Father, do you think a just God, on whose power we rely, requires us to abandon powers of our own? Do you think that questioning God's holy word is a sign of reverence—or disrespect?"

Sometimes I felt myself smiling at my John's discomfiture. How satisfying I secretly found it! Sometimes he'd disappear for hours of prayerful brooding, and once, when he returned, he had declared at supper, "Methodism is a robust religion, children." Then he turned from Faith and the boys to look at me. "It has always urged a fearless examination of the soul and passionate expression by men *and* women," he continued. "Methodism is a broad, strapping faith. If it can be broad enough to accommodate itself to the prairie, it is surely not too narrow to make room for people's questions."

Standing by the open grave, I looked across the group of mourners and saw my father's head bent low in respect. How grateful I was for the final resting place of my coverlet! How joyful I felt about the change in my own father! In the quiet, observing my father's bowed head, I recognized the power that had always lain in my own hands, and I saw that I had questions of my own: Did life perhaps come in small stitches, in the humble patches of the everyday? Was it something to bind and patch, to remake and refurbish, to honor and cherish?

After a time of silence, my father explained that, when we felt ready, we could take up a handful of dirt, inhale the promise in it, and then sprinkle it over Birdie's grave. After I did so, I turned to leave, finding comfort in the thought of Grandma Birdie lying close to little Charlie Curtis.

Afterward, I knew Alberta Tanner's service hadn't been the kind my John had studied in the pages of his Scripture. In fact, John wondered aloud if it had been a proper funeral at all.

When I said that perhaps you could tell a proper funeral by whether or not it returned people to God, John slipped his arm around my waist and nodded.

Ellen Gordon

After we girls put down our sewing and the women followed, after Celia's grandma died, after Biddy Bostick's front steps proved to be stiff competition for Albert Biggs's window, I had hope that Millbrook was becoming as interesting as Philadelphia.

But then Millbrook quickly returned to its old predictable self: Daddy winding the clock at the end of the day; Mama boiling down the spoiled apples into apple molasses; the stagecoach driver's new beaver hat being the only news in a week.

To my mind, I was grateful for all the things that finally happened. But I'd never expected that the Irish boy would be the cause of them.

John Common

Truth to tell, I had never met anyone as clever as my sister.

When the Irish boy returned to town looking for Celia, Faith and I learned that he'd been hired by a laundry in South Hadley. He'd learned about starches and blueing compounds, about cleaning calicos with ox-gall or wheat-bran washes. Mostly he'd prospered from his skills with numbers: the number of white shirts brought in and due out for the day; the amount of soap it took per gallon of wash water; the number of towels he could crowd on a line at one time and the amount of time it took them to dry.

He'd come looking for Celia because of my sister's letter of reference. The laundry where Sean Hungerford worked was in a school called Mount Holyoke Female Seminary, and its mistress, a Miss Mary Lyon, had been scouting for a poor girl with a longing for learning to receive a scholarship. Sean had suggested Celia, and then Miss Lyon had declared that a girl who could write such a fine letter of reference as my sister should be invited to come, too. Miss Lyon said Celia and

Faith could both come and help out in the laundry or the pie room, catching up on lessons for a year or two until they were ready for classes with the rest of the girls.

Both Faith and Celia were elated, but Faith plunged right ahead with a plan. "We'd better get to work, John. If we're going to college, we're going to need dormitory beds, aren't we?"

Ellen Gordon

To my mind, there was no one like Faith Common. She invited us girls to help build the dormitory beds she and Celia would need for Mount Holyoke. Her brother John and her father and her mother and some of her mother's friends helped, too. I enjoyed the drama of Vera Cramer and Liddie Martin running across the Whites' lawn hauling boards to set on sawhorses, of Biddy Bostick loading her apron up with nails, of Amanda Putnam pulling the jagged teeth of a saw across a board.

It felt good to have a hammer in my hand. *Whack.*

It felt good to poise the arm of a hammer high above a board. *Whack.*

It felt good to eye the distance between hammerhead and nail. *Whack.*

"But why are we building *three* dormitory beds, Faith?" I asked.

"You'll have to ask John," Faith said. "It was my brother's idea."

I didn't quite understand the gleam in Faith Common's eye when I approached her brother.

John put down the pencil that he held between his teeth. "You'll need someplace to sleep when you come to *visit,* won't you, Ellen?"

I couldn't argue with that invitation. And I couldn't

argue with the secret invitation Faith issued only to me, the invitation to sew.

It was Faith's idea for us to fashion the quilt out of the squares we had stitched before the schoolroom fire. Together we huddled over the trapezoidal wings of birds, the triangular steeples of churches, the square steps of stacked hay.

We talked about all that had happened and all that might. We gloated over the fact that Lucy Putnam had been caught heading out of town with Amos Read and that her mother had shipped her off to a finishing school in Maine. We hoped the rumor about me might come true. Mrs. Putnam had suggested that I take over the primary school after Thanksgiving until they could find a new teacher. We talked about the plays the children could write and the speeches they'd memorize and what I'd wear to school each day. At the time I couldn't know that Bishop Common would donate a set of used hymnals to use as readers or that Faith's brother John would serve as music master or that the profits of the Benevolence Fair would be used to purchase slates and a globe.

Now, almost finished with the quilt, I marveled at what I'd never expected to drop from the lips of Faith Common: words of praise for sewing.

"What I once despised for its monotony, Ellen," she said, "I'm beginning to appreciate for its rhythm. What I once hated for its repetition, I'm beginning to understand as design. Our quilt has an appeal like the geometry we were forbidden to learn," she concluded. "Proportion and balance. Pattern and design."

And, as I observed the arrangement of quilted blocks that was nearly completed, I had to agree.

"Ellen," Faith asked, "would you mind if I gave this quilt to someone?"

"*Who?*"

"I can't tell, Ellen, but it's someone who needs it in the

same way we girls needed it. To remember that the things *everybody knows* aren't always true."

To my mind, our stitching had accomplished that purpose for us. "Sure, Faith," I said. "Give the quilt to whoever might need it."

"Ellen," said Faith, her mind skipping dozens of paces ahead of me, "this quilt, in fact, has given me new questions for my copybook. Questions about stitching."

"*Stitching*? You've been asking questions in your copybook about *stitching*?"

She nodded. Then she thumbed through her copybook until she found the page she wanted.

As I peered down into the questions she had written in her firm, regular hand, I saw her questions had moved beyond those we girls had practiced in our copybooks at school; these new questions were far harder for me to grasp:

When a girl looks to another girl for support, does she in some way begin to support herself?

When women look to other women for support, do they not in some way begin to support a shared destiny?

"What do you think, Ellen?" Faith asked, earnest urgency on her face.

My mind was swirling with scraps and swatches of ideas that I could not piece together. To my mind, my friend had moved somewhere beyond me. "I don't know, Faith," I said. "I just don't know."

John Common

Looking back, I remembered that the reins felt good in my hands. Faith, the noisy one, was on one side of me, and

Celia, the quiet one, was on the other. Truth to tell, I felt twice blessed.

Jacob had helped me load the three dormitory beds onto the back of the wagon, and then, after it began to grow dark, we slipped our cargo between the ropes and the mattresses. Before she climbed onto the seat, Faith passed something into the hands of Rufus Thomas, and I knew what it was. It reminded me of what Rufus had said that day in the barn. About how somebody else's truth didn't have to be yours.

As I flicked the reins and headed out the Silas Enders Trail, the fireside hues of red and orange and gold lit up the dark sky like Mother's embroidery stitches. I saw my sister throw off her bonnet and Celia throw off hers, their faces gleaming like candles in the darkness, and I knew that somehow all of us were now what Rufus had once said: friends who had helped one another get a tad more free. Truth to tell, as I heard the jingling bells and the snapping reins picking up the pace for the final leg to South Hadley, a quiet faith settled over me: it felt like a balm, a kind of heartsease.